I0748286

# BOOKS BY AVA MARIE SALINGER

### CONTEMPORARY ROMANCE WRITTEN AS A.M. SALINGER

FALLEN MESSENGERS
SHORT STORY COLLECTION

# WICKED

## AVA MARIE SALINGER

# COPYRIGHT

# FALLEN MESSENGERS GLOSSARY

Aerial: An angel or demon who can control wind.

Alchemist: A human who can create new matter or manipulate existing matter into new forms. Emits a scent of powdered iron.

Aqueous: An angel or demon who can control water.

Argent Lake: Home of the Naiads.

Argonaut Agency: Organization responsible for law and order in the supernatural and magical communities. Headquarters in New York. Agents include angels, demons, and magic users.

Astrea Sea: Home of the Nereids.

Black Fates: The Keres. Goddesses of Death. Tenebra, Kes, and Orena.

Bloodsand: A black tree with red veins that grows in the Nine Hells. Created by warlocks who made pacts with the Underworld after the Fall. Can be used to summon war demons from the Nine Hells.

Blossom Silver: A silver derivative that can heal injuries caused by demonic weapons or black magic. Made by the Naiads.

Cabalista: Demonic organization. Agents include demons only. Headquarters in London.

Dark Blight: A powder black-magic users use in their rituals and which is poisonous to angels and other magic users. Made by Shadow Empire alchemists from the heart of a Dryad.

Demi: The offspring of a God of Heaven/God of the Underworld and a human or a being possessing divine powers. Can take on any appearance.

Electrum: Naturally occurring alloy of gold and silver, as well as copper and other trace elements. Used extensively by Argonaut in their weapons. Combined with steel, titanium, and Rain Silver to make their bullets.

Empyreal: The highest order of angels or demons, with powers equal to those of a Demigod.

Enchanter/Enchantress: A human who uses illusion

magic. Emits a scent of cedar.

Fiery: An angel or a demon who can wield Heaven or Hell's Fire.

Fractured Soul: A human's damaged soul core, extracted from the body – a powerful source of magic.

Furies: The Erinyes. Goddesses of Vengeance. Tisiphone, Megaera, and Alecto.

Ghoul: An evil spirit who consumes the flesh of humans. Emits a scent of rotting meat.

Glitterfang: A pale powder white-magic users employ in their rituals and which is poisonous to demons and black-magic users. Made by Nereids.

Hesperides: Nymphs of the West. Goddesses of the Evening. Guardians of the Sacred Tree. Erytheis, Hesperia, and Arethusa.

Hexa: Guild of magic users. Agents include magic users only. Headquarters in Seattle.

Incubus: A male demon who gains power from sleeping with humans and divine entities.

Ivory Peaks: Home of the Dryads.

Khimer: A creature born of the fusion of a Reaper and a living being.

Lucifugous: A heliophobic demon who abhors light and who can control darkness.

Mage: A human who uses an arcane staff to focus their magic powers. Emits a scent of Juniper.

Magic Levels: Classification of magic users based on their abilities, with Level Six being the weakest and Level One the strongest.

Messengers: Those belonging to the Third Sphere of Heaven and Third Hierarchy of Demons.

Moirai: The Fates. Goddesses of Destiny. Clotho, Lachesis, and Atropos.

Order of Rosen: Religious order affiliated with the Catholic Church. Agents include angels only. Headquarters in Rome.

Potamos: A male Nymph.

Rain Silver: A liquid-silver derivative that can injure and kill demons. Made by the Nymphs.

Rain Vale: Home of the Nymphs.

Reaper: A soul collector and guide of the dead. Emits a

scent of camphor.

Reaper Seed: A drug that can intoxicate most beings and which is fatal in high doses. Mined by Lucifugous demons in the Shadow Empire. Potent hallucinogen for Lucifugous demons.

Shadow Empire: Home of Ghouls, Lucifugous demons, and Dark Alchemists.

Sorcerer/Sorceress: A human born with powerful soul core magic. Uses the energies around them to manipulate magic. Emits the scent of Valerian.

Soul Core: A living being's life force. Red for demons, white for angels, and dirty gray for humans.

Spirit Realm: Home of Pan, the Gods of the Underworld, and lesser spirits.

Stark Steel: Strongest and most magic-resistant metal on Earth. Found exclusively in the weapons and armor of the Fallen.

Succubus: A female demon who gains power from sleeping with humans and divine entities.

Terrene: An angel or demon who can control earth and its derivative metals.

The Fall: An unexplained event five hundred years ago

that resulted in an army of angels and demons falling to Earth.

The Fallen: Angels or demons who fell to Earth.

The Nether: The space between Heaven, Earth, and the Nine Hells.

The Abyss: A forgotten realm beyond the Nether from where there is no escape. Also know as the Eater of Souls.

War Demon: Demon soldiers created for battle. Remnants of an ancient war between Heaven and Hell. Banished to the deepest parts of the Hells.

Warlock: A human who draws power from demons and the Hells and converts it to magic. Emits a scent of sulfur.

Wizard/Witch: A human who learns to use magic through spell books, and who utilizes potions and rituals to access their soul-core magic. Emits a scent of Frankincense.

# UNBOUND

AVA MARIE SALINGER

# UNBOUND

CASSIUS BLACK CLOCKED THE FOUR MEN SHADOWING him minutes after he'd left the headquarters of Cabalista. He pretended not to notice them as he headed east from Liverpool Street Station, too weary to fathom the reason why he was being tailed.

People rarely needed a motive to antagonize him these days. Most had regarded his existence as a stain upon this world even before the battle that had taken place three weeks ago, in the tunnels beneath London. The one where he had had to reveal his status as the most powerful angel on Earth in order to save countless lives and kill the sorceress who had terrorized England and Europe for a quarter of a century.

The fact that quite a few of the magic users and otherwordly beings whose skin he'd saved that day were now intent on making him out to be public enemy number one hardly came as a surprise to Cassius. He'd been stabbed in the back too many times in the past by his supposed allies to trust they would ever change their ways.

Since they couldn't justify picking a fight with him, they'd found other methods to wear him down. Official ones he couldn't ignore. Like the almost daily interrogations he'd been subjected to by the various supernatural agencies who governed the Fallen ever since he killed Tania Lancaster and ended her reign of terror.

The debrief session at Cabalista had been particular brutal today. He'd found himself struggling to maintain his composure as he was forced to stand before the demonic council and its leader and answer their never-ending questions for nearly three hours, his ire restrained by the thinnest of threads.

Russell Gilmore, the current head of Cabalista, was an otherworldly whose arrogance knew no bounds. His mistake in the tunnels had almost cost them the battle, a fact Cassius knew the demon would never acknowledge. Instead, Gilmore had made it his mission to portray Cassius as the one responsible for the deaths of the two Cabalista demons they had lost to the clash with Tania and her sect.

A light rain started falling across London, peppering his face with cool drops. Cassius frowned. He knew from the vibes he'd gotten from the rest of the Cabalista council that Gilmore would not get his own way. That the council members were choosing to indulge the demon at Cassius's expense was something he was prepared to overlook for now.

*Besides, there's no way I'm going to let that asshole conduct his fake witch hunt to a satisfactory conclusion.*

He soon came in view of the towering white steeple of Christ Church. The men kept trailing him, their presence a warm spot on the back of his neck. He headed past Old Spitalfields Market and entered a road lined with eighteenth-century merchant buildings and Georgian townhouses.

They caught up with him in a narrow brick lane one street over. The place was almost deserted at this time of day, the few people who passed the mouth of the footpath hastening their steps when they saw the men surrounding Cassius.

Cassius eyed his would-be attackers with a neutral expression.

He knew two of them were demons from their sulfurous scent. The other two, wizards whose soul cores reeked of Frankincense, were Level Three magic users at best.

"Care to tell me exactly what I've done to deserve your attention?" Cassius said quietly.

The men glanced at one another, as if they couldn't quite believe he'd had the audacity to ask the question.

"Do we need a reason to loathe you?" the first demon said with a smirk.

Cassius prayed for patience. An afternoon spent indulging Gilmore and the Cabalista council meant he didn't have his usual reserve of self-restraint. All his hard work these past few weeks would be in vain if he lost his cool now.

The demon moved, as fast as light.

Cassius rocked back on his heels as the otherwordly's fist connected with his face, his jaw snapping to the side from the force of the impact. He turned his head and met the demon's hateful gaze with narrowed eyes.

The guy had used enough force to kill a human.

The ground trembled beneath Cassius's feet as the second demon called forth his Terrene powers. The wizards started murmuring spells under their breaths. Alarm shot through Cassius when a faint crack split the asphalt next to him. The air grew heavy with malice.

*Are these guys stupid?!*

Cassius scowled. The demons and the wizards were acting with reckless abandon.

*I have to stop them before this goes too far!*

Power pulsed through Cassius. He fisted his hands and let enough of it slip through to brighten his skin and eyes, a warning to the men preparing to attack him that he would not hold back.

The demons and wizards stilled. Something shifted in their gazes. Something that told Cassius things were about to get ten times worse. He reached for the dagger strapped to the small of his back, knowing he would have to be careful not to kill them. The last thing he needed right now was to be accused of murdering two magicians and a couple of demons. Never mind that it would be an act of self-defense.

The hairs suddenly rose on his arms. Cassius blinked as he sensed the presence of a powerful demon closing in on them.

A figure swooped down from the sky and landed lightly at the end of the lane. He folded his gray wings and studied them with a piercing stone blue gaze. Heat rippled through the air as he headed their way.

"What are you doing?"

The demons and wizards startled. Cassius stared.

The man closing in on them now radiated a shimmering haze that sparked with orange glows at the edges, the warm waves ruffling his light blond hair. Cassius didn't have to be a genius to know he was looking at the barest hint of hellfire.

There was only one being on earth who could readily access it.

And that was Victor Sloan, the Fiery demon who fell to Earth nearly five hundred years ago, when the Nether ripped apart and brought an army of angels and demons down upon the unsuspecting humans and their greatest cities.

"I said, what are you doing?" Victor repeated in the same low, silken tone, his pupils flaring crimson with demonic power.

Cassius knew this little demonstration was more for the benefit of his attackers than his own. He'd known Victor for several hundred years. Unlike the fools who'd ambushed him, the Fiery wasn't the kind of man who needed to put on a show of force to command respect.

"We were just passing through when this asshole picked a fight with us," the first demon said, his tone defiant.

Victor looked at Cassius. "Is that correct?"

Cassius sighed. "No." He tucked his dagger back in its sheath, the energy throbbing through his soul core abating as he curbed his powers.

"I didn't think so either." Victor's gaze lingered on Cassius before shifting to his attackers. "How about you make yourself scarce before I decide to follow this up with your respective agencies?"

The demons and wizards glanced uneasily at one other.

A wave of hot air blasted through the alley, warming Cassius's skin. Victor arched an eyebrow at the four men.

"Or would you rather I deal with you right now?"

The four men turned and disappeared hastily down the footpath.

"Is your face okay?" Victor asked.

Cassius gazed from his attackers' fading figures to the demon beside him.

"It's fine," he murmured dismissively. "It'll heal in no time." He hesitated, wary. "How did you find me?"

A chagrined expression came over Victor.

"I saw Russell talking to those men after you left the council chambers. I could tell they were up to no good when they followed you out of the building."

Cassius grimaced and rubbed the back of his neck. "Your boss is a real jackass."

Victor smiled faintly. "I know. And I'm sorry. I doubt he realized they would go this far."

Cassius wasn't surprised by the apology. Victor was one of the few people who had ever treated him civilly since the Fall. Though their paths had crossed on many an occasion in the last few centuries, they had been but passing acquaintances up until two months ago, when Cabalista and the other agencies called on Cassius to help them find Tania Lancaster.

Few people in the world knew that the organizations who governed the Fallen and human magic users secretly relied on Cassius to deal with their most challenging affairs, this despite making no secret of their dislike for him publicly over the years. Although Cassius was well within his rights to refuse to assist them, he knew helping them out from time to time kept them from persecuting him twenty-four seven. Besides, most of the cases they hired him for were ones where human lives were at risk. However much the world hated him, Cassius had never been able to turn his back on it.

To Cassius's surprise, working with the multi-agency task force that had been put together to tackle Tania Lancaster and her sect had been less of a chore than he'd expected it to be. He knew he had Victor and a few key figures from the other organizations to thank for that. Though he wouldn't exactly call them his friends, they weren't his enemy either.

"Do you want to go for a drink?"

Victor's question sent surprise shooting through Cassius. He masked it behind a steady stare.

"You don't owe me anything, Victor. On the contrary, I'm grateful for your support these past few weeks. Especially today."

Victor was the only one who'd asked him if he'd wanted to take a break during the endless questioning by the demonic council that afternoon. The demon may have been Gilmore's second in command, but he didn't bow to the Cabalista head nor blindly follow his orders, unlike some of the other council members.

Victor would have no trouble overpowering Russell in a fight. Though Russell was a formidable Aerial demon in his own right, a Fiery's abilities could not be easily outdone by any power on Earth. Any power except for the one Cassius had recently demonstrated during his battle with Tania and her sect. Strangely enough, Victor had been the least bothered out of everyone who'd witnessed Cassius's latent abilities that day.

It was almost as if he'd been expecting it.

Since Cassius had no interests in agency politics, he didn't know the reason why Victor wasn't the current head of Cabalista. The demon was more than capable of assuming the role. Not only was Victor a born politician, he was level-headed, pragmatic, and more attuned to the political undercurrents in the various otherworldly and magical societies than Gilmore would ever be. Cassius suspected the other agencies would appreciate working with Victor rather than the current Cabalista head. He was busy mulling over this and debating whether to politely bid goodbye to Victor and take his leave, when the demon spoke.

"I'm not asking you to go for a drink because of what just nearly happened," Victor said quietly. "I'm doing it because I enjoy your company."

Cassius's pulse stuttered.

This time, there was no mistaking the interest in Victor's eyes.

The concept of angels and demons as asexual beings had pretty much been shattered after the Fallen came to Earth. Not only were the otherwordly keen patrons of the pleasures of the flesh, they were also open to same sex relationships and having multiple partners. None of the Fallen retained any memories of their lives prior to the Fall and who their mates had been, if they'd had any. Still, surprisingly few had ever settled for a long-term engagement since their untimely arrival on Earth, especially with humans. The weaker race's lifespan was too painfully short in the eyes of the quasi-immortals who had fallen through the Nether; a relationship with a human man or woman would only result in regret and heartache for the otherwordly left behind.

Cassius would be lying if he said he wasn't attracted to Victor. Angels and demons were breathtakingly beautiful creatures and had been the subject of much adulation by mankind following the end of the Hundred Year War that had seen human magic users battle the otherwordly who had destroyed their cities.

It had been some time since Cassius had been with anyone, man, woman, or otherwordly. Once his partners found out he was the Cursed Angel, they invariably turned their back on him. He'd never imagined someone like Victor would be interested in him.

*Then again, we have spent quite a lot of time together lately.*

"Come, it's not far from here." Victor twisted on his heels and headed back the way he'd come, his dark cashmere coat flapping around his long legs.

Cassius hesitated before going after him, a little annoyed the demon had presumed he would follow and equally thrilled at the command.

The place Victor took him to was not what he'd expected. Located in an old distillery at the edge of Spitalfields, the pub boasted a soaring, vaulted ceiling crisscrossed with metal beams and pretty arches spanning exposed red brick columns. The floor was aged wood and the soft light of the overhead chandeliers made the polished walnut and dark oak furniture gleam with understated elegance.

Victor led Cassius to a secluded booth at the back of the room. A waitress appeared moments after they sat down. She placed two freshly drawn half pints of beer on the table, flashed a smile at them, and slowly walked away, the swing of her hips deliberately exaggerated.

"I think she's hitting on you," Cassius murmured.

Victor smiled faintly. "Anna was actually flirting with you."

"I doubt that." Cassius hesitated. "Are you a regular here?"

"Yes." He indicated Cassius's glass. "Try the beer. It's the best in the city."

Cassius cast a dubious look at him before taking a sip of the brew, conscious of the demon's eyes on him.

"It's nice," he said, surprised.

"Do you want to take a look at the menu?" Victor handed him one of the cards propped between the bottles of condiments inside the basket on the table. "The food's good too."

Thirty minutes later and Cassius found himself sitting in front of a generous serving of steak and kidney pie and a mountain of chips.

Victor tucked a napkin on his lap. "What's wrong?"

"I thought this was just meant to be a drink," Cassius said warily.

Victor's mouth tilted in a faint smile. "So?"

Cassius frowned. "We appear to be having dinner."

Victor propped his elbows on the table and leaned in slightly.

"Are you allergic to dinners?"

Cassius blinked at the blatant teasing light in the demon's eyes and his seductively low voice. Heat punched through his gut. He swallowed, his pulse quickening at the spark of attraction lighting the air between them.

"No," he managed, surprised the word didn't come out strangled. "It's just…this is kinda strange."

Victor raised an eyebrow. "How so?"

"Someone like you doesn't hang out with someone like me," Cassius blurted out. "Especially somewhere like here."

Faint lines marred Victor's brow. "What's wrong with this place? Or you, for that matters?"

"There's nothing wrong with the place," Cassius mumbled. "It's just too…normal for you. You're a Ritz kinda guy. And I'm not somebody anyone in their right mind would want to be seen with."

Victor blinked, startled. "Pardon?"

Cassius blew out a heavy sigh. "I'm saying you're too sophisticated for this place." He indicated the pub with a wave of his hand. "I mean, you are *the* Victor Sloan, the strongest, and quite likely nicest all-around guy on the planet."

Victor stared. He burst out laughing in the next instant.

The deep, throaty sound sent a delicious shiver down Cassius's spine and drew admiring stares from several tables. Victor was the single most attractive man in the place and everyone knew it.

"I'm sorry," Victor chuckled. "That was hilarious."

Cassius bristled. "It wasn't that funny."

Victor grinned. "It kinda was. You seem to have a very high opinion of me. That should work in my favor."

"How so?" Cassius asked, puzzled.

The smile that stretched Victor's mouth made Cassius's belly clench with a bolt of desire. The demon leaned in close and brought his mouth to Cassius's right ear.

"I'm not as virtuous or as nice as you seem to think I am, Cassius," he murmured.

The hairs on Cassius's body rose as Victor's breath washed across his skin. He shivered, his heartbeat accelerating. The sultry wave of heat that pulsed off Victor told Cassius the demon had sensed this and liked it. A lot.

"What you said just now, about you not being the kind of person anyone would want to hang out with? You're wrong." Victor drew back slightly.

Cassius's breath locked in his throat.

Their lips were but a hairbreadth apart. This close up, he could see the steel gray flecks in Victor's irises and the smoldering redness at the back of his pupils.

"I've been looking at you for a long time," Victor admitted quietly. "I know what brought you to London was not the happiest of circumstances but still, I'm glad you're here. Because I finally get to do what I'd wanted to do since the first time I ever laid eyes on you."

"Which is what?" Cassius breathed.

"Ask you out."

Cassius froze. "*What?!*"

Victor grinned at his outburst, sat back in his chair, and took hold of his knife and fork.

"I'm asking you out, Cassius. As in, I want to date you."

Cassius sucked in air.

"Have you lost your freaking mind?!" he hissed under his breath, glancing around to see if anyone had overheard their conversation.

"Nope," Victor said cheerfully. "Now, eat." He pointed at Cassius's plate.

Cassius opened his mouth to argue, stopped, and blew out a heavy sigh. He picked up his cutlery and dug into his meal, Victor's confession ringing in his ears.

To his surprise, the next few hours passed in a flash. Victor's charm was magnetic and his voice mesmerizing. Cassius couldn't help but fall under his spell as they wiled away the time over more drinks and spoke about the past. Talking with the demon was as easy as breathing and Cassius felt utterly comfortable in his company.

It wasn't long before he returned to the subject that had been preoccupying him all evening.

"Were you serious? About what you said before?"

The pub had grown noisy in the last hour, people coming in to have a drink and catch a meal with friends after work. Despite the brouhaha around them, Victor's attention remained steadfastly focused on Cassius.

"Do you mean about asking you out?"

Cassius hesitated before nodding, his stomach twisting at the thought of Victor laughing and telling him it had all been a joke. For some reason, Cassius didn't want that to happen. He stiffened when Victor reached across the table and tipped his chin up gently with his fingers.

"What are you—?"

The rest of Cassius's words died in his throat as Victor leaned over and pressed his mouth to his. The world faded around him.

This kiss was heat. It was electric. It sparked and sizzled and set him alight from the top of his head to the tips of his toes. It was everything Cassius hadn't realized he'd been missing and more.

Victor's eyes darkened to azure as he explored Cassius's lips, gently molding and brushing their mouths together, learning the shape of Cassius. Cassius found himself unconsciously chasing his touch, his head angling to make the most of Victor's sensual kiss, his body leaning in to maintain contact.

Cassius didn't realize he'd been holding his breath until Victor lifted his mouth off his. He stared dazedly at the demon before touching his lips with his fingers, wondering if he'd imagined it all. The hotness of his flesh told him otherwise.

"Don't look at me like that," Victor groaned.

Cassius blinked, the clamor around them finally registering as awareness returned.

"Don't look at you like what?"

Victor's voice dropped an octave. "Like you want more."

Cassius flushed, conscious of the fullness in his crotch. A single kiss from the demon had gotten him hard.

Victor's expression turned serious. "And the answer is yes, just in case you still had doubts."

Cassius sobered. "Why?"

Victor covered Cassius's fisted hand with his own. "Why not?"

Cassius frowned, unable to mask his frustration any longer.

"I'm the last person you should be hanging around with, Victor," he said bitterly. "You should stay away from me if you want to become the head of Cabalista."

The demon arched an eyebrow. "Why can't I do both?"

Cassius sucked in air. It was the first time he was hearing Victor admit he aspired to the position currently held by Gilmore. He swallowed at the other man's unruffled expression.

*Damn. How the hell is he so confident?*

"I want you." Victor's touch and gaze burned into Cassius. "And I know you want me too. Go out with me."

&.

DUSK WAS FALLING WHEN CASSIUS PULLED UP IN FRONT of a pair of towering, black, cast-iron gates. The cream-gravel driveway beyond them curved to the left, the foliage from the thick trees lining it obscuring the property at the end.

A wry half smile stretched his mouth as he looked along the secluded lane he'd just driven down. Somehow, he wasn't surprised Victor's home was in Highgate. The epitome of wealth for those who wanted to work in London while still enjoying country style living, the former Victorian village boasted some of the most expensive zip codes in the country.

It suited the demon.

The gates opened with a faint electronic whirr before he had a chance to press the call button on the intercom. Cassius glanced at the camera atop the wall to his left.

*Guess he's expecting me.*

Butterflies swarmed his stomach as he rode his motorbike up Victor's drive.

It had been two weeks since Victor had asked him out. They'd been on several dates since then, mostly in the City of London. Though they'd shared many a torrid kiss during that time, Victor never made a move to take him to bed. Cassius knew the demon was biding his time, stoking the desire that ignited between them whenever they touched.

Tonight was the first time Victor had invited him over to his home. Even though he hadn't made his intentions explicit, Cassius was conscious the demon intended to have sex with him.

Cassius would be lying through his teeth if he said he wasn't looking forward to it. Victor was always calm and composed. Cassius's instincts told him this attitude wouldn't extend to the bedroom; the way Victor sometimes looked at him was so carnal he couldn't help but shiver and yearn for the promise in the demon's eyes.

He was dying to see Victor lose control.

An impressive, gray stone Neo-Gothic Victorian mansion loomed into view. Cassius parked next to Victor's Jaguar and switched the motorbike engine off. He was admiring the pretty facade with its crenelated parapets and tall, leaded windows when the front door opened.

Victor appeared on the porch.

Cassius's mouth went dry.

The demon was wearing a long-sleeved, open neck black silk shirt that highlighted his broad shoulders and champagne-colored trousers that made his legs look like they went on for miles. The familiar citrus scent of his aftershave teased Cassius's nostrils, the fragrance masking the faintest hint of sulfur emanating from his soul core.

Hunger stirred inside Cassius.

Victor looked and smelled good enough to eat.

The demon's lips curved in a smile that made Cassius's stomach flip-flop.

"I'm glad you found the place okay."

"I'd be hard pressed to miss it," Cassius said, masking his nerves behind a steady tone. "It's the only property on this road."

He climbed off the motorbike and took out the bottle of wine he'd brought from the storage compartment, conscious of Victor's gaze roaming his body. He'd opted for a dark blue shirt and cream chinos for their dinner date tonight.

Victor pressed a light kiss to his mouth when Cassius joined him on the porch.

"You look great."

Cassius tried hard not to swallow convulsively when he met the demon's smoldering gaze. "So do you."

"Come on in."

The proprietary hand Victor laid on Cassius's lower back as he guided him inside his home had Cassius's pulse quickening. He relished the subtle ways Victor laid claim to him since they started dating. Cassius wasn't a clingy lover by any means. It had just been a damn long time since he'd experienced the kind of attention Victor so readily showed him.

The inside of Victor's home was even more impressive than the exterior. The color tones were vivid blues, dark grays, and gold, the elegant furnishings and soft lighting providing a sophisticated contrast to the moody hues. It was a masculine decor that oozed good taste and money.

Cassius's heart fluttered when he observed the ornate, winding staircase dominating the main foyer. Victor's bedroom was undoubtedly upstairs. He wondered if he would finally get to see what it looked like tonight.

"Let's eat," Victor murmured with a smile that told Cassius he'd guessed his filthy thoughts. "I'll show you around later."

Cassius followed Victor down a hallway to the left, his cheeks warm. Victor led him into a beautiful sun room that overlooked the extensive, terraced gardens at the rear of the property. Movement down on the lawn drew Cassius's gaze. He didn't have to squint to see the two creatures walking daintily across the immaculate grass, his otherworldly vision piercing the gloom easily.

"Are those peacocks?"

"Yes." Victor chuckled at Cassius's expression. "Before you let your imagination run wild about my extravagant habits, they came with the property."

Cassius pursed his lips. "I wasn't going to say anything."

Victor guided Cassius to his seat and drew the chair back. "You didn't have to."

Cassius hesitated before sitting down. Victor's attentiveness was something he was still getting used to. He stiffened when he felt Victor draw close.

"You're right," the demon murmured into his ear from behind, his breath dancing hotly across Cassius's skin. "My bed is upstairs. And I fully intend to have you in it tonight."

Cassius shivered, his dick thickening at the scorching promise.

Victor straightened. "But first, dinner."

He took the bottle of wine Cassius had brought and disappeared from the room, only to return with a butler's tray holding several serving dishes covered with silver cloches and a bottle of champagne in an ice bucket.

"I hope you like venison."

"I do." Cassius's eyes widened when Victor removed the domes. "Did you make this?" He stared at the immaculately presented food the demon had uncovered.

The meal looked good enough to be served in a Michelin-starred restaurant.

"I did. I like cooking."

Cassius bit his lip.

Victor smiled faintly. "Are you laughing at me?"

"I'm struggling to imagine you in an apron," Cassius confessed.

Victor chuckled. "I look pretty good in it if I say so myself."

"I bet you do."

They gazed at each other, awareness rippling between them. Cassius's breathing accelerated as the air grew charged with sexual tension. Victor broke eye contact first and turned to open the bottle of champagne.

Cassius didn't remember much about the meal. By the time Victor tidied the dishes away and showed him to the library for dessert and coffee, his body was so wired he knew a single touch from Victor might make him explode.

He was standing at the bay windows and staring out into the night to calm his nerves when Victor came inside the room. The demon put their servings of cheesecake down on the desk and brought the coffees over.

"Here."

"Thanks," Cassius murmured, accepting the drink.

A sigh left him when he took his first sip. Victor had made the coffee just the way he liked it, black and sweet. They stood in silence for a while, their gazes on the dark landscape outside.

"This place is beautiful," Cassius finally said.

"I was lucky," Victor admitted with a wry half smile. "I knew the previous owner. When he told me he was contemplating selling it and moving to the States, I secured the property before he could put it on the market." The demon grimaced. "I paid him way more than it was worth at the time, but I really wanted to live here."

"I can see why."

Cassius finished his drink and turned to set the empty cup down on the desk. He tensed when he sensed Victor's presence at his back. Victor's breath ruffled his hair and tickled his skin. Cassius shivered and sighed when he felt Victor's lips brush his nape.

Still, Victor didn't lay his hands on him.

*What's he waiting for?*

Victor stilled. Cassius flushed when he realized he'd

said the words out loud. He froze when Victor pressed his face in his hair.

"I'm afraid to touch you."

The demon's tortured confession made Cassius tremble.

"Why?" he mumbled.

"Because I don't want to hurt you."

Victor slipped strong arms around Cassius's waist and pulled him against his body. Cassius shuddered when he felt the rigid length of Victor's erection nudge his butt. A gasp tumbled from his lips when Victor's teeth found the sensitive flesh of his nape.

"What I feel for you? This hunger?" the demon growled, gently nipping at Cassius's skin. "I fear it will consume us both. That we will be scorched by it and never recover."

Cassius closed his eyes and angled his head to the side, inviting Victor's kiss.

"Then so be it," he breathed, shivers racing down his spine. "Burn me, Victor. I want to feel your heat."

The demon groaned, clasped Cassius's chin in a punishing grip, and twisted his head to the side so he could take his mouth. Cassius welcomed the savage kiss, his lips parting eagerly under Victor's tongue.

He wanted this. Wanted everything Victor's kiss heralded. Craved it all so badly he feared he would lose his mind if Victor didn't deliver on his sinful promise.

Victor's hands roamed Cassius's chest and quivering abs in possessive motions, fingers kneading and exploring the hot, hard flesh they found. Goosebumps broke out all over Cassius's skin at the lust surging through his veins, his entire being focused on the man who was wreaking sweet havoc on his body.

A stifled moan rose up in his throat when Victor's hand found his raging erection. Cassius bucked his hips, pushing his straining cock into Victor's grasp. Victor responded by palming him firmly through his chinos and stroking his arousal.

Cassius dimly registered the sound of his belt being undone and his zipper being pulled down, too enraptured by Victor's torrid kisses and his wicked touch to care much about anything else. Then Victor's fingers were on his naked cock, one hand holding his throbbing length with aching tenderness while the other pushed his chinos and briefs down his hips.

Victor broke their kiss, leaned across the table, and dipped two fingers in one of the cheesecake slices. He brought the thick cream to Cassius's lips and tightened his grip slightly on Cassius's shaft.

"Suck them," he ordered in a low gravelly voice.

Victor's filthy demand had Cassius's hole twitching. He opened his mouth and swallowed Victor's fingers to the knuckles, his tongue wrapping sensuously around Victor's digits as he did exactly as he was told.

A feral sound left Victor as Cassius suckled him. He crowded Cassius against the desk, probed his cleft with his erection, and rolled his hips, his hand moving on Cassius's dick.

They gasped and groaned, pleasure dancing through them.

Cassius moaned and panted around Victor's fingers

as Victor stroked his ardent flesh. Victor kissed and bit his nape, the table rocking slightly as he thrust his dick against his ass, mimicking the act of sex.

Sweat beaded Cassius's upper lip as Victor took him higher and higher. Tension tightened his body and pooled in his belly, heralding his orgasm. Victor slipped his fingers out of Cassius's mouth and pulled away slightly.

Cassius sucked in air when the demon dipped inside his cleft and stroke the wet pads across his pucker.

"*Ah!*"

Victor's hand clenched on Cassius's erection, causing him to hiss.

"Does that feel good?"

"Yes!" Cassius moaned. "That feels amazing! Don't stop—*oh fuck!*"

Cassius rose on his tip toes, a guttural rasp tumbling from his lips. Victor had nudged his opening and pushed inside, his fingers made slick from Cassius's spit. Cassius's passage burned and throbbed at the penetration, body clamping down tightly on the thick intruders.

Victor bit down on Cassius's shoulder.

"Shit! You're so tight," he growled. "I can't wait to feel you around me!"

A buzzing sound filled Cassius's ears as Victor finger fucked him and rubbed his aching erection. He came on a loud shout, his dick spurting hot cum all over Victor's hand and the table, his back passage spasming around Victor's thrusting fingers.

Victor waited until Cassius had stopped shuddering before pulling out of his body and letting go of his spent cock. He pressed a gentle kiss to Cassius's sweat-slicked nape and turned him around.

"Let's go upstairs." The demon's gaze scorched Cassius as he took his hand, his erection tenting his trousers.

Cassius nodded tremulously, electric aftershocks still rippling through his body. He allowed himself to be led out of the library and up the stairs.

Victor's bedroom was at the end of the west hall. Cassius caught a glimpse of an eggshell blue clawfoot tub and an elegant bathroom through the double doors on his left as Victor guided him to the super king-size bed dominating the parquet floor.

Victor stripped him of his clothes with an urgency that made Cassius quiver with anticipation, his hands dancing across the flesh he exposed, as if he couldn't quite believe what he was seeing. He pushed Cassius down on the edge of the bed.

Cassius gasped and bounced once, the dark blue satin sheets rustling under him. Victor towered over him, the demon's sulfurous scent strong with arousal. He stripped off his shirt and cast it on a chaise lounge. His hands were on the zipper of his trousers when Cassius stayed his fingers.

"Let me," Cassius murmured.

Victor swallowed and nodded.

Cassius leaned in and carefully undid the zipper with his teeth.

Victor groaned and dropped his head back when Cassius freed his swollen cock.

Cassius's belly clenched as he explored Victor's throbbing length with his fingers, his touch light and teasing. Victor's cock was long and thick, the veins covering the silky surface standing out tautly with his arousal, his trimmed pubes tickling Cassius's fingers.

Cassius licked a hot strip from the root of Victor's cock all the way to the glistening tip. Victor cursed, his right hand finding Cassius's hair, his fingers sinking in none too gently.

Cassius repeated the motion over and over again, laving Victor's trembling flesh with his spit. Victor tolerated his wicked ministrations for long seconds before taking hold of his dick and guiding the tip to Cassius's lips.

"Please," the demon said roughly.

A thrill shot through Cassius at the crimson light blazing in Victor's pupils. He was right. Victor losing control was every bit as hot and as filthy as he'd hoped it would be.

He stared at Victor from under his lashes, opened his lips, and took him in.

An incoherent sound left Victor. His other hand found Cassius's head.

Cassius set the rhythm as he bobbed his head to and fro, working Victor's thick organ deeper inside his mouth. Victor's toes clenched on the floor. He steadied his stance and gave in to his instincts, his hips moving in deep rolling motions that sent his rigid shaft sliding slickly through Cassius's hungry lips.

Cassius lost himself in the moment, all his senses focused on pleasuring the man in front of him. It wasn't long before Victor's gasps grew more urgent. Cassius fondled the demon's tense balls and scraped the rugged skin lightly with his nails.

Victor stiffened, his head falling back, the tendons in his neck cording. He exploded on Cassius's tongue with his next thrust, his salty seed flooding Cassius's mouth and throat, his savage grunts ripping across the bedroom.

Cassius swallowed greedily.

Victor panted as he came down from his high. He lowered his head and met Cassius's sultry stare, his own hot enough to scald. Cassius slowly let go of Victor's cock. He gasped when Victor gripped his chin and leaned down to take his mouth in a possessive kiss.

"I just sucked you," he mumbled against the demon's lips.

Victor smiled and stroked a thumb across Cassius's mouth.

"I hope you'll do that again before morning comes."

Cassius's cheeks grew warm. He nodded, feeling oddly shy for some reason. Victor's expression grew even more heated. He got down on his knees and spread Cassius's thighs open.

"Victor, you don't have to—" Cassius started.

He stopped abruptly, his eyes widening.

An immense, floor-to-ceiling, gilded mirror stood opposite the end of the bed. Cassius hadn't noticed it in the low lighting. The soft reflection the chandelier cast on the silvered surface made it almost glow in the gray blue room.

"That's right," Victor said huskily. "I want you to watch me blow you. And later on, we're both going to watch as I fuck you over and over again."

Cassius's stomach clenched at the torrid scenes Victor painted with his words. Then Victor's mouth was on his dick and Cassius lost himself to pleasure.

Watching their reflection in the mirror as Victor blew him was every bit as salacious and titillating as the demon had hinted it would be. It wasn't long before Cassius came on a loud shout, sweat beading his face and his hips pumping furiously as he ejaculated. He shivered as Victor swallowed his cum, the demon's lips making his throbbing flesh twitch as he sucked and slurped.

Victor finally let go of his spent dick with a wet pop.

"Hmm," he teased, drawing a moan from Cassius as he took a final lick of the sensitive tip. "Thank you for dessert."

Cassius covered his flushed face with his hands and groaned.

"I can't believe you just said that!"

Victor laughed softly, rose, and maneuvered Cassius up the bed as he climbed onto the mattress.

"It's the truth. You're the finest sweet course I've ever had."

"Stop it!" Cassius mumbled, his ears flaming.

Victor kissed the hot tips gently. "How about we get back to the main meal?"

The demon rained kisses across Cassius's face and throat before making his way slowly down his chest. Cassius shivered and shuddered and moaned as Victor explored every inch on his body. Victor rolled him over before continuing his ardent inspection, his fingers, lips, and tongue dancing hotly across Cassius's quivering back and legs.

By the time Victor drew him up on all fours and shifted him so they faced the mirror, Cassius was a whimpering mess. Victor grabbed a bottle of lube and a strip of condoms from the nightstand, dropped them on the bed, and moved in behind Cassius.

Cassius stared dazedly at their reflection in the dimly lit room, the shadows around them emphasizing their figures where they knelt on the bed. His heart thundered in his chest and his cock throbbed between his thighs as he registered the lust in his own eyes and the color staining his cheeks, his excitement at his submissive posture plain to see in the shallow pants falling from his lips.

Victor's pupils glowed crimson behind him, his chest heaving with his own ragged breathing. Cassius could tell from his strained expression that he was holding himself back by the thinnest of threads.

The demon coated his hand liberally with lube, parted Cassius's cleft, and pushed two fingers inside him. Cassius sucked in air and bit his lip.

Victor held his gaze in the mirror as he slowly thrust in and out, stretching Cassius's passage, his face feral with hunger.

"Victor?" Cassius panted.

"Yeah?"

"Hurry!"

Victor gnashed his teeth, scissored his fingers, and pushed a third finger inside Cassius's hole. Cassius hummed and danced back on Victor's hand, the sting and burn fading as Victor prepped him thoroughly. Victor pulled out a moment later, sheathed his straining erection with a condom, and coated the rubber with lube.

He crowded Cassius's back, stretched his ass with his hands, and pressed the thick tip to Cassius's twitching opening.

They both groaned as Victor punched inside, his dick stretching Cassius's passage oh so deliciously as he entered him. Cassius breathed through his mouth and forced his body to relax as Victor pumped his hips in a gentle motion, his eyes on their reflection.

Seeing and experiencing Victor's penetration at the same time was sexy as fuck.

Victor's sweat splashed onto Cassius's back when he was finally seated fully inside his body. The demon closed his eyes, a wave of heat pulsing from his core as he reined himself in.

Cassius moaned when Victor's cock grew even hotter and thicker inside him.

"Move," he begged. "Fuck me, Victor. Fuck me like you want—*Ah! YES! Just like that!*"

Cassius's shout echoed around the room as Victor did exactly that, his fingers closing punishingly on Cassius's hips, his body rocking to and fro as he started pumping his dick in and out of Cassius's hole.

Bolts of electrifying pleasure shot through Cassius's back passage and spread through his body as Victor thrust passionately inside him, Victor's cock sliding tantalizingly over his prostate. His mouth opened on lustful moans and cries, his hand finding his oozing cock. He dropped his head as he started stroking himself, dizzy with pleasure.

Victor fisted a hand in his hair and pulled his head back up.

"Keep looking in the mirror, Cassius," the demon commanded in a heated growl. "Look as I make you scream."

Heat throbbed from the demon's soul core as he fucked Cassius slow and deep, pleasure painting red flags on his cheekbones, his eyes dark but for his crimson pupils. Cassius welcomed it all, his entire body growing hot as Victor's powers danced through him, his passage burning sweetly from Victor's lovemaking.

Victor rose slightly off the bed, braced his feet against the mattress, and started fucking Cassius with savage grunts where he crouched behind him, his movements growing forceful and his hands biting into Cassius's hips. The angle brought the head of his cock flush against Cassius's prostate, drawing even louder cries from him as he punched his sweet spot with every thrust. Dazzling spots of lights flashed across Cassius's eyes.

He didn't think he could take much more of this insane pleasure.

"Can you see it?" Victor panted. "Can you see me fucking you, Cassius?!"

Cassius focused on their reflection. He gasped lustfully when he glimpsed Victor's slick dick moving in and out of him. Victor cursed when Cassius clenched his hole. He accelerated his motions, the bed squeaking beneath them as he rammed his cock in and out of Cassius's passage.

Tension tightened Cassius's spine and balls. He squeezed his dick with his hand, wanting to prolong the ecstasy he was experiencing.

"Come for me, Cassius," Victor growled. The demon leaned down, closed his teeth on Cassius's back, and rolled his hips in a hard thrust.

Cassius's breath locked in his throat, the sweetly savage bite finally sending him over the edge. He came on a vicious shout, his vision flickering and his passage spasming violently as he spurted cum all over the sheets.

Victor gnashed his teeth and went rigid behind him, body taut and head thrown back as his own climax crashed through him. His hips pistoned his ejaculating cock in and out of Cassius's trembling hole in the next instant, his movements unrestrained and erratic, his mouth open on wild grunts and gasps.

Cassius rode the storm with Victor and watched it all, his insides pulsing with violent pleasure, Victor's dick massaging his swollen prostate.

Their pants sounded loud in Cassius's ears when Victor finally stilled a moment later, his hands loosening slightly on Cassius's hips. He pulled out of Cassius, looped an arm around Cassius's chest, and drew him up against him.

Cassius moaned as Victor turned his head to the side and took his mouth in a scalding kiss. Foil rustled. Cassius blinked.

Victor was still hard. Cassius's mouth went dry as he watched Victor discard the used condom and sheathe his rigid cock again. Victor crowded Cassius's back and guided his erection to Cassius's loose opening.

"Ready for round two?" The demon rained kisses on Cassius's nape and shoulders, his hot gaze meeting Cassius's eyes boldly in the mirror.

Cassius swallowed convulsively. The soreness of Victor's penetration was already fading, his seraphic powers swiftly soothing his pleasantly used insides.

Victor snaked a hand around Cassius's hip and stroked his half-hard length. Cassius hummed and closed his eyes, body thrusting automatically into Victor's skillful touch.

Victor smiled. "I'll take that as a yes." He entered Cassius in a single, slow thrust.

Cassius lost track of time as Victor made love to him over and over again, the hours whiling away slowly while their cries and grunts and moans echoed around the bedroom, the desire filling their veins never ending. The demon's heat scorched Cassius just like he'd feared it would, his soul core throbbing with intoxicating pulses of power where they physically connected, making their orgasms even more intense. Cassius welcomed it all, his sweat-slicked body trembling as Victor took him with possessive savagery, relishing the passion burning them both. It wasn't until the sky lightened on the horizon that they finally collapsed on the bed, Cassius's head dropping heavily on Victor's chest where he'd been riding him.

Victor danced gentle fingers up and down Cassius's back as Cassius shuddered and shivered with aftershocks of pleasure, his dick pulsing with echoes of his own climax deep inside Cassius's body.

"Thank you for the meal."

Cassius narrowed his eyes and lifted his head to stare down at the demon, his breathing ragged.

"Will you stop saying that?"

"Why?" Victor rose slightly and took Cassius's mouth in a light kiss. "Teasing you is such sweet fun."

Cassius's chest tightened at the warm light in Victor's eyes. He swallowed.

"I was wrong about you," he mumbled. "You're not the all-around nice guy I thought you were."

Victor laughed at that. They both sucked in air and groaned when the motion made his spent cock shift inside Cassius. Victor pulled out gently, took Cassius's hand, and dragged him off the bed.

"How about we clean up and have breakfast? I make a mean Eggs Benedict."

Cassius followed the demon into the bathroom, his heart light and his soul at peace for the first time in years.

## THE END

# BEWITCH

## AVA MARIE SALINGER

# BEWITCH

*Great. Just great.*

Suzie Myers narrowed her eyes slightly at the barrel of the gun inches from her nose.

It was late Saturday night and she'd just been about to close up *Occulta*. Dane Wilder, her head bartender, had left but a moment ago with Gary Evaneski, their doorman. Though the pair had gone to great pains to pretend they were headed their separate ways, Suzie knew they would end up together at Dane's place in Japantown.

After eighteen months of stolen glances and circling one another like two bears debating whether to fight or fuck, the wizards had finally succumbed to their mutual attraction and were now unofficially dating. Or, as Lisa Burnett, one of *Occulta*'s other bartenders liked to put it, Gary was dipping his wick in Dane's honey pot with the aggressive enthusiasm of someone who intended to make up for lost time.

*We really need to expand Lisa's vocabulary. Maybe I*

*should give her some books to read.* Suzie swallowed a forlorn sigh. *And if someone doesn't use* my *honey pot soon, I'm gonna shrivel up like a dried prune.*

Zach Mooney's broodingly handsome features flashed before her eyes then. She clenched her teeth.

It had been a week since she'd last seen the Argonaut demon. Seen being a metaphorical word. Her cheeks warmed when she recalled the scalding kiss they'd shared in front of the entire bar. He'd said he'd call but she hadn't heard from him since.

"Goddamn tease," she muttered to herself.

An irate voice intruded upon her dismal thoughts.

"Hey, didn't you hear us, bitch?! I said give us everything in the cash register!"

Spit peppered her face. Cold metal pressed into her cheek, leeching the warmth from her skin. Suzie ignored the weapon digging into her flesh and focused on the guy holding it.

His pupils were large, black circles in sunken orbits set in a pale, sweaty face. Though he was likely in his late twenties, he looked two decades older and had the gaunt appearance of someone who was sick. But it wasn't an illness that was making his hand shake and sending sporadic twitches coursing through his skinny body. He was an addict. And, judging from what Suzie could smell from him, his favorite poison was Reaper Seed.

Though Bostrof Orzkal had purged San Francisco of the devastating drug smuggled from the Shadow Empire, elements of the underbelly of the city still had some supplies left over and were selling them to the highest bidder, the scarcity racking up prices to exorbitant levels. This had seen a rise in crime in certain parts of town as those dependent on the drug looked for alternative means to fund their addiction.

The gunman's two companions looked no better, the rank odor wafting from them carrying the chemical scents of a cocktail of street drugs.

*They must have been staking the place, waiting for Dane and Gary to leave.*

Suzie chewed her lip as she considered her options. The trio had barged through the front door of her bar presuming she wouldn't be able to put up much of a fight without her staff around. After all, everyone in the city knew the bartenders and doormen who worked at *Occulta* were wizards and witches of a certain caliber.

In the end, she chose the least troublesome of her choices.

"How about I let you walk out of here? We'll pretend none of this ever happened and I won't tell the cops on you."

The man holding the gun stiffened at her calm tone. He stared at her like she'd grown another head.

"Are you crazy?!" He dug the barrel deeper into her face and let out a bark of deranged laughter before cocking his head to address his friends. "Hey, did you hear what this whore just said?!"

Suzie lowered her brows as the gun ground into her cheekbone. "Watch the face, dipshit."

The man froze.

Stars exploded in front of Suzie's eyes as he

backhanded her across the face. Her head snapped to the side. She blinked, stunned.

*Fuck. Is it the drugs that made him so fast?!*

She could tell he was no magic user. And he definitely was not an otherwordly. Something hot trickled down her chin, distracting her. Suzie wiped it and stared numbly at the blood on her thumb. Heat bloomed in her belly.

"I said to watch the face, asshole!" she snapped.

The man's expression turned ugly. Movement flashed at the corner of Suzie's eyes. She caught his arm before he could strike her again.

The guy cursed and jerked back. His eyes rounded when he saw the faint radiance dancing across her fingers where she'd grasped his wrist.

Suzie squeezed until she felt bone grind against bone.

He cried out, the gun tumbling from his suddenly limp fingers. It clattered noisily onto the ground. Metal hissed as his companions flicked open their switchblades. A predatory gleam overcame their dull expressions as they closed in on her, their gazes raking her denim shorts and T-shirt clad figure with fresh interest.

Suzie shuddered in disgust. Fire licked her veins as she drew on her magic. A bolt of anger tightened her stomach. The last thing she needed was for her bar to be wrecked all over again.

*Dammit. Looks like I'm gonna have to go with the second option after all.*

"Need a hand?"

Suzie's head whipped around, as did the three men's.

A different kind of heat rippled through her when she saw the Aqueous demon who'd just strolled inside *Occulta*. Her gaze wandered over chocolate brown hair she wanted to sink her fingers into, blue eyes that simmered with a hint of redness and danger, a sexy smile that made her toes curl, and a body she yearned to explore with her mouth and hands.

The man she hadn't been able to get out of her mind for the past two weeks was just as devastatingly hot as she recalled. Suzie swallowed, the heat pooling low in her belly having nothing to do with magic and everything to do with desire.

The last time she and Zach Mooney had been in the same space, their tongues had been glued together and there had been nary a hairbreadth between their straining bodies.

The demon's gaze stayed locked on hers as he exited the foyer, the crimson glow that darted in the depths of his dark pupils hinting at his otherwordly nature. He leaned a nonchalant hip against a booth close to the entrance, ignored the intruders gaping at him, and studied her broken lip with a faint frown.

"You okay?"

Suzie shook herself out of the lustful daze she'd fallen into. "Yeah. Give me a minute."

The three men exchanged panicked glances. She had to give them due credit. Despite the drugs coursing through their systems, it was clear they could tell Zach wasn't human.

Light flared across the bar, etching everything in sharp relief and chasing the shadows away. The men cursed and squinted. The little color they had left drained from their faces when they saw the white orb that had exploded into existence above her right palm.

The guy whose wrist she still held glared at her as if she'd committed some ungodly sin. "You're—you're a witch?!"

Zach bit back a smile. Suzie wrinkled her nose.

Though she'd wished to keep her identity as a Level One witch a secret from the agencies who governed the otherworldly and magic wielders in the city, she'd had no option but to reveal her powers a few weeks back, when Cassius Black, the most feared and ostracized angel on all the continents, had showed up at *Occulta* with his merry band of Argonaut agents and practically destroyed her bar after they were attacked by a group of black magic sorcerers.

Cassius's own status as a legendary Empyreal had also become public knowledge during the battle that had almost cost him his life. Suzie's mother had once told her about the time she had witnessed Cassius's true abilities, but she'd long thought it hyperbole brought on by Stephanie Keller's dementia. A once powerful witch who'd helped Cassius bring down Tania Lancaster, the sorceress and black magic necromancer whose sect had terrorized Europe for a quarter of a century, Stephanie had broken the pact pressed upon everyone who had seen Cassius's true form during one of her less lucid spells when she'd revealed that particular secret to Suzie.

If not for her mother's achievements and the high regard in which she was still held by her former companions in Hexa, Suzie knew Stephanie might have ended up in trouble for breaking the covenant all had taken on the fateful day Cassius felled Tania Lancaster.

"Better grit your teeth," Zach warned the men gawking at Suzie as if she were a monster. "This is gonna hurt like a bitch."

"Wait!" the guy who'd been holding the gun mumbled. "We'll leave! Just don't—*aargh!*"

The spell bomb struck him in the chest and carried him straight across the bar. He crashed into the wall next to Zach just as his companions charged Suzie. She ducked beneath their blades, front kicked one of her attackers in the gut, and elbowed the other one in the face. Bone crunched. The man cried out and fell on his ass, blood gushing from his shattered nose.

A hand closed around Suzie's throat. Cold steel pressed against her heart.

Zach straightened where he still stood near the entrance, his expression darkening. Lassoes of water now bound the guy who'd slid down to the floor next to him.

"It's alright." Suzie's cool gaze never left the man holding her captive. "I'm almost done."

Magic crackled around her. Her attacker yelped and released her, the sparks stinging him. His knife fell from his hand when her hair lifted around her head in a halo. His mouth rounded in horror.

Suzie scowled. "You picked the wrong bar to rob, fucker."

She flicked her fingers.

The man screamed as an invisible power picked him up and drove him to the tall, vaulted ceiling.

Zach winced when he smashed into a metal beam. "Easy, tiger."

The man's horrified shout was cut off when Suzie shoved him straight back down into the hardwood floor. Boards splintered under the impact. She cursed.

The guy groaned and grew still.

Zach sighed. "I told you to go easy on him." He stiffened in the next instant.

His figure blurred.

Suzie jumped when gunfire shattered the fraught stillness. Acid churned her stomach as the awful echo died down around her.

The man whose nose she'd broken had lunged for the weapon on the ground and fired a shot at her. Except it wasn't her the bullet had struck.

"Ouch." Zach brushed away the flattened disc that was all that was left of the slug that had slammed into his shoulder when he'd moved at lightning speed to cover her. It clinked onto the floor, the metal still steaming from its impact against the demon's hardened flesh.

Suzie sagged, the relief shuddering through her making her legs weak. The only things on this Earth that could hurt an otherworldly were Stark Steel, the divine metal making up the Fallen's armor and weapons, or devastatingly powerful magic.

Relief turned to anger.

She stormed out from behind Zach, her magic powering up a blazing sphere.

"Maybe you should dial that down a bit," the demon suggested in a placatory tone. "You only just fixed up the place."

Suzie gritted her teeth and ignored him.

The guy with the smashed up nose screeched when magic enveloped the gun he still held. Metal crumpled. So did two of his fingers. His scream became an incoherent gurgle.

"Oh wow," Zach observed leadenly. "You are *pissed*."

"He shot you!" Suzie snarled where she stood above the man writhing on the ground in agony.

She kicked him in the crotch for good measure. The guy's eyes rolled back in his head.

"I'm fine. See, it didn't even scratch me." Zach indicated the hole in his shirt and the unbroken skin beneath it.

Suzie's nails dug into her palms when she clocked the slight red mark the bullet had made. "That's gonna bruise."

"It'll heal in no time," Zach protested.

Irritation had Suzie rounding on the demon. "Why are you defending these assholes?!"

Zach stared at her for a moment. Suzie blinked when shackles of water secured the hands and feet of her two remaining, senseless attackers, the cuffs forming so swiftly she almost missed them.

"I'm not defending them per se."

She wrinkled her brow at his hesitant tone.

The demon scratched the back of his head, his

expression growing sheepish. "How am I supposed to have my wicked way with you if you end up in jail for aggravated assault?"

Suzie's stomach flip-flopped. She opened and closed her mouth soundlessly, too stunned to speak for a moment.

The guy she'd slammed into the ceiling groaned and looked at them like they'd lost their freaking minds. "Dumb fucks," he mumbled.

Her eyes shrank to slits. She took a threatening step toward him.

Zach closed a hand on her arm and took his cell out of the rear pocket of his jeans. "How about you go make yourself a drink while I call the cops?"

He cast a cold glance at the man who'd insulted them. The guy squealed as the shackles holding him prisoner tightened, drawing thin cuts into his flesh.

It was past midnight by the time Suzie was finally able to lock up the bar.

"Thanks," she told Zach ruefully as they strolled into the main area. "Your friends made this easier than I thought it was gonna be."

"No problem," the demon murmured.

The San Francisco PD guys who'd turned up had known the Argonaut agent. They'd taken her deposition there and then instead of insisting she go back to their precinct.

Suzie inspected the damage to the floorboards. They would need replacing. Again.

"Dane is gonna kick my ass when he sees this on Monday," she muttered.

"It wasn't exactly your fault," Zach said.

She frowned at the demon's slight emphasis on the word 'exactly.'

His lips tilted in a faint smile when he clocked her expression.

"Where's your first aid kit?"

"Behind the bar."

He found the box, wrapped some ice in a towel, and sat her down in a booth. She hissed when he carefully cleaned her broken lip.

Zach paused and arched an eyebrow. "Want me to kiss it better?"

Suzie wrinkled her brow at his dry tone. It was bad enough that they were sitting so close their knees were touching and she could smell his cologne. Both were doing all kinds of crazy things to her breathing.

"You're enjoying this, aren't you?"

He smiled. "You have quite the temper." He sobered, his eyes darkening a little. "Although, I hate to think what would have happened if I hadn't been here tonight."

Suzie blinked. A muscle was twitching in Zach's cheek. She raised a hand to his face, unable to stop herself. He stilled at her touch. She flushed and made to snatch her fingers away.

"Sorry. I—"

Zach closed his hand over hers. "Don't be."

Suzie's breath stuttered at his husky voice and the crimson points of light in the depths of his pupils. His skin was hot. So hot she feared he would burn her.

Zach's lashes came down as he appeared to battle

against some inner instinct. The redness had faded from his eyes when he opened them again.

Suzie couldn't help the twinge of disappointment that darted through her. The demon took a shallow breath and pressed the makeshift ice pack to her lip.

"Why didn't you call?" she blurted out.

Her pulse raced as she waited for his answer, the air between them so thick with sexual tension she was finding it hard to catch her breath.

"You didn't give me your number."

Suzie startled. "What?!"

Zach shrugged. "I mean, I could have found it out through Argonaut but I didn't think you'd appreciate that." He gave her a lopsided smile. "It would start our relationship on the wrong footing."

Suzie's stomach lurched at his words. She stared into his eyes and saw only the truth. She'd hoped this wild attraction between them was more than just lust. Zach evidently wanted the same thing.

She racked her brain for details of their last meeting and grimaced. "Shit. I really didn't give you my number." She searched his face. "Is that why you came here tonight?"

"A week is a long time to make a demon wait for a third kiss."

Suzie blinked. Their first kiss had happened in her apartment, in front of Zach's entire Argonaut team. Her cheeks warmed at the memory. Her belly clenched in the next instant. There was no mistaking what she was reading in Zach's eyes.

He'd come here with more than just a kiss in mind.

"Looks like my honey pot won't dry up after all," she mumbled under her breath.

"What?"

"Nothing." Suzie chewed her lip out of habit and winced when she reopened her wound. "Dammit. How are we supposed to kiss now?"

Zach chuckled and continued icing her flesh. "There are plenty other places I could kiss you."

Suzie sucked in air as a slew of torrid images flashed before her eyes. He grinned like he'd read her mind. Her pulse quickened.

"You better deliver on that promise tonight," she said hoarsely.

The demon grew still at her words. His smile faded. Something else replaced the amusement in his gaze. Something that made Suzie's heart pound in anticipation and her sex throb with a surge of heat and wetness. Her breath hitched a little when he leaned in.

"Is that an invitation?"

His husky words washed across her lips, his eyes so close she could count every gray speck in his blue irises. Redness flared in his pupils. The faint smell of sulfur teased her nostrils along with the scent of his arousal.

The little control Suzie possessed snapped with a sound she swore she heard.

She grabbed Zach's face and kissed him.

He froze for a heartbeat before dropping the ice pack and raising his hands to sink his fingers in her hair. He angled her head and swept his tongue past her teeth, his lashes lowering over a gaze that simmered crimson with desire. Suzie groaned and closed her eyes when she tasted a sliver of her own blood on his tongue. Then he wrapped his thick, hot flesh around hers and all her thoughts scattered to the winds.

Her nipples hardened and her pussy ached as they kissed with barely controlled hunger. Suzie gasped when Zach grabbed her waist, lifted her onto the edge of the table, and filled the cradle of her thighs with his hips. She hooked her arms around his neck and plastered her body against him, her mouth as demanding as his. He groaned when the weight of her full breasts pressed into his chest. A shudder shook her as the solid ridge of his erection nudged her crotch.

Suzie's heart thundered like a freight train when the demon tugged her T-shirt out of her denim shorts, his movements as frenzied as the hot gaze he raked her with, his tongue lashing hers with strong, lustful strokes. Her breath froze when he danced his hands up her rib cage. He skimmed the satin covering her mounds and gently stroked his thumbs across her nipples.

Suzie arched and cried out, heat stabbing her core from his sensual touch. Zach swallowed the sound greedily and repeated the motion again and again before pinching her hardened nubs and tugging. She hissed at the pleasure pain, her sex growing slick with arousal.

He lowered his head to her throat and inhaled deeply. "Fuck, you smell divine." He shivered. "I can't wait to taste your pussy."

The fire in his pupils drew a needy moan from her

lips and had her knees clenching tightly around his thighs.

"Soon," he growled against her mouth. He rocked his hips, grinding his cock into her crotch. "Soon, I'm going to be buried so deep inside you you won't know where I begin and you end."

Suzie dropped a hand between them and palmed his meaty rod. "You promise?!" she gasped, dizzy at the feel of him.

Zach cursed. "Don't worry. I'm going to give you all of me."

Suzie's heart fluttered at his ardent vow. She tugged his lower lip between her teeth and gave him a playful bite. "I can't wait."

Zach shuddered. "Let's head over to your place."

Suzie giggled when he lifted her off the table, grabbed her waist, and walked her to the side exit, his touch hot and urgent. They made for the private entrance to her second-floor apartment, their hands all over one another, their lips meeting in torrid kisses as they tumbled through her front door.

Choked off laughter left Suzie when Zach lifted her over his shoulder in a fireman hold and practically ran up the stairs. He crossed the open plan living area briskly, climbed the steps to the mezzanine level and her bedroom, and put her down, his fingers making the most of her flesh as he slid her along his body.

"Shower," Suzie murmured, glancing at the door to her en-suite. "I need to wash those men's touch off me."

Zach hooked his fingers in the waistband of her shorts and tugged her close. "I'll help." He walked her backward into the bathroom, mouth busy kissing her and hands expertly stripping her T-shirt up and over her head. He attacked his own next.

Suzie gulped at the hard planes and ridges of his muscular torso, his sculptured six-pack, and the sharply defined V highlighting the treasure trail dipping past the top of his jeans.

He flashed her a sexy smirk, balled his T-shirt, and dropped it on the floor. "Like what you see?"

"Uh-huh," she managed in a strangled voice.

"Good." His tone turned husky and his gaze smoldering. "Cause I like what I see too." He hooked a finger under the shoulder strap of her bra, slipped it down her arm, and freed her left breast.

Suzie gasped when he palmed her hot flesh and carefully rubbed a thumb across the dusky nipple.

"Pink," Zach breathed. He stared at the hard nub as if it were a treasure. "I knew they'd be pink." He unhooked her bra, dropped it on the floor, and weighed her breasts reverently in his hands before lowering his head and sucking her left nipple into his mouth, his fingers teasing and squeezing her other mound and its proud crest.

Suzie clutched his shoulders and moaned, the pleasure storming through her rendering her dizzy. Every lash of Zach's tongue against her nipple made her sex pulse and drew a shaky sound from her throat, so much so she feared she would come just from having him suck her breast.

He lowered his hands to her shorts, popped the top button, and pulled the zipper down. Suzie shivered as he worked the denim and her panties over her ass and down her hips. He let go of her breast, peeled her clothes off her legs, and stepped back, his chest heaving with his ragged breathing.

His pupils flared scarlet as he took in her naked form, his heated gaze raking every inch of her flushed flesh.

"You're beautiful." Zach danced a finger down her throat and breast.

Suzie panted and trembled as he grazed her quivering belly. He stopped just shy of the ash blond curls covering her sex and flashed her a wicked smile.

"Tease," she whispered.

He chuckled and unbuckled his belt.

Suzie stared, her heart beating so fast she thought she would faint. The sound of the shower filled the bathroom when he reached behind her and turned it on, his chest skimming her torso with tantalizing heat. He started lowering his zipper, stopped, and gave her a grin that should have been illegal in every state.

Suzie fisted her hands. "I swear to God, if you don't pull that zipper down right now and show me your dick, I'm not letting you anywhere near me!"

Zach laughed at her growl. Then he did exactly what she wanted.

Suzie pressed her thighs together and tried not to squirm when he freed his impressive erection, her pussy so sopping wet it felt like she'd come already.

*Oh sweet Jesus!*

The demon was bigger and harder than she'd imagined he would be, the skin over his shaft flushed and silky smooth except for the sculptured ridges of his veins. His cock visibly throbbed at her hungry stare. She licked her lips.

She wanted him inside her so bad she was willing to get down on her knees and beg him to take her there and then.

Zach backed her under the hot spray, his gaze smoldering as if he'd read her thoughts. He pinned her against the tiled wall and crushed his mouth over hers. Suzie's lips parted eagerly under his tongue, the slight throbbing from her split flesh all but forgotten.

He explored her mouth for a long, torrid moment, his chest hard against her tingling nipples, his erection probing her belly with an insistent pressure even as he pressed a thick thigh between her legs.

Suzie moaned and wrenched her lips from his. "So, I always wanted to know something!" she gasped.

He groaned and licked the corner of her mouth. "Really, questions? *Now?*"

Suzie tugged his hair.

Zach sighed and drew back slightly. "This better not be a quiz on astrophysics."

Suzie chewed her lip and hesitated for a moment.

"A demon's tongue," she finally blurted out.

Zach stilled. A lazy smile curved his lips, the teasing light in his eyes telling her he knew where this was going and he was going to enjoy every minute of seeing her squirm her way through it.

"What about a demon's tongue?"

"Is it—" Suzie faltered and swallowed, "is it true what they say?"

He arched an eyebrow. She punched him lightly on the arm.

"You're gonna make me spell it out, aren't you?" she grumbled.

Zach chuckled. "You started this, cupcake."

She glared and waved a hand vaguely. "What I mean is, can you do stuff with your tongue a normal human can't?"

Zach's face crunched up. He bit his lip hard, shoulders quaking with his mirth.

Suzie rolled her eyes and sighed heavily. "Well, can you or can't you?"

The smile he gave her was categorically criminal and had her pulse rocketing into the stratosphere. "If you mean have I got a snake's tongue, the answer is no. If you're asking if a demon's tongue is more...*malleable* than a human's, then the answer is yes."

"Shit," she mumbled hoarsely. Her sex throbbed, causing her hips to twitch and ride his thigh.

Zach cursed at the sinful friction. He tipped her head back, kissed her jawline, and worked his way hungrily down her throat. His demonic power washed over her in a wave of tantalizing sulfur.

Shackles of water formed out of thin air and bound her wrists above her head.

"Wait!" Suzie protested. "I want to—*ah!*" She arched into his touch as he palmed and kneaded and kissed her aching breasts. "I want to touch you!"

"Later." Zach flicked a nipple with his tongue and wrenched a moan from her mouth. "If you touch me right now, I won't be responsible for my actions."

Suzie shivered at the sensual threat lacing his thick words. She couldn't think of anything she wanted to see more than this demon losing control.

*Would he rut? Would he fuck me senseless everywhere I can be fucked? Would he keep going even if I beg him to stop and squeeze every drop of pleasure from my body?*

Tension spiraled through her at the primal imagery playing across her inner vision. Her pussy spasmed on the first wave of her climax.

Zach shuddered and lowered a hand to cup her sex. "Your scent. It just got stronger!" he growled.

She moaned at the intimate touch. He stroked her slick folds with his palm before working his fingers between them to her slit. She cried out when he thrust two digits inside her, her orgasm so swift it took her by complete surprise.

Zach held her close as she rode his fingers, her hips jerking and her body writhing with her convulsions. Her insides spasmed again and again around him while her sultry cries and gasps echoed across the bathroom.

It was a while before she relaxed against him, the tension oozing out of her until her limbs felt as thick as molasses. She emerged from the sweet havoc he'd wreaked upon her body and opened her eyes languidly, her thundering heart finally slowing down.

The demon's expression had her breath catching all over again. He nuzzled her cheek and pressed a soft kiss to her lips.

"I think I'm gonna get addicted to your O face," he confessed huskily.

Suzie flushed. "Not fair."

Heat flared deep inside her as she drew on her magic. She broke the bands of water holding her prisoner, twisted a startled Zach around, and slammed him against the wall.

"My turn."

He grinned as she explored his throat and his shoulders with her fingers and lips. Though the demon could easily overpower her, he stayed a willing prisoner under her curious touch. A shudder raced through him when she caressed his chest and squeezed his nipples. Suzie closed her teeth on one of his dark nubs and tugged.

Zach swore, hips jerking and thick cock stabbing her belly.

Suzie shivered when his sex pulsed against her skin. She lavished his flesh with loving bites and sucks and worked her way down his six pack. She danced her hands down his treasure trail and finally grasped his straining erection.

Suzie stilled, full of wonder at his silken heat and the defined map of veins under her fingertips.

"*Fuck!*" Zach hissed as she carefully explored him. He dropped his head back against the tiles and swallowed heavily.

The way he dug his nails into his palms told Suzie the demon was hanging on to his self-control by the barest thread. She probed his length and girth for a torturous minute, her fingers dipping to cup and test his heavy balls. Zach panted and groaned, precum pearling his flushed slit.

Suzie licked her lips as she stared at the musky

evidence of his pleasure, her pussy heavy and tingling and her heart racing all over again.

"I want to taste you." She dropped to her knees, opened her mouth, and swallowed the head of his swollen cock without waiting for his reply.

She might as well have let off a bomb the way Zach reacted. His hands found her hair in a painful grasp, his neck cording as tension rippled through him.

"I'm not gonna last long if you do that!" he said harshly.

She let go of his dick with a wet pop and scraped her nails lightly up and down his turgid shaft.

"That's the whole idea, Mr. Demon."

Zach groaned when he met her sultry gaze. "I can tell I'm going to have my hands full with you, Witch."

Suzie smiled, flicked her tongue across his leaking slit, and took him inside her mouth. The demon hissed and shuddered as she started blowing him slow and deep, her tongue slicking his throbbing flesh with her spit and his precum. He widened his stance, held her head in strong hands that trembled, and guided her to pleasure him just the way he liked it.

Suzie breathed through her nose and relaxed her jaw when Zach finally gave in to his instincts and started fucking her mouth with increasingly savage thrusts, his grip no longer gentle where he clutched her face, his grunts guttural with passion. She looked up and met his scorching gaze as she took him deeper, his cock sliding into the tight confines of her throat.

Zach's pupils flared. His lips curled back on a feral

expression. "I'm gonna fill you with my seed, Witch!" he growled.

Her fingers clenched on his thighs as he rutted with wild abandon, her lips sucking his pulsing flesh with every forceful push and pull of his hips. Zach threw his head back and gnashed his teeth, his balls twitching. He stiffened a moment later and exploded on her tongue and down her throat with a guttural shout.

Suzie swallowed and gulped his hot cum greedily, close to coming herself at his wondrous taste and his bewitching scent. She moaned, spread her thighs, and cupped her sex. She slicked her fingers with her juices and stroked the wet pads across her swollen clit, eager to release the tension building back up inside her body.

Zach pulled out of her mouth, yanked her to her feet, and pressed her back to the wall, his eyes wild. He was still ejaculating, his cock spurting out sticky strings of cum that splashed against her thigh.

"What—?!" Susan mumbled.

"Sorry," Zach said hoarsely. "I'll be coming for a while!"

She gasped when he lowered himself to his knees, grabbed the back of her thighs, and hooked her legs over his shoulders. Then his hands were stretching her folds open, his face was in her sex, and his mouth was on her clit.

She cried out as he sucked her throbbing flesh and ate her pussy, his clever tongue lashing her sensitive nub and throbbing opening with sensuous strokes that robbed her of her sanity. She came once. Twice. Three times.

Still he pleasured her, his fingers digging into her thighs and his pants full of hunger where he devoured her.

"Stop!" Suzie finally whimpered. Her toes clenched in mid-air as an exquisite tingling spread through every inch of her body, setting her nerve endings on fire. "I—I can't anymore!"

Zach paused and licked his lips. "Not enough." His gaze grew hooded as he traced her slit with his tongue, drawing a broken moan from her. "I haven't had enough of you yet!"

Suzie stiffened when he spread her open and pushed his tongue inside her. Her mouth rounded on a shocked "*Oh!*"

She clutched his head and gasped when she felt him thicken and lengthen.

Zach unleashed his demonic power and secured her wrists above her head once more as he started thrusting in and out of her sex.

"Oh God! That's—! Yes! *Yes!*" Suzie panted.

She squeezed her eyes shut so she could focus her entire being on where the demon was fucking her with his tongue. Something hot and silky flicked her nipples and danced across her quivering belly. She blinked her eyes open and shivered at what she saw. Bands of water teased and aroused her aching flesh, the manifestations morphing to translucent fingers and hands that mimicked Zach's touch.

Her eyes flared when his tongue grew stouter and longer still, stretching her even wider. "*Zach!*"

He met her startled gaze and carried on fucking

her, his pupils glowing a deep vermilion, his tongue repeatedly scrapping her G-spot.

Tension coiled through Suzie, languorous waves of pleasure that ebbed and flowed with every sinful movement of his tongue deep inside her, so deep she felt him caress her womb. Blood roared in her ears.

She lost track of time. Of space. Of self.

Her orgasm when it came shattered her into a million pieces. The world went a blistering white, the only sounds piercing the blinding haze her own thumping heartbeat and her distant scream of ecstasy. She felt Zach withdraw from her body at some point and whimpered when her insides clung hungrily to him.

The next thing she knew he was washing her hair and body, his touch tender and his lips raining soft kisses over her face. She finally found her voice after he finished showering and was patting them both dry with a towel, her racing pulse now a steady thrum.

"I think I kinda had an out of body experience back there," Suzie mumbled.

Zach grinned. "You mean you came so hard you passed out?"

She shook her head numbly. "Seriously, I heard angels sing, saw the pearly gates, even got a whiff of ambrosia."

The demon chuckled. "I would stay away from those Greek gods if I were you. Besides, we only just got started."

Her gaze found his thickening cock. She swallowed, her interest perked once more. "I can see that. By the way, what was that earlier?" She met his confused gaze and chewed her lip. "You came for a long time."

"I guess it's not common knowledge among humans," Zach drawled, "but demons can ejaculate for over a minute when they have strong orgasms."

"Oh." Suzie blinked. Somehow, this revelation was making her sex throb all over again. "Wait. Does this mean I rocked your world just now?"

"Yup, you did." Zach tipped her chin with a knuckle and dropped a kiss on her nose, still amused. "Want a snack?"

She stared. "Are you being literal or figurative?"

He laughed. "As much as I enjoyed having you *eat* me, I actually meant food. You're gonna need more energy before we continue."

Suzie flushed. She got the added bonus of seeing the demon buck naked in her kitchen while he made them pastrami sandwiches. They kissed, flirted, and retired to the mezzanine with loaded plates and a bottle of beer each.

Sitting in her bed eating and chatting about inconsequential things was never a scenario she'd ever have envisaged when she'd thought about spending the night with Zach. Suzie's chest tightened a little at how easily their conversation flowed and how natural it felt to have him lying in her bed and feeding her chunks of meat and bread.

Desire soon thickened the air between them. Zach wiped a trace of mustard from her lip, licked his thumb, and took her plate from her hand. Her breath caught at the flash of crimson in his pupils and his sulfurous scent when he turned to place their plates on the floor. The sheet shifted on his groin, revealing his straining erection. Her mouth went dry as she scanned his thick length, not quite believing she'd taken him in her mouth. Heat pooled between her thighs. Her sex throbbed and grew heavy with an ache only he could assuage.

Zach grasped her ankles and tugged her down the bed until she lay flat on her back. He braced her hips with his knees and her shoulders with his hands before raking her body with a torrid gaze. He closed his eyes and angled his head, his nostrils flaring as he caught the scent of her arousal.

"So goddamn sweet." His eyes pinned her to the bed when he opened them once more, the hunger in the crimson depths sending a shiver of need down her spine. "I could smell and taste you for hours."

Suzie's pulse stuttered when he took a bottle of beer from the nightstand and tipped it over her body. She gasped as cold liquid splashed onto her chest and trickled down her belly. It pooled in her navel before trailing farther south, soaking into her soft fuzz and oozing through her silken folds. Zach leaned down and carefully licked her breasts clean before laving her nipples with his clever tongue.

The demon took his sweet time working his way along the wet trail he'd created, his fingers steady as he touched and caressed every inch of her, his attention one hundred percent focused on driving her out of her mind.

By the time he laid face down on the bed and

pushed her thighs open, Suzie was a moaning, whimpering mess. Her fingers clenched in the sheets above her head as he parted her folds and traced her slit with his tongue. His breath danced teasingly across her swollen clit.

He blew out a puff of hot air over her sensitive flesh.

Suzie let out a guttural sound, heels digging into the bed and hips jerking at the exquisite sensation. Zach growled in approval and repeated his torturous ministration. It wasn't until she was begging and writhing fitfully beneath him that he finally relented and gave her what she was asking for.

She came at the first flick of his tongue.

Zach pinned her hips with his strong hands and continued sucking and licking her as she convulsed, her sex drenching his lips with the evidence of her climax. He slipped three fingers inside her spasming passage, ate her clit, and finger fucked her pussy through a second then a third climax.

By the time he rose on his knees and slipped a condom over his shuddering length, the bedroom was drenched in a thick spoor of sulfur and the musky scent of her orgasms. A sheen of sweat covered Suzie's face and body as she met Zach's hooded gaze, her flesh tingling and her heart racing faster still at what was still to come.

The demon sat back on his heels, grabbed her calves, and tugged her close. He slipped a pillow under her back and angled her hips so her slit was poised at the perfect angle to take his cock. Suzie whimpered when he spread her legs and lifted them high up in the air.

Zach leaned forward, braced the back of her calves with his shoulders, and stretched her even wider. Her breaths shuddered in and out of her lungs as he stilled and studied her where she lay open and trembling beneath him, his gaze simmering with a banked heat that would soon explode and consume her.

She should have felt embarrassed at the vulnerable way he'd positioned her, like a sacrificial virgin about to have her body plundered by a hungry deity. Yet, she couldn't help but feel powerful beneath his torrid stare.

She was the reason he was so hot and hard.

She was the reason he was slowly losing his mind to lust.

She was the reason a demon as powerful as him was about to let go of his iron self-control and rut to his heart's content.

"Zach," she whispered.

He shivered and leaned down to take her mouth in a blistering kiss before nudging his cock through her opening. Suzie gasped at the thickness of his penetration, his shaft stretching her entrance with exquisite tension.

Zach froze and gnashed his teeth when she squeezed him lightly.

"Fuck! If you do that—!" He groaned and dropped his head.

A bead of sweat dripped off his nose and splashed onto the base of her throat.

"I can't help it," Suzie whimpered, her heart

slamming against her ribs. She clenched again and drew another curse from his lips. "More! I want more of you!"

A savage sound left the demon. He grabbed the back of her ankles, stretched her legs straight and wide, and rolled his hips in shallow thrusts, his gaze scorching her like she knew it would as he sank into her body

Suzie hissed and fisted her hands in the sheets, her sex throbbing and expanding to accommodate his impossible girth. He entered her inch by rock solid inch until he was in to the hilt and filling her to the brim.

They stilled and gazed hotly at one another, their chests heaving with their pants while their bodies savored this first mating.

"You okay?" Zach asked huskily.

Suzie nodded tremulously.

"It doesn't hurt?" the demon asked insistently. He rocked his hips gently.

She swallowed, too overwhelmed to fully describe what it felt like to be possessed by him. Though it seemed like he would split her in two, her body had adapted to his size as if she'd been made to fit him.

"It aches."

A muscle jumped in his jawline. He frowned and started to pull out. "I'm sorry, I'll—"

Suzie grabbed his hips to still his motion and shook her head vehemently. "It aches because I want more! Move, Zach! I want to feel you even more!"

Zach's nostrils flared. He growled and flexed his hips.

"Oh! *Oh yes!* Just like—" Suzie stiffened, her eyes rounding in shock. "I'm gonna—*oh God I'm gonna—!*"

He swallowed her scream as she shattered around him, her insides pulsing violently and sucking his flesh even deeper. Suzie shivered and shuddered, her mind numb and her fingers clenching on Zach's hips until her knuckles blanched. He thrust through her convulsions, his grunts warming her neck as he buried his face in her throat.

"Suzie! Suzie!"

She gasped when he suddenly straightened and pulled her up with him. He sat back on his heels, hooked her arms across his shoulders and locked her legs around his waist. His hands found her ass as he pumped his cock hard and deep inside her, his mouth blindly seeking her lips, his breaths coming in labored pants.

Suzie melded their tongues together and felt the first wave of yet another orgasm tickle her nerve endings. They fucked with a carnal hunger that shook her to the core. A hunger that would not be quenched.

She had never had sex like this. So raw. So primal. So...*animal.*

She knew then that no man could ever satisfy her like Zach could. That no one could teach her so much about her own body in a single night like he was doing at this very minute.

Her passage grew tighter and slicker, her sex

clinging to his thick rod as he pounded her pussy, his flesh slapping wetly against her aching flesh.

Zach's fingers dug painfully into her ass cheeks as he neared his climax. His movements grew uncontrolled. Coarse grunts left him as he sank his teeth in her shoulder and rutted wildly, his powerful hips lifting her off the bed with every frenzied thrust.

He cursed and groaned before stiffening.

Suzie felt his cock swell and pulse deep inside her as he twitched and ejaculated. She suddenly wished he hadn't worn a condom.

What would it feel like if he spilled his scalding seed inside her sex just like he had done in her mouth?

His release lasted a long time. Suzie shuddered when the demon finally relaxed against her.

Zach was still hard.

He dropped his face in the crook of her neck. "Sorry, I don't think I can stop."

He proved his words with a sinful roll of his hips.

She gasped as his cock plundered her tingling sex.

"Then don't." She grasped his face and kissed him.

Zach groaned. He pulled out carefully and discarded the used condom. Suzie's stomach clenched as he went to grab a second foil from the nightstand. She took hold of his wrist. He gave her a puzzled look.

"I'd rather you didn't use that," she said quietly.

His pupils flared. "What?"

She flushed. "I'm on the pill. And it's the wrong time of my cycle."

Line furrowed Zach's brow.

"I'm clean if that's what you're worried about."

He shook his head. "It's not that." He cupped her chin and pressed a soft kiss to her lips. "Demon seed can hurt a human."

Suzie stared. "Hurt? How?"

Zach grimaced. "Most women say the orgasm it gives them is too strong."

Her pussy pulsed a flood of hot wetness between her thighs. "You're kidding, right?!"

"I am not," Zach said solemnly. "And before you ask, it's different from a blow job," he added just as she opened her mouth to voice that very question.

"Why isn't this common knowledge?" she mumbled.

He shrugged. "Because demons choose not to sleep with human females if they can avoid it. And if they do, they always use protection."

Suzie swallowed, her pulse pounding. Her gaze dropped to his erection. "What if I really want it?"

Zach narrowed his eyes. "Did you just drool a little?"

She wiped her mouth distractedly with the back of her hand, her eyes locked on his dick as if it were the Holy Grail. "What if I want it so bad I'm willing to beg?"

Zach groaned. "Are you listening to yourself right now?"

"Not really." She traced the demon's weeping slit with a finger.

He cursed and jerked his hips.

Suzie licked the silken liquid she found there and grinned salaciously. "Let's do it." She pushed Zach down on the bed and mounted him.

"I really don't think this is a good idea," he said in a strangled voice. "You passed out when I tongued you—"

She fixed him with a stern stare and deliberately rubbed her slick slit along the back of his throbbing cock. "Dear Mr. Demon, this witch demands to be filled to the brim with your pleasurable seed."

Zach shivered. Redness exploded in his pupils. Suzie gasped when he grasped her hips and raised her above his turgid cock. Her breath locked in her throat as he impaled her in a single, savage thrust. She exhaled a guttural sound, her sex pulsing and stretching around the demon's impossibly hot, bare shaft.

"Don't say I didn't warn you!" he growled.

Her only reply was to brace her hands on his chest and rock her hips, her body moving instinctively into the beginning of a dance that was as old as time. Zach hissed, his belly clenching with tension as she started riding him. He stroked her waist and raised his hands to knead her lush breasts, his fingers teasing and tugging her nipples.

Suzie's breath caught again and again as she danced up and down Zach's cock, every stab of his thick length eliciting the most exquisite feeling inside her sex as she grasped him with her heat.

"You feel so good," Zach grunted. "*Fuck!* Your pussy is so hot and tight!" He clenched his fingers on her ass and started thrusting up while she rose and fell with wild abandon, her breasts swaying and her lips parted on sensual cries.

The bed rocked as they rutted with increasing

savagery, the sounds they made feral. Pleasure sparked down Suzie's spine. The way Zach's hips jerked and his neck corded told her he was about to crest the same wave.

Tension tightened every muscle in Suzie's body as she met the demon's scarlet gaze, the pulses of fire in his pupils matching their sinful mating and the wild beat of their hearts.

A white haze filled Suzie's world as she tumbled into an oblivion filled with scalding pleasure, her sex clenching so tight she feared she would strangle Zach's shaft. She heard his guttural cry a moment before his seed gushed against the entrance of her womb.

Fire filled Suzie's body, a violent eruption that began in her convulsing passage and wreaked havoc upon her senses. The ecstasy storming her insides robbed her of breath as it deepened and stretched into a never-ending ocean of the most exquisite sensations.

She wasn't sure how long her orgasm lasted. All she knew was that Zach held her tightly throughout it, his cock pulsing strong and deep as he continued to ejaculate inside her.

Suzie came to sometime later and found Zach's gently stroking her damp cheeks with his fingers. She was lying in his arms, her ribcage shuddering as she tried to draw oxygen into her starving lungs.

"Did I pass out again?" she panted.

"You cried," Zach murmured, his expression contrite.

Suzie grabbed his fingers and pressed a shaky kiss to his palm. "In pleasure," she said adamantly.

Zach frowned. "You looked like you were in pain." He grimaced. "I mean, at one point, I thought your pussy was going to bite my dick off."

She chewed her lip guiltily. "That was also in pleasure."

"Are you sure?" the demon said suspiciously.

She nodded and snuggled closer to him. "Demon seed is magic."

Zach's lips twitched.

"How about we go another round and I prove it to you?" she said brazenly.

Zach sobered. "You're kidding right?"

He danced a hand down her body and dipped his fingers inside her wet pussy. She moaned at the slight soreness.

"You're still full of my cum." His pupils reddened, his voice growing heavy.

"Do that again," she breathed.

Zach arched an eyebrow. "Like this?"

He thrust back inside.

"Whoa!" Suzie gasped. "I'm all tingly still!"

Zach groaned and pressed his forehead against hers. "You're gonna be the death of me, you know that, right?"

She squirmed encouragingly against his hand. "They do call sex the little death."

"I feel like I'm gonna need stamina pills," Zach mumbled.

She grasped the solid rod of his erection where it dug into her hip and gave it a playful tug. "Your stamina looks pretty good to me, Mr. Demon."

"How about I make us another sandwich?"

Suzie pursed her lips and grabbed Zach's face. "Listen pal, are you trying to distract me? Because, I assure you, the only thing this witch is craving is one demon's fabulous cock, capiche?!"

She squeezed his fingers with her pussy.

He cursed and rolled her onto her back. "Surely, you mean one fabulous demon's dick, right?" He settled in the cradle of her body, passion staining his cheekbones a dull pink.

"Sure, whatever you say." She angled her hips and hooked her legs around his waist, her belly quaking in anticipation.

"I'm starting to feel like you just want me for my body," Zach said testily as he positioned the head of his cock against her quivering slit.

"Your body. Your dick. Your tongue," she mumbled. "I like everything about you! Now hurry up and enter me!"

They both groaned as he did just that, his shaft sinking into her slick sex with more ease than it had done before.

"How about my mind and my dazzling personality?" Zach gasped. Sweat beaded his nose as he bowed his back and started thrusting.

Suzie moaned and clenched around his rigid length. "I like those too!"

She hooked her arms around his shoulders and sought his mouth frantically, her pelvis tilting up and down to match his pumping motion.

Zach obliged and fused their lips together. "And my

heart and soul?" he murmured after delivering a blistering kiss that made her see stars.

Suzie's chest tightened at what she read in his beautiful eyes.

"I love those too," she breathed.

He stilled and held her gaze for a moment, somewhat stunned. "You do?"

She bit her lip and nodded tremulously.

Zach blinked. "Oh." He gave her a goofy smile.

"Zach?" Suzie said after a breathless moment.

"Yeah?"

"Move." She sucked in air as he grinned and complied with her request, his movements growing energetic. "Oh! Yes! *Just like that!*"

THE END

# ENCHANT

AVA MARIE SALINGER

# ENCHANT

JASPER COBB HISSED AS REUBEN FLETCHER THRUST inside him, his ass stretching slickly to accommodate his lover's thick cock. Reuben's fingers were locked tight on Jasper's head, grasping his hair in a punishing grip that had his neck and spine arching at a delicious angle where they knelt on the bed. Not that he minded the ruthless way the angel was claiming him.

Despite his puritanical image and his lofty status as the director of the San Francisco branch of the Order of Rosen, the organization of angels allied with the Catholic Church, Reuben was in no way a straitlaced creature when it came to the bedroom. Theirs was a relationship based on mutual trust and respect, and one hundred percent wicked sexual gratification.

Jasper wouldn't have it any other way and he knew Reuben wouldn't either, regardless of the prudish outward appearance the angel chose to project upon the world of man.

When Reuben called, Jasper came. And when Jasper

needed a savage fuck, Reuben delivered. Though they'd both agreed they could date other people when they'd first become sex friends, Jasper's gaze had never strayed to another since that time, just as he knew Reuben had remained true to him. Which was saying something considering angels and demons had no qualms having several bed partners at any one time. Their races had never been one for serial monogamy, not even before the Fall.

Jasper's muddled thoughts scattered to the four winds as Reuben possessed him the way he loved to be taken. Hard and rough and fast, the exquisite ache that accompanied Reuben's ardent penetration only serving to heighten the mind-numbing pleasure pooling in his belly. His hand found his aching cock where it bobbed against his stomach, his body jerking with every hard pump of the hips pistoning against his ass.

Reuben tightened his hold on his hair, a warning not to touch himself. Jasper bit his lip and slowly lowered his hand to the bed, knowing his orgasm would be all the more powerful if he obeyed Reuben.

*If I'd known this fucker was such a control freak, I would have had second thoughts when he'd approached me.*

"Focus, Jasper." Reuben's hand bit into the demon's waist where he held him steady. His thrusting hips slowed to a stop, the savage pounding Jasper had been thoroughly enjoying abating with a suddenness that had a whimper of protest falling from his lips.

*Make that third thoughts!*

The demon gnashed his teeth in frustration, his hands fisting in the satin sheets beneath them. His passage spasmed around Reuben's shaft, his climax so close he could taste it.

"Move!" Jasper bit out.

Reuben yanked his head back until his neck tendons corded and ached.

"What's the magic word?" the angel whispered in Jasper's ear before sinking his teeth in his lobe.

Jasper cursed, cum shooting out of his dick at the pleasurable sting. His hole clenched around Reuben where the angel filled him to the brim. The way Reuben shuddered told the demon he was close to losing his composure too.

"Say it, Jasper," the angel ordered in a hard voice.

"I swear to the Nine Hells, I'm gonna kill you when we're done this time!" Jasper snarled.

Reuben ignored his threat. "I want the word, demon." His breath coasted his nape a second before he bit him with enough strength to bruise his flesh.

Jasper gasped and jerked at the sharp prick of the angel's teeth. He inhaled raggedly, body close to exploding from ramped up sexual tension. There was only one way he would obtain the release he craved.

"Please," he whispered.

He closed his eyes, hating how his voice sounded.

Like he couldn't do without the angel. Like he needed him so badly he was willing to beg for his pleasure.

Reuben stilled at Jasper's softly spoken plea. "That's a good demon."

For a second, Jasper thought he felt the angel's lips ghost lovingly across his back as he relaxed his commanding hold on his hair. Then there was no more time to think. All he could do was feel as Reuben clutched his hips, hitched his ass higher, and resumed their fierce mating dance. His every thrust ground the broad head of his dick against Jasper's prostate and sent pulses of red-hot ecstasy rocking through his soul core.

The pulses expanded. Merged. Became a sea of violent sensations.

The demon came on a guttural cry, his vision exploding with bright sparks as he ejaculated with untamed force, his belly clenching so tight he gasped at his twinging muscles. Reuben rutted against him, mouth open on husky groans and grunts, the bed rocking under his powerful thrusts. He reached around Jasper's body and clasped his pulsing cock.

Jasper moaned out a protest, head drooping forward. A demon's release was longer than any otherworldly's when they were overwhelmed by pleasure, their ejaculation sometimes lasting well over a minute. He was at his most sensitive right now and couldn't endure being touched.

*This asshole!*

Sweat dripped from his face as he looked down the length of his body to where Reuben's fingers moved skillfully on his aching flesh, the sight of his lover's large hand stroking him to a fresh erection almost too much to bear.

Reuben knew just how to touch Jasper to make him hard in seconds.

The angel brought Jasper to another soul searing

orgasm before he finally climaxed, his cum flooding Jasper's back passage in sharp spurts until it spilled over and trickled down his thighs in hot, sticky strings. The musky scent had Jasper's head spinning as they both twitched and jerked with aftershocks of pleasure.

They collapsed on the bed a moment later, limbs tangled and chests heaving with their ragged breathing, the angel's heavy weight a comforting pressure on Jasper's back as he stretched their arms above their heads.

Reuben pressed a soft kiss on Jasper's left shoulder. "I thought you said you were gonna kill me after we were done."

"I'm still thinking about it," Jasper panted when he could speak again, too sated to move.

Reuben chuckled, the vibrations shaking his chest where it warmed Jasper's back and causing his cock to shift enticingly inside his ass.

"You realize you say that every time we fuck, right?"

"Shut up," the demon grumbled.

He bit back a protest when Reuben pulled out of him and climbed off the bed, secretly wishing the intimate moment would last longer. Reuben returned with a couple of cool, damp towels. He rolled Jasper on his back and proceeded to clean him intimately.

Jasper stiffened a little before surrendering to the angel's attentive ministrations. Though they'd been together for two years, it still surprised him when Reuben treated him so warmly after the act of sex.

The angel was the first lover he'd had who'd ever acted this way.

The demon's face tightened, irritation shooting through him. He hated the feelings Reuben evoked in him at times like this. Hated the angel's kindness. His tenderness. It made Jasper feel weak and vulnerable, emotions he refused to assign to himself.

They were both fierce warriors who had shed lakes of blood in the millennia of their existences, Reuben in the Heavens and Jasper in the Hells.

Love. Affection. Devotion.

Those words shouldn't exist in their vocabulary.

Jasper folded his arms behind his head and watched his lover from hooded eyes, vexed still at the unwanted fondness he felt for the angel.

"What?" Reuben's touch raised sparks on Jasper's skin as he wiped his body clean of sweat. He arched an eyebrow. "You like seeing me take care of you?"

A cruel smile twisted Jasper's mouth. "I like seeing you at my feet, where you belong." He pressed his foot against Reuben's chest.

Reuben's eyes darkened with a nameless emotion. He danced a hand down Jasper's thigh and around the back of his calf, causing the demon to tense and twitch.

Jasper's breath caught when Reuben took a hold of his ankle and lifted his foot so he could kiss his toes. A hot feeling tightened the demon's chest. One he wished to deny. Words of protest crowded the back of his throat.

The look Reuben gave him strangled them.

"Don't." Jasper tugged his foot from Reuben's grasp, his brow furrowing in a heavy frown.

Reuben held fast. "Don't what?"

"Don't say it!" Jasper growled.

Reuben sighed. "It's been two years, Jas. You know how I feel about you. When are you finally going to admit that you love me too?"

Jasper's heart stuttered at the angel's confession and question. It wasn't the first time he'd said those words and it wouldn't be the last. Still, he couldn't bear it when Reuben got like this. All solemn and inflexible, like a Stark Steel blade that would never yield. It wasn't what he'd signed up for when Reuben first approached him and asked him to come to his place. He remained mute, knowing Reuben would take his silence for what it was.

A rejection of his feelings.

The expression that flitted across the angel's face as he rose to go in the bathroom had Jasper's stomach clenching on a wave of self-loathing. Reuben looked resigned, like he hadn't actually expected an answer.

It made Jasper want to rage at him.

He knew he was being an asshole. He'd proven that enough even before he became the director of the San Francisco branch of Cabalista, his legendary temper and tendency to shoot first and ask questions later earning him an unsavory reputation over the last few hundred years.

Still, it was his skills as a warrior and his ability to lead the men and women in his charge even under the most harrowing of circumstances that had allowed him to climb the pecking order of the organizations that had formed to govern the Fallen and the human magic users who had flourished during the Hundred Year War.

Despite his achievements, Jasper was aware he likely owed his position as bureau director to Victor Sloan. The Fiery demon and head of Cabalista was an old friend who had always supported him over the centuries. Jasper wasn't anywhere as good at playing politics as Victor was. The few times he'd attended formal functions to mingle with those in power had ended with him sporting a hungover from the Nine Hells and having to live with Victor's teasing for days on end. Still, he knew Victor had likely pulled some strings to get him the job in San Francisco.

Jasper's heart twinged a little as Victor's face swam before his eyes, his unrequited affection for the powerful demon a sore that had festered too long in his soul. To his surprise, the pain and bitterness he always experienced when he thought of the man he could never have had all but abated as of late.

He'd wondered if it was because Victor had finally broken up with Cassius Black, the angel who had held the Fiery's attention ever since the Fall and the only man Victor had had a long-term relationship with.

Shunned by humans and the Fallen alike for the ominous color of his wings, Cassius was someone Jasper had loathed at first sight. He'd known at their very first meeting that he'd won Victor Sloan's heart without even trying. Jasper could only watch with helpless impotence as Victor fell deeper and deeper in love and in lust with the beguiling angel over the centuries that followed.

It didn't help that Cassius's quiet strength and calm demeanor were the completely opposite of Jasper's smart mouth and brash attitude. They were like oil and water, never meant to mix and best kept apart.

Still, Cassius was now technically his and Reuben's ally. The dark-winged angel had relocated to San Francisco a couple of months back and had almost immediately become embroiled in a battle with far reaching consequences for humans and Fallen alike. Though Jasper still resented the angel to some extent, Cassius had more than proven himself when they'd fought alongside one another to handle a threat that had almost ripped open the Nether once more.

Jasper and Cassius would never be best friends, but he could at least tolerate the angel's presence now.

"A penny for your thoughts?"

Reuben's voice stirred him from his gloomy ponderings. His lover had finished showering and was getting dressed.

"It's gonna cost you more than a penny for me to tell you what I'm thinking about," Jasper grumbled. He glanced at the clock on the nightstand. "Aren't you gonna be late for your meeting?"

"No." Reuben leaned across the bed and dropped a kiss on Jasper's mouth. "I'm never late for my meetings. And you didn't answer my question."

Jasper narrowed his eyes a little.

*He's not thinking about flying over to his office, is he?*

Even though he was the director of the Order of Rosen, Reuben would still need special permission to use his wings in the absence of an emergency.

The angel smiled, as if he'd read Jasper's mind. "I'm a good driver."

Jasper grimaced. "I can't believe you said that with a straight face. You're a menace behind the wheel."

Reuben chuckled and pressed another kiss to his lips.

"I was thinking of Cassius," the demon mumbled.

Reuben's smile faded. "What about Cassius?" He straightened and crossed his arms across his chest, his brow furrowing.

Jasper stared, not quite sure what he was reading on his lover's face. His stomach flip-flopped. "Wait. Don't tell me you're jealous?"

Reuben's eyes shrank to slits. "I know he's not your type, so no."

Jasper raised an eyebrow, enjoying this game. "Who's my type?"

"I am."

Jasper choked at the angel's quiet arrogance. "Who the heck said you were my type, asshole?!" he spluttered.

"Your body did," Reuben said with a haughty smile. "Multiple times. In fact, your mouth, your dick, *and* your hole loudly proclaimed I was your type five times last night, never mind the two orgasms I just gave you." He headed into their closet and came out with cufflinks and a tie. "Plus, you said yes when I asked you to move in with me."

Jasper scowled. "We *moved* into a new place. Don't make it sound like I crawled into your cage." He watched Reuben fumble the cufflinks and tsk-tsked.

"Give it here." He climbed off the bed and padded over to the angel buck naked.

Reuben stilled and let him do up his cuffs. "You make a good wife."

Jasper punched him in the arm. "What the fuck do I see in you?!"

"Ouch." Reuben chuckled. "My dazzling smile and my charming personality?" He cocked an eyebrow. "Plus, you forget I have a dick that can satisfy your every need." He did his tie up and shrugged into his suit jacket while Jasper grumbled under his breath. "By the way, Brianna messaged me yesterday. She's meeting up with Galliad and the others at *Occulta* Saturday night. She said we should come."

Jasper's ill thoughts faded. "Everything got sorted with her daughter?" he asked gruffly as he adjusted the knot in Reuben's tie.

"Yeah. It's a shame we weren't around for the fight with that mage, but it looks like Brianna got plenty of help from Cassius and Morgan, as well as the Dryads."

Morgan King was Cassius's current lover and a powerful Aerial angel in his own right. As for Brianna Monroe, the director of the San Francisco Hexa bureau had been through a turbulent time lately, after her daughter Eden ran away from home and fell prey to a group of bloodcursed sorcerers led by a powerful mage. Jasper and Reuben had been away on business in Europe and had landed in San Francisco two days after the battle ended.

"We should go to *Occulta*. There's someone I want us to check out when we're there."

Jasper wasn't fooled by Reuben's light tone. He frowned at the angel's broad back as he walked out of their bedroom.

*This again?!*

☙

"You realize my daughter is still in high school, right?" Brianna Monroe ground out.

Cedric Esteban bobbed his head respectfully. "Of course. I am more than willing to wait until Eden is eighteen for us to formally wed. We shall call it an engagement for now."

Eden Monroe choked on air.

Charlie Lloyd smiled in his beer at their exchange.

It had been ten days since Argonaut and Hexa's showdown with *Ouroboros* and the Hartman sisters at an abandoned amusement park on the Pacific coast. News of the epic battle and the rumored rising of a new bloodcursed mage had already begun to filter through the grapevine that connected the agencies which governed the otherworldly and magic users in San Francisco.

"Twenty!" Brianna barked.

"Twenty-five," Malik Garcia snarled. "And after she graduates from college."

Eden spluttered, eyes rounding. The teenage bloodcursed mage looked like she wanted to dig a hole and crawl right into it. Charlie could sympathize. He had already had to stop himself from rolling his eyes half a dozen times.

"Well, this is a surprise," someone said coolly.

Charlie stiffened and looked over his shoulder.

Jasper Cobb and Reuben Fletcher stood next to their booth.

Jasper sneered at Morgan. "I heard you and Cassius got your asses handed to you by a mage and her sister."

"I see fake news spreads like wildfire," Morgan retorted nastily.

Reuben smiled. It didn't quite reach his eyes. "So, it isn't true?"

Morgan lowered his brows.

Irritation quickened Charlie's pulse. Though their paths had only crossed sporadically since he'd started working for Argonaut, Jasper and Reuben had always rubbed him the wrong way. There was something about them that set off his survival instincts, like prey in the presence of predators. Besides, he'd heard enough unsavory rumors about the two bureau directors to know he should steer clear of them.

Reuben glanced at him. A mysterious smile flitted across his face before his gaze shifted to Brianna.

Charlie stiffened. *What the hell?!*

Jasper and Reuben chatted briefly with the others before heading for the bar.

"I still can't believe those two are a couple," Julia Chen said.

"Reuben's a saint," Morgan muttered. His eyes found Charlie. A resolute expression hardened his face.

Charlie's stomach plummeted. He knew that look.

"Excuse me." He rose and beat a hasty retreat in the direction of the restroom before Morgan could speak.

Charlie knew the angel had been about to demand he take the Argonaut promotion exam to level up his status as a magic user. For reasons he couldn't fathom, his team seemed hell bent on him becoming a Level One enchanter.

They'd become even more zealous in their endeavors ever since he mastered the Altered Mind box they'd seized from Lucille Hartman and her black magic sorcerers. To Charlie's surprise, even Cassius had joined in their attempts to convince him he was more than capable to rise up the ranks.

*And there I thought he was the smartest one of all of us.* He sighed as he flushed the toilet. *Why do they think they know my own magic better than me?*

He came out of the stall, washed and dried his hands, and turned to find Reuben and Jasper blocking the exit. His pulse spiked.

There was no one else in the restroom except the three of them.

*Fuck. I didn't hear them come in.*

Charlie swallowed. He clenched his jaw in the next instant.

*Wait. Why am I letting these assholes intimidate me?*

"Could you move, please?" he said in a voice that came out more steady than he thought it would.

Jasper cast an irate look at Reuben. "I really don't know what goes through your head at times. He's not the solution to our problems."

Reuben's gaze stayed riveted to Charlie's face. "We don't have problems, Jasper. What we have is a unique situation. One I believe he fits perfectly."

Charlie's heart started to race. His instincts were telling him he should get the hell out of there.

"He's just a scared little kid, Reuben," Jasper grumbled. "And I feel no attraction to him whatsoever."

"That's because you've never seen the real him," Reuben murmured. "Or been close enough to smell him."

Charlie blinked. *What the hell are they talking about?!*

He lowered his brows. "I have no idea what's happening here, but I would appreciate it if you two would move your sorry asses so I can be on my merry way. Feel free to indulge into whatever this—" he waved a hand at them, "*this* is after I'm gone."

Jasper's eyes darkened at his derogatory tone. A hint of sulfur blasted out of him.

Heat bloomed in Charlie's core as he instinctively drew on his magic. He widened his stance and fisted his hands.

"Word of warning," he ground out. "I'm not as weak as you think I am!"

He hoped they didn't notice how hard his heart was pounding or that he was clenching his knuckles to stop his fingers from trembling.

Reuben's astute gaze told the enchanter he'd noticed all those things and more. "I don't think you're weak, Charlie. On the contrary. And we're not here to attack you. We have a...proposition for you."

"You mean, *you* have a proposition for him." Jasper raked Charlie with a disparaging gaze. "I have no interest in arrogant boys still suckling at their mother's tits."

Ire tightened Charlie's jawline. "Yeah, like *I'm* the arrogant fucker here, dipshit!"

Jasper blinked, shocked. Reuben coughed discreetly and masked a smile behind his hand.

Charlie cursed inwardly. Truth was, he wasn't anywhere the sweet, quiet guy Morgan and the rest of his team thought he was. Sure, he got along well with all of them, but there was one thing he tried real hard not to show them.

His true personality.

It pissed him to no end that Reuben and Jasper had managed to provoke him enough to demonstrate what a temperamental asshole he could be.

Reuben started toward Charlie.

Charlie stiffened and took a step back.

Reuben halted. "I'm not going to hurt you, Charlie."

Charlie swallowed, annoyed with himself at his reaction.

Though Reuben hadn't done anything to earn his distrust, he felt super self-conscious in his presence. His skin prickled when Reuben stopped in front of him. The angel had a few good inches on him and he had to tilt his head to meet his gaze.

His breath stuttered.

He'd never been this close to Reuben before. The angel's eyes weren't just blue. They were a stunning Aegean that reminded him of a tumultuous sea. And they were boring into him like they could see straight through his soul.

A slow heat coiled through Charlie's veins. His gaze dropped to Reuben's mouth.

His mind screamed *Danger!*

His body ignored it.

The angel's lips moved, forming words he barely heard above the rush of blood in his ears.

Charlie blinked dazedly. "What?"

Reuben's lips twitched in amusement. "I said, could I see your phone?"

Charlie had to think for a second. He fished his cell out of his back pocket, fumbled, and almost dropped it.

Jasper sneered. "Butter fingers."

"No one's talking to you, shithead," Charlie snapped.

The demon scowled. Charlie resisted the urge to stick his tongue out at him.

Reuben looked like he was enjoying their exchange. His fingers touched Charlie's when he took the device from him. Electricity lit Charlie's skin. A shiver of dread and excitement skittered down his spine.

Reuben pretended not to notice his blatant response to his touch and brought up his contact list. He typed in an address.

"Why don't you come over for a chat tomorrow night? Say six?"

He leaned in and slipped Charlie's phone in his back pocket, so close their chests brushed. Charlie's breath hitched as ozone and a smell he couldn't fathom flooded his nostrils. His cock twitched when Reuben's fingers skimmed his ass.

He exhaled shakily, arousal slamming into him hard.

Reuben grew deathly still. Jasper straightened

where he'd been leaning against the far wall, his gaze fastening on Charlie like a laser. Crimson flared in his dilating pupils.

Charlie froze.

He didn't need to be a genius to realize he now held Reuben and Jasper's undivided attention. And that the angel and the demon were staring at him like he was dessert.

His instincts screamed at him to run.

The air thickened with a delicious mix of ozone and sulfur. The scent locked Charlie's limbs in place and made his belly spasm on a wave of lust. He fisted his hands.

*What's happening to me?!*

Reuben lowered his head. His hot breath washed along Charlie's throat. Charlie trembled. He couldn't stop himself from tilting his chin to grant the angel access to his skin.

A low growl of approval rumbled from Reuben's chest. He inhaled deeply and shuddered. "Jesus, you smell divine!"

He moved, his lips a hairbreadth from Charlie's jawline.

Charlie's heart thundered as he met the angel's searing gaze. All he had to do was turn his head and their mouths would meet. His chest rose and fell heavily with his ragged breathing.

*This is crazy. I should push him away!*

Reuben's eyes darkened. "The feelings you have for Morgan will never be returned."

The angel's words jolted Charlie out of the lustful

spell he'd fallen under as effectively as a bucket of icy water. He recoiled, shock and anger rallying inside him. Reuben grasped the back of his head with a hand and his hip with the other, immobilizing him.

Charlie pressed his hands against the angel's chest, his face hot. "What the fuck do you mean?!"

He might as well have tried to move a mountain for all the effect he had on Reuben.

"One only needs to watch the way you look at Morgan to know you like him," Reuben observed.

Though the angel's words were cool, his touch was not. And it wasn't pity Charlie was reading in his eyes.

"Don't worry," Reuben murmured. "Only people who have an…interest in you would notice."

Charlie clenched his jaw. He couldn't deny Reuben's words. Not when the angel could so easily read him.

His feelings for Morgan were…complicated. He'd blamed them on a crush at first, certain the way his stomach fluttered and his pulse quickened whenever he was around the beguiling Aerial would soon be a thing of the past. Angels and demons were stunning creatures after all and many a human had fallen for their charms over the centuries since the Fall.

But when he started dreaming about Morgan. When he woke up with his bedsheets drenched in cum and his cock hard at the thought of the angel, he knew he was in trouble.

Because what he felt for Morgan wasn't simple lust. His desires were twisted. Dark. Perverse. They were so depraved he knew he would shock Morgan if he described every obscene sexual act he'd fantasized about over the years he'd known him.

He didn't just want Morgan to make love to him. He wanted to be possessed. To be dominated. To experience total, humbling submission. He wanted to be broken and made whole again. To hurt and to come so hard his mind would shatter and he wouldn't be able to think for hours. He wanted to be fucked raw and defiled in every way a man could desecrate another man.

"What I can offer you." Reuben glanced at Jasper. "What *we* can offer you, is something different. It won't be conventional by any means. But I think it will satisfy all of our mutual…needs."

Charlie's stomach fluttered at the banked heat in the angel's eyes. He stared, certain he knew what Reuben was saying but wanting him to spell it out nonetheless.

"I—what do you mean?"

Reuben saw through his lie. He brought his lips to his ear. "You know exactly what I mean, Charlie."

Charlie shuddered as the angel's hot breath skimmed his flesh.

Jasper approached. His nostrils flared and his head moved like he was scenting Charlie. The light in his eyes deepened to a rich vermillion. He walked around them, a predator stalking his prey.

Charlie trembled when he felt the demon at his back, his heat scorching him even though they weren't touching.

Jasper's breath ghosted his nape as he inhaled deeply. "Is this what you meant by he fits us?"

Reuben dipped his chin at the demon's low growl, his gaze still locked on Charlie's.

Confusion clouded Charlie's mind, dampening the insane hunger coursing through him. "What—what is he talking about?!"

Reuben raised a hand and stroked Charlie's lower lip with his thumb.

"He means your scent."

Charlie stilled, his attention captivated by Reuben's touch. His flesh tingled and throbbed, as if he'd stuck his finger in an electric socket.

"Did you know animals can pick out compatible mates by smell alone?" the angel said huskily.

Charlie blinked. *Mates?!*

"It's how demons and angels select humans to share their bed with." Reuben smiled tightly. "Not just any human will do, Charlie. So, how about I give you a taste of what could be yours?"

Charlie's eyes widened at his words. Then Reuben's mouth was on his.

Need. It stormed Charlie's senses, so sudden he shivered and gasped. Reuben explored his lips thoroughly before sweeping inside his mouth. Charlie moaned at the dizzying sensation of the angel's tongue lashing against his. His hands found Reuben's shoulders, his fingers digging in demandingly.

Jasper clasped Charlie's hips and pulled him against his body, chest to back, crotch to butt. Charlie panted when he felt the thick ridge of the demon's erection probe his cleft. Jasper tilted Charlie's neck to the side and went to town on the pulse beating frantically there with his mouth, his fingers roaming Charlie's ass and hips in exploratory sweeps before working their way up his sides to his chest.

Charlie's cock jerked out a sliver of precum as the angel and demon kissed and touched him with a possessiveness that scorched his sanity.

The scent of his arousal seemed to drive them crazy.

Their kisses became desperate. Their touch rough.

It was as if they wanted to rip him apart and consume his flesh.

And damn if Charlie didn't want them to do just that.

The angel and the demon's fingers met on his chest. His abs. His ass. A ragged moan danced up his throat when they pinched and tugged his nipples. Jasper worked his hardened nubs while Reuben dropped his hands lower. The angel trailed a finger down Charlie's erection and swallowed his cry with a passionate groan.

Then he was pushing them across the room to the wall.

Jasper grunted as he slammed back first in the tiled surface. His hands never left Charlie's body and neither did his lips. The sound of a buckle being undone and a zipper yanked down registered dimly on Charlie's dazed mind as the demon drove him out of his mind with his touch and mouth.

Cool air washed across his naked cock. It was replaced by the scalding depths of Reuben's mouth as the angel dropped to his knees and swallowed his erection in one fell swoop, his face taut with lust.

Charlie whimpered, overwhelmed by everything that was happening to him. He wasn't a virgin by any means. But this? This right here?

This was straight out of his filthiest fantasies. And it felt just as good as he'd thought it would.

*No!* His hips jerked as Reuben sucked his dick with powerful contractions of his jaw, the first wave of his orgasm dancing across his nerve endings. *This feels—Oh God! It feels ten times better!*

He weaved his fingers in Reuben's hair and started thrusting, helpless to stop his body's instincts to rut. The angel made an approving sound and caressed his twitching balls.

Jasper cupped Charlie's jaw and twisted his head to the side so he could take his lips. Charlie expected him to be rough. And he was, at the start. Then his mouth gentled. Softened. Grew probing.

Charlie trembled when he tasted sulfur on Jasper's tongue. There was something else there. A flavor he couldn't define. One that had his hand rising to clasp Jasper's hair so he could lock their mouths together and explore it to his heart's content.

The demon's hooded eyes turned to crimson pools that would devour him, just like his lips and tongue were threatening to swallow him whole. Gone was the scornful man who had insulted him earlier.

This demon wanted to fuck him, just like the angel whose mouth he was filling with his cock.

Sweat beaded Charlie's face as a savage tension tightened his spine. His thrusts became erratic, the slick sound of his cock sliding through Reuben's lips only serving to heighten his pleasure.

Jasper swallowed his shout when he went rigid and climaxed seconds later. Reuben gulped greedily, his tongue and lips lashing Charlie's dick hotly as he ejaculated in his mouth.

It took a while for awareness to return. Charlie panted heavily as he finally emerged from the blinding heights his orgasm had taken him to, his body twitching with aftershocks of pleasure.

*Did that—did that just happen?!*

One look at Reuben's satisfied expression and the hungry light in Jasper's eyes told him he hadn't imagined the mind numbing act they'd just performed together.

Someone banged on the restroom door, startling him.

"Hey, everything okay in there?"

"Ye—yeah!" Charlie said in a strangled voice. "Everything's peachy!"

"That was more than just peachy, kid," Jasper muttered against his neck.

Reuben rose, tucked Charlie's dick back in his pants, and zipped him up.

"Six o'clock tomorrow. I'll make dinner."

Then he and Jasper were gone. Charlie sagged

against the wall, his breathing still uneven. A couple of wizards came in, their gazes trailing over their shoulders as they watched the bureau directors leave. They halted when they saw Charlie.

One of them frowned. "You sure you're okay, kid?"

Charlie swallowed and nodded jerkily, too overcome with emotion to berate the man for calling him a kid. The wizard glanced at his companion and shrugged.

Charlie looked at the mirror filling the width of the wall to his right, wondering what it was about his expression that had given them cause for concern. His stomach flip-flopped.

His cheeks were flushed and his eyes wild. Blood pounded heavily in his veins and his tingling cock at the naked lust in his gaze.

He had the look of a man who'd just been thoroughly fucked.

Charlie raised a trembling hand to his swollen lips. He shivered.

The heat of Reuben and Jasper's kisses was still there.

It hadn't been a dream after all.

*I MUST BE CRAZY.*

Charlie rested his forehead on his knuckles where he clutched the steering wheel of his Volvo. The memory of last night's sensual encounter danced across his inner vision in graphic technicolor detail once more, like it had done a hundred times already since yesterday.

He still couldn't believe Reuben had blown him. Or that Jasper would likely have fucked him senseless if they hadn't been interrupted. Somehow, he sensed the demon wouldn't have been half as gentle as Reuben had been with him.

*And damn if that doesn't turn me on.*

Charlie looked accusingly at his erection.

He'd been in state of near permanent arousal since he'd left *Occulta* last night. Even masturbating several times hadn't relieved the restless ache in his belly and balls.

Which was why he was parked in a private garage beneath the exclusive Marina District apartment complex housing Reuben and Jasper's condo, about to walk in the lion's den like a meek, sacrificial lamb.

*Well, not entirely meek.*

He'd surmised from Reuben's words that the angel and the demon wanted to have a threesome with him. He was willing to grant them their wish, if only for one night.

Charlie took a shaky breath, climbed out of his car, and headed for the elevator before he could change his mind. He came out on the tenth floor and checked out the thick expanse of black carpet leading to the pair of imposing, gray double doors at the far end.

A wry grimace twisted his lips as he made his way over to them.

*Of course, their apartment takes up the entire top two floors of this building.*

His pulse quickened when he stopped in front of the condo. He wiped sweaty palms on his chinos and pressed the bell.

Jasper opened the door seconds later.

Charlie's mouth went dry.

The demon was wearing a teal shirt that matched his eyes, dark, faded jeans, and a scent that immediately sparked Charlie's nerve endings.

"What?" Jasper said suspiciously.

Charlie lowered his brows. "I was gonna tell you you look nice, but I guess I won't since you're being a dick." He barged past him and shoved the bottle of wine he'd brought in the startled demon's hands.

Jasper blinked. "Oh." He closed the door. "Er, thanks." His appreciative gaze skimmed Charlie's black shirt and cream chinos. "You scrub up nice yourself."

Charlie blinked. He pinched his own arm. "Ow."

Jasper stared at him like he'd lost his mind. "What the heck did you do that for?"

Charlie wrinkled his nose. "I wanted to check I wasn't dreaming just now."

Jasper's brows met. "You're a prickly little shit, aren't you?"

"Takes one to know one," Charlie retorted.

"Well, wonders will never cease," someone drawled.

Charlie looked around. Reuben was crossing the foyer barefoot. He wore a gray dress shirt that highlighted his fair hair and pale trousers that hugged long, powerful legs.

"I think that's the second time I've ever heard Jasper compliment someone," the angel said with a smile that made Charlie's pulse quicken.

The demon scowled at his lover. "Shut up."

"Dinner will be ready in a bit," Reuben said, unfazed. "Why don't you pour us some of that wine, Jas?"

Jasper grumbled and led the way through their condo, the tips of his ears reddening slightly at the pet name. Charlie bit his lip to stop himself from smiling. Somehow, dinner with the angel and the demon didn't seem half as daunting as it had been minutes ago.

He looked around curiously as he followed them. He'd imagined Reuben and Jasper's place to be austere and minimalistic. It was anything but. Though the apartment was built along clean, modern lines, the furnishings were rich and eclectic, the sophisticated color tones projecting a masculine warmth that made it clear the condo wasn't just a house but very much a home for the two powerful otherwordly who occupied it.

Charlie accepted the glass of wine Jasper offered him. "When did you guys move in here?"

"A year ago." Reuben cocked his head at Jasper. "It took some time to convince him it was a good idea for us to live together."

"Yeah, well, you're still on probation," the demon muttered, taking a sip of his wine.

Charlie couldn't help but study the strong column of his throat as he swallowed. He caught Reuben watching him and shifted his gaze, embarrassed.

"You can look all you want, Charlie," the angel said quietly.

Charlie stiffened. Jasper shot Reuben an ambivalent look.

Charlie became convinced then that this had all been Reuben's idea and that the demon was merely tagging along to indulge his lover. A pang of disappointment darted through him at that thought. He blinked, startled.

*Since when do I want this jackass's attention?*

The jackass arched an eyebrow as Charlie stared at him.

"Like what you see, kid?" he taunted.

"Bar that sassy mouth of yours, yeah, I like what I see, demon."

Jasper stilled at his blunt riposte. His pupils expanded, the dark depths filling with a crimson light.

The air thickened with sexual tension.

Reuben's chuckle broke the fraught moment. "How about we save that for after dessert?"

Charlie swallowed, able to breathe again.

Reuben's presence made him hyper aware. But Jasper's?

There was something about the demon that knotted his insides and scraped his nerves raw. He'd thought it was because he disliked him. But now, he wasn't so sure.

The two of them were alike. Much more alike than he'd ever care to admit.

"What are you making?" Charlie asked distractedly. He joined Reuben at the range.

"We're having foie gras with caramelized pears and a balsamic sauce for appetizers, and seared duck breasts with a cherry glaze and Belgian endives for our main course."

Charlie's mouth watered as he watched the angel put the finishing touches to a meal worthy of a Michelin star restaurant.

"Oh, and Jasper made chocolate truffle cake for dessert," Reuben added with a warm smile.

Charlie froze, his wine glass halfway to his lips. His wide-eyed gaze found the demon where the latter rested his hip against the counter next to Reuben.

"You bake?"

Jasper crossed his arms at Charlie's shocked tone. "Yeah, I bake. So what?"

Charlie bit his tongue.

Jasper scowled. "Are you laughing?"

"No," Charlie choked out.

Reuben's shoulders trembled.

"Stop it!" Jasper punched the angel lightly in the arm.

Charlie couldn't help himself. He burst out laughing.

The angel and the demon stared, surprised. Their expressions turned more heated as they watched him.

Charlie wiped his eyes. "What?"

Reuben cleared his throat. "Your scent. It seems it gets stronger when you experience a strong emotion."

Charlie sobered. "Oh." He squinted at them warily. "We're still eating, right?"

"We're not animals who can't control ourselves," Jasper scoffed.

Charlie's gaze dropped. He arched an eyebrow. "Your erection says otherwise."

"Let's eat," Reuben said brightly as Jasper narrowed his eyes.

The food was as delectable as Charlie thought it would be. Though a hint of sensual tension still danced between the three of them, they made light conversation as they ate. To his surprise, Charlie found the topics stimulating and he ended up talking far more than he normally would when in company.

It wasn't until they'd finished dessert and retired to the lounge with their coffees that Charlie finally remembered why he was there in the first place. He walked over to the glass wall spanning the length of the room and stared out at the bay to calm his nerves.

"This is some view," he muttered.

The Golden Gate Bridge rose to his left, its lights painting an orange glow across the dark waters beneath.

"It is," Reuben concurred.

The angel was sitting on a wine-red Chesterfield chair. Jasper perched on the armrest, a hand draped possessively across his lover's shoulder as they both watched Charlie.

Charlie's pulse quickened. He finished his drink, took the seat opposite them, and put his empty cup on a side table. He leaned his elbows on his knees and folded his hands together before taking a shallow breath.

"One night."

Reuben blinked. "Pardon?"

Charlie's fingers clenched. He forced himself to meet their stares unblinkingly. "If you want a threesome, I'll give you one night."

A strange look came over Jasper. He seemed almost…disappointed.

Reuben cocked his head to the side. "I think you're misunderstanding something, Charlie. What we want isn't just one night with you." He stroked Jasper's thigh.

Charlie's gaze focused on his long, strong fingers. He couldn't help but wonder how they would feel on his body.

It took a moment for the angel's words to register.

"What?" He blinked, his confused gaze swinging between the two men. "What do you mean?"

It was Reuben's turn to rest his elbows on his knees. He steepled his hands under his chin.

"We require something more…permanent."

Charlie flinched. "But—why?!" he blurted. "The two of you are perfect together. Why would you need a third person in your relationship?!"

Reuben stilled. Jasper's eyes widened.

"You think we're perfect?" the demon asked stiltedly.

"Well, yeah." Charlie waved a hand. "You're the grumpy asshole and he's the saint. You're salt, he's sugar. You complement one another, like a thorn does a rose."

Jasper's mouth thinned. "I don't know whether to thank you or smack you right now."

Reuben stayed quiet, his eyes full of a nameless emotion.

"I love Jasper," he finally admitted with a candidness that shocked Charlie. "And he loves me, however much he may deny it."

A muscle twitched in the demon's jawline. The angel ignored his vexed look.

"There's something he needs that I can't give him." Reuben paused. "Something we *both* need to make this relationship...perfect, like you say. We want to see if you're the third piece of our puzzle."

Charlie's heart pounded heavily against his ribs as he digested Reuben's words. He couldn't quite believe his ears. After all, what could he possibly offer them?

He didn't realize he'd said the words out loud until Reuben replied.

"You're someone who can tame Jasper's rough edges. Who can make him less scared of expressing the softer side of him. And his dominance."

Jasper recoiled as if he'd been slapped. "Wait! What do you—?!"

"You know what I mean, Jas," Reuben said in a tired voice. "I told you you could fuck me but you still refuse. It will take more than my mouth to satisfy your rut."

The demon opened his lips to voice a protest. He faltered and lapsed into a frustrated silence.

"As for me, I will gain pleasure from watching the two of you together," the angel told Charlie.

Charlie flushed. He was annoyed all of a sudden and he didn't even know why. "You mean, you won't participate? You just want to sit there like some kind of voyeur and look on as Jasper fucks me?!"

His anger wasn't lost on Reuben.

The angel smiled tightly. "Oh, I'll participate alright. In fact, I would like both of us to take you." He arched an eyebrow. "At the same time." He paused as Charlie drew a sharp breath. "That's if you're up to it, of course. We would never do anything without your consent."

Charlie's mouth dried. His hole clenched.

He'd never experienced a double penetration. The thought to taking two cocks inside his ass, let alone that of the angel and the demon before him, should have scared him senseless and had him bolting out of their apartment.

Yet he found he couldn't move. Didn't *want* to move.

What Reuben was suggesting and Jasper seemed very much on board with despite his wavering look from earlier was exactly the kind of sexual fantasies he'd indulged in. He knew instinctively that they would break him and satisfy him in ways he'd only ever dreamt of. That the pleasure and pain he would experience in their arms would soothe his hungry, twisted soul.

Charlie swallowed and closed his eyes.

*I must be certifiably insane to even be entertaining this— this craziness!*

He opened his eyes to find Reuben and Jasper watching him, bodies as still as stone. What he read on their faces had him voicing an answer he never thought he could give.

"Yes," he breathed. "I would like that too."

Reuben blew out a soft sigh. Jasper's hand clenched on the angel's shoulder, his eyes darkening with what looked like relief.

Charlie blinked. He hadn't realized they'd been so tense. It gave him a taste of the power he had over them. A power that made his cock throb and his ass ache.

"How about I start the show?" Reuben said.

Charlie stared, confused.

The angel raised a hand to the back of Jasper's head and brought him down for a kiss.

Charlie's cock immediately hardened as he watched the two men's mouths meet hungrily. Their scents swirled around him, mesmerizing currents that robbed him of the ability to form a coherent thought.

Jasper stood and started to strip. Fire lit the depths of his eyes as he locked gazes with Charlie.

Charlie's breathing accelerated when the demon was completely naked.

Jasper was beautiful. His golden skin was toned to perfection and his every muscle sharply defined, as if a God himself had sculpted his body into existence. The sight of his cock had Charlie swallowing a curse.

He was long and thick, the silky surface of his shaft ridged with veins that pulsed. Jasper flashed him a mocking smile, like he'd read his mind. He climbed on Reuben's lap and kissed the angel.

Blood pounded in Charlie's skull as he watched the two make out. Reuben's hands caressed and kneaded Jasper everywhere. His chest. His nipples. His abs. His back. His taut ass. His thighs. He knew exactly where to touch the demon to make him shiver and groan.

Reuben clasped Jasper's cock and started rubbing him briskly. Jasper cursed and dropped his face on his lover's shoulder, hips rolling powerfully to thrust his erection through the fingers pleasuring him. Reuben flashed a heated look at Charlie over Jasper's shoulder.

"Remember all his good spots."

Charlie swallowed and bobbed his head jerkily, his cock doing press-ups behind his zipper.

This was hands down the hottest thing he'd ever seen.

He knew now why Reuben wanted to watch Jasper fuck him. It was sexy and sinful and so titillating he could come just from looking at them.

Reuben slicked his fingers with Jasper's precum and dipped them inside his cleft. Charlie shuddered as the angel spread his lover's ass open, exposing his hole. Jasper arched and thrust his cock against Reuben's abdomen, making a mess of his shirt.

"Your fingers!" The demon clutched the back of the chair with his hands. "I want them inside me!" he ground out.

Reuben complied, like he'd been waiting for the rough command.

A buzzing sound filled Charlie's ears as he watched Reuben slip three fingers inside Jasper. The demon's hole swallowed the thick digits greedily. Shudders shook him as he started riding the angel's hand.

Reuben let him pleasure himself for a minute before taking his fingers out.

Charlie felt Jasper's moan of protest to his core.

The demon climbed off Reuben, like he was used to this game. The angel undid his zipper and freed his erection, color high on his cheekbones.

Charlie almost swallowed his tongue.

Reuben was even bigger than the demon.

"Turn around, Jas," he ordered silkily.

Jasper twisted on his heels. His pupils were scarlet pools of lust as he met Charlie's eyes, his lips parted on excited pants. He gave himself a few brisk rubs, his engorged cock dripping precum on the hardwood floor.

Reuben clasped Jasper's waist and sat him back down on his lap. He worked his large hands under the back of the demon's knees and lifted him over his dick.

An incoherent sound left Jasper as Reuben impaled him, the angel's thick shaft stretching his hole deliciously open until he was in to the hilt. Reuben buried his face in the side of Jasper's neck, his cheeks flushed and his eyes bright with desire. He sank his teeth in the demon's flesh and started thrusting.

Jasper clutched the arm rests with white-knuckled hands, his erection jerking and slapping against his belly as Reuben pounded his ass. His mouth opened on low, guttural grunts that raised goosebumps on Charlie's skin and sent a prickle of pure need down his spine.

Charlie couldn't look away from the wicked act being performed before him. From Reuben's hard length ramming Jasper's body. From the demon's spasming entrance and his proud, leaking erection. Lust twisted his belly.

He wanted it to be him. He wanted to be the one being fucked right now.

Jasper. Reuben. Both of them. He didn't care.

He just yearned to be filled to the brim and taken hard and fast until he screamed in pain and pleasure.

Charlie palmed his erection through his chinos and bit his lip hard when he felt the slickness of his precum. He was soaking wet.

Jasper's glazed eyes found his. Even Reuben stared at Charlie as he fucked the demon, the seraphic glow lighting his pupils pulsing with every roll of his hips.

Charlie was on his feet before he realized what he was doing. He closed the distance to the two men in a couple of strides, clutched Jasper's face, and leaned down to kiss him.

Jasper groaned. His gaze grew hooded as Charlie pushed inside his mouth. He welcomed him with relish, his pants of pleasure washing over Charlie's tongue.

"Touch him," Reuben ordered, voice thick and slurred with passion.

Charlie ran his hands down Jasper's throat to his chest. He wrenched his mouth free, dropped to his knees, and sucked Jasper's right nipple in his mouth.

Jasper stiffened. His breath hitched and his head dropped back against Reuben's shoulder.

Charlie lavished the demon's hard nubs with his fingers and lips and tongue and teeth before working his way down his six-pack and his quivering abs. The musky scent of Jasper's precum filled his nostrils as he drew level with his throbbing cock. He trailed his nails up and down the demon's twitching shaft and flicked the leaking slit with the tip of his tongue.

Jasper jerked. "Fuck!"

Charlie took his time exploring his length before taking him in his mouth. He wrapped his tongue along the demon's impossible girth and started sucking, his heart pounding and his own dick so full and tight he felt he would explode at any second.

Jasper moaned and gasped as he was thoroughly pleasured front and back. Charlie's jaws ached as he swallowed the demon steadily into the velvety depths of his throat. Jasper smelled like sin and tasted like Heaven, his precum so intoxicating Charlie could happily suck him for days.

Reuben's fingers bit into the demon's thighs as he accelerated his thrusts.

Charlie matched him beat for beat, his head bobbing aggressively as he deep-throated Jasper.

Jasper grasped Charlie's hair. "I'm gonna come!"

Charlie resisted the demon's attempt to pull him off.

"He can take it, Jas." Reuben's gaze met Charlie's. "Just come."

"But he doesn't know—!" Jasper's breath locked as Charlie cupped his trembling balls and squeezed.

His mouth opened on a silent scream as he climaxed.

Charlie gulped and swallowed the hot cum flooding his mouth and throat. Jasper groaned and hissed as he convulsed, his dick throbbing with violent pulses. His seed soon spilled out of Charlie's overfull mouth. Charlie let go and cradled the demon's jerking shaft in a gentle hand as he continued ejaculating, his pulse racing.

*Is this what Jasper meant?!*

"A demon's orgasm can last over a minute," Reuben confirmed. "That's only if they've been pleasured well." He pressed soft kisses to Jasper's nape.

Charlie did the same to Jasper's mouth as his release stormed through him. The demon finally relaxed in their arms. He blinked sweat out of his eyes and looked at the cum filling Charlie's palm and spilling onto the floor.

"You should—you should clean your hand," he mumbled.

"I will." Charlie wiped a slick lock of hair from Jasper's brow and gazed into his beautiful eyes. "That was delicious."

The demon's pupils rounded, the fading redness in the dark depths flaring to life once more.

"I could suck you for hours," Charlie confessed, a little shocked at his bluntness.

Somehow, it felt important that they be honest with one another.

"Is that a promise?" Jasper said gruffly.

Charlie smirked. Reuben pulled out of Jasper and wiped the demon intimately with some tissues before cleaning Charlie's hands.

Charlie stared, his heart thumping. The angel was still rock hard.

Reuben smiled at his expression. "Let's go to the bedroom."

They headed upstairs and down a corridor to a large, masculine room with double aspect views over the bay and the bridge. Charlie's breathing accelerated when he saw the huge bed dominating the hardwood floor. He spotted an elegant closet and a luxurious bathroom to his right and eyed the tall mirrors dotting the walls.

Reuben let Charlie go and headed over to an arm chair. He stripped, dropped his clothes on the floor, and sat down. He focused a heated stare upon them, his hand dropping to his erection where it jutted proudly from his trimmed pubes.

Charlie dragged his hungry gaze from the angel's stunning body and watched Jasper approach, his pulse racing.

❧

CHARLIE'S EYES WERE GUNMETAL GRAY POOLS OF LUST Jasper could easily drown into. Color painted his cheekbones a dull pink and his lips were parted on shallow pants. Jasper didn't have to look down to see how turned on the enchanter was.

He could smell it.

The same intoxicating scent that had had his cock hardening in an instant in the restroom in *Occulta* last night, to his everlasting surprise. His belly clenched.

He could make out a faint waft of cedar that marked Charlie as one possessing enchantment magic.

But there was something else. Something sweet and tart. Something that was pure Charlie. And it had his blood boiling with desire all over again despite the fact that he'd just been thoroughly serviced.

Having Reuben take him while Charlie watched was a sensual experience that would live with him for a long time. He wasn't a stranger to the most perverse debauchery. There were things he'd seen in the Hells that would make the most hardened whore blush. Yet, the encounter just now still made his ass twitch and his cock throb.

*It seems Reuben is truly far more discerning when it comes to these things.*

Jasper stopped in front of Charlie. The enchanter raised his chin and met his gaze unflinchingly.

"Are you scared?" the demon asked gruffly.

Charlie blinked. "Should I be?"

Jasper bit back a smile. *Sassy little thing.*

Truth be told, he enjoyed their repartee. There were not many people who could engage with him as wittily as Charlie could. The enchanter clearly didn't like backing down from a challenge.

Jasper raised a hand and trailed a knuckle down Charlie's cheek to his mouth. "I could easily hurt you, you know." He pressed his thumb in Charlie's lower lip, grinding the soft flesh against his lower teeth.

"I don't mind if you hurt me." Though his words were brazen, Charlie's voice quavered a little.

Something loosened in Jasper's chest at the hint of vulnerability in the enchanter's tone. A tightness he hadn't been aware of.

He blinked as a shocking truth resonated through him.

He didn't just want to fuck the man in front of him.

Jasper wanted to protect Charlie. To cherish him.

He shivered when the enchanter's tongue darted out to taste him.

Then his hands were on Charlie's face and he was crushing their mouths together.

Charlie responded immediately, his lips parting to welcome Jasper's demanding tongue. His gaze grew hooded. He grabbed Jasper's hips and pulled him closer. Pleasure dilated his pupils as he ground their erections together.

Jasper hastily unbuttoned Charlie's shirt and stripped it off his shoulders and down his arms, his fingers trembling so powerful was his need to take him. Charlie's chinos and boxers followed. He tumbled Charlie down on the cool satin sheets, their mouths meeting again and again, lips and tongues entangling messily.

Jasper grasped Charlie's wrists and yanked his arms above his head before lowering his full weight upon the enchanter. Charlie groaned, clearly enjoying the sensation of their flesh making contact even as he sank into the mattress. His thighs dropped open, welcoming Jasper in the cradle of his body.

The hot stickiness of his precum slicked Jasper's belly.

The demon shuddered, the enchanter's beguiling scent flooding his nostrils.

*Shit! I want to enter him right now!*

But he couldn't do that just yet. Plus, they needed to give Reuben a show.

Jasper glanced over at his lover and found him stroking the solid length of his cock at a leisurely pace. Reuben's hungry gaze pierced him. The demon shuddered.

The angel had been right. They both needed this.

Charlie freed his wrists and clutched Jasper's face. "Fuck me!" He nipped at Jasper's lip, his touch urgent.

Jasper gnashed his teeth. "Not yet." He addressed Reuben. "How about you tie him up?"

Charlie gasped when Reuben unleashed his Aerial powers and bound his wrists to the bed posts with fetters of wind. His hot gaze moved from Jasper to the angel and back. His hips jerked and his flushed cock throbbed out a jet of precum.

"I want to come!"

It took everything Jasper had to hang on to his self-control then. He could tell how badly Charlie's arousal was affecting Reuben too from the way his breathing had turned fast and shallow.

Jasper kissed Charlie before he could say something that would make them both lose their composure. Charlie moaned lustfully in his mouth.

The demon roamed his hands down the enchanter's throat and across his chest, exploring muscles and skin much different from his own and Reuben's. Charlie wasn't skinny by any means, nor was he brawny.

He was just…

*Perfect.*

Jasper's lips and tongue followed the path his fingers had taken, strangely humbled by that thought. He kissed, licked, bit, and tugged Charlie's nipples, relishing the way he trembled and shuddered and groaned in his arms. By the time he traced Charlie's cock with teasing fingers, precum had pooled on the enchanter's tense belly and he looked like he would detonate at any second.

"Hurry!" Charlie's knuckles whitened as he fisted his hands.

Jasper flashed him a savage smile, grabbed a couple of objects from the nightstand, and lay face down on the bed. He slicked his fingers with lube, hooked Charlie's right thigh over his shoulder, and swallowed one of his balls in his mouth.

Charlie cursed.

Jasper dipped his hand under his twitching sac and found his pucker.

Charlie tensed and trembled. Jasper played with his taut folds before slipping a finger inside, his lips and tongue teasing the enchanter's cock with powerful sucks and flicks.

"Ah! *Yes!*" Charlie started squirming and thrusting.

*Soon. Soon, I'll eat his hole and fuck his ass with my tongue!*

Jasper's cock throbbed deliciously at that thought. He took Charlie's shaft inside his mouth and started blowing him at the same time he pushed a second finger in him. Charlie's entrance spasmed around him. His hole slowly relaxed.

Jasper pushed a third finger inside.

"Oh!" Charlie clenched his passage hard. "That feels —that feels good!"

Blood pounded in Jasper's ears and his cock as he started finger fucking the enchanter. He couldn't wait to sink his dick inside him.

Charlie's pants and moans and cries filled the room as he danced on the bed, hips undulating to drive his cock in Jasper's mouth at the same time he squeezed his fingers greedily with his ass. His scent deepened as he neared his climax.

"Coming!" He squeezed his eyes shut, his knuckles whitening as he dug his nails in his palms where Reuben still held him captive. *"Oh God! I'm—!"*

A strangled sound left him when Jasper pulled off his cock and removed his fingers from his ass.

"What—?!"

He blinked dazedly as Jasper slipped a rubber ring on his erection and pushed the beaded stick attached to it inside his engorged shaft.

CHARLIE'S BREATH LOCKED IN HIS THROAT AS FIRE LICKED his cock inside and out. He stared at the toy as Jasper's tongue traced a slick path from his root to his plugged off tip.

The demon flashed him a dirty smile. "You're not allowed to ejaculate until we tell you to."

*Fuck!*

A feverish excitement sent Charlie's heart thundering in his chest. He gasped when the shackles of wind holding him prisoner maneuvered him on the bed. He found himself on his hands and knees near the edge of the mattress.

His eyes rounded when Jasper crowded his back, parted his ass, and pushed the head of his cock inside his hole.

*"Ah!"*

A buzzing sound filled Charlie's ears as Jasper penetrated him, the exquisite sting and burn making him bite his lip.

The demon was big.

He jerked and twitched when Jasper punched against his swollen prostate. Pleasure stormed him in violent waves. Charlie cried out as his erection throbbed and his ass contracted with strong spasms.

Jasper cursed when Charlie's passage sucked him in to the hilt. "Jesus, you're tight! Your hole is gonna bite my dick off!"

It took the enchanter a moment to realize he'd just had a dry orgasm. He panted heavily and blinked sweat out of his eyes when he caught movement ahead.

Reuben had risen from the chair and was approaching the bed, fingers busy on his slick rod and face taut with lust. He stopped in front of Charlie, cupped his chin, and slipped a thumb through his lips.

"Take my cock, Charlie."

The angel pressed the broad head of his shaft to his mouth. Charlie shivered and opened up. Tension stretched his jaw as Reuben filled him.

Jasper slapped his ass hard, making him gasp and

jerk. Reuben slid inside farther. His fingers found Charlie's hair, his grip savage.

Charlie's breath hitched, the sharp sting of pain and the burn of pleasure coming from both ends of him making his fingers clench on the bedsheets.

"You're gonna have to do this yourself," Reuben said silkily.

Charlie blinked and met the angel's smoldering eyes.

Jasper leaned down and skimmed his lips along Charlie's nape. "Fuck yourself on our cocks, Charlie," he growled, sinking his teeth in his tender skin.

Charlie shivered at the prick. He knew now why Jasper still hadn't moved.

Reuben's dick punched the back of his throat when he shifted forward. Jasper filled his hole when he moved back.

Heat coiled through his body as he started rocking to and fro just as they'd commanded, taking them in the scalding depths of his mouth and ass.

This was the perfect game of push and pull. Of penetration and submission.

It was wicked and filthy and felt so damn good he never wanted it to end.

His stomach clenched when he caught their reflections in one of the mirrors. He could see it all. The bulge of Reuben's cock stretching his cheeks and expanding his throat. His trapped cock swaying and bobbing against his belly. Jasper's pale knuckles on his hips and his engorged dick slipping in and out of his hole.

But it was the expression on his own face that had the most delectable tension spooling through Charlie's body. He looked like a man who was being fucked raw and enjoying every second of it.

Charlie groaned as another dry orgasm licked his nerve endings. He stiffened and came on a guttural cry, the sound muffled by Reuben's thick organ.

His cock spasmed with sharp twinges, the ring and beads preventing him from ejaculating. Reuben's fingers tightened punishingly in his hair. Jasper made a feral sound and slapped his ass, his palm smacking hard enough to leave a handprint.

Charlie shuddered in pleasure pain and started moving again.

It wasn't until he came a second time that Reuben and Jasper finally surrendered to their own instincts. They grasped his body with a desperate touch and fucked him brutally just like he'd secretly wished they would, their cocks threatening to split him open at both ends as they rammed inside him.

The wet sounds of their blistering lovemaking filled Charlie's ears, the slick slaps of flesh inside flesh as intoxicating as they were lewd. His heart hammered violently against his ribs as his entire body tightened painfully. Tears sprung to his eyes.

The next climax would wreck him, he was sure of it.

To his surprise, Reuben's thumb found his lashes and tenderly wiped the wetness away.

Jasper reached under Charlie's body and removed

the cock ring and plug. The demon kissed his back. "Come, Charlie!"

They climaxed together, the angel and demon stiffening and shouting out gutturally as they spilled their hot seed inside him. Charlie convulsed and jerked, his spurting dick painting the sheets with cum even as they filled his throat and hole with their release. His head swam dizzily as he rode the violent tides of the most incredible orgasm he'd ever experienced for what felt like endless minutes. He lost track of time. Of self.

Charlie was vaguely aware of Reuben and Jasper pulling out of him some time later while his hips jerked with intense aftershocks of pleasure. They tumbled him on his side and sandwiched him between their bodies, their hands skimming his twitching flesh as they waited for him to come down from his giddy high.

Charlie opened his eyes dazedly when Reuben kissed his forehead.

"Did you enjoy that?" the angel murmured.

Charlie swallowed and nodded, too spent to speak. He flushed when he felt Jasper touch his hole. The demon's cum was oozing out of him.

Reuben smiled. "Good."

Jasper clasped Charlie's jaw and turned his head around to take his mouth in a sweet kiss, his pupils crimson pools of desire. He moved Charlie onto his back and knelt above him, his knees denting the mattress by his hips while his hands pressed down next to his shoulders.

Charlie watched breathlessly as Reuben sat up and moved behind the demon.

Both of them were hard again.

Reuben rained kisses down Jasper's spine, parted his ass, and punched his cock inside him. Jasper gasped and arched.

Charlie licked his lips as they started fucking above him, their feral grunts quickening his pulse. His spent cock stirred. His gaze found Jasper's dick.

He raised a hand and touched the demon's shaft.

"*Oh!*" Jasper hissed.

Charlie stroked his throbbing length and started rubbing himself.

Jasper's pupils dilated.

"I— I want to try something," Charlie said breathlessly.

Reuben and Jasper slowed and stopped moving. They gave him a puzzled look. Charlie took a deep breath. His soul core pulsed with heat. Magic filled his veins.

The lush scent of a tropical forest exploded around them as the dark enchantment weaved its spell. Reuben and Jasper's eyes widened when luxurious foliage covered in dew shimmered into existence, their forms solid and real. Vines and creepers multiplied rapidly across the floor and ceiling and shot onto the bed. The calls of birds and wild beasts surrounded them.

Warmth flooded Charlie's face at Reuben and Jasper's surprised stares. "I've always wanted to fuck in the middle of a jungle," he mumbled.

"I like it," the angel said, his sharp gaze lingering on the realistic manifestations crowding the bedroom.

Jasper nodded.

Reuben gripped the demon's hips and started pounding his ass once more. Jasper swayed and moaned, his fingers whitening on the bed sheets. Pleasure painted red flags on his cheekbones.

His gaze locked on Charlie's hand where he was rubbing his own cock briskly. "I want to suck you!"

Charlie's heart stuttered. He scooted up, knelt in front of Jasper, and brought his cock to the demon's eager lips.

Jasper swallowed him to the hilt.

Charlie cursed and grasped the demon's head.

Reuben leaned across Jasper's back and sought Charlie's mouth with his lips.

The three of them rutted with wild abandon amidst the dazzling colors and smells of the jungle. It wasn't long before they came, Jasper greedily taking in Reuben and Charlie's seed while their shouts echoed against the trees and thick canopy. The demon ejaculated long and hard before the three of them collapsed on the bed in a tangle of limbs, chests shuddering and breathing ragged.

Reuben and Jasper started kissing and touching Charlie again. Charlie reciprocated, his magic manipulating the vines to stroke and tease Reuben and Jasper's flesh. Their groans and the way they twitched and shuddered under his ministrations told the enchanter they enjoyed the novel sensation.

Reuben palmed his cock to a fresh erection as

Jasper maneuvered Charlie onto his back and knelt above his head.

Charlie stared at Reuben as the angel spread his thighs open and crowded the cradle of his body. He shivered when Reuben hitched his legs around his hips and pressed the broad head of his shaft against his hole.

Charlie licked his lips in anticipation.

Finally, he would get to experience the angel's penetration.

Reuben's mouth was a thin grimace of pleasure pain as he pushed inside. Charlie gasped when his passage stretched deliciously to accommodate the angel's thick length, his hole loosened by Jasper's lovemaking and slick with the cum still inside him. He shivered when Reuben slid in to the hilt.

The angel was even hotter and bigger than the demon.

Reuben growled and started rocking his hips, his fingers digging painfully in Charlie's waist as he stuffed his ass hard and good. Charlie barely had time to draw breath before Jasper grasped his jaw and pushed his cock inside his mouth where he hovered above his face.

Charlie breathed through his nose as they started fucking him slow and deep. His heart swelled with an indescribable feeling when he met the angel's and demon's bright eyes.

He was the reason for their pleasure-glazed expressions. For their lips parting on harsh breaths and broken grunts. For their hands clinging to him with passionate strength. For their cocks being so thick and full.

Charlie lost himself to their intense lovemaking once more.

He came once. Twice.

Still they thrust inside him, their movements growing uncontrolled.

Their scents swamped his senses when they finally climaxed on animal shouts, their cum gushing inside his throat and hole. They barely gave him a moment to rest when they pulled out of him and proceeded to claim him again and again in every position Charlie could imagine.

On his back. Against the wall. Squatting and riding them. Lying on his front, their hands driving his head into the mattress as they crushed him with their weights and rutted inside his well-used ass. They formed a fuck chain, Reuben taking Jasper while Jasper pounded Charlie's hole with him on all fours then lying on his back.

They used toys on him. Made him moan and hiss in pleasure pain. Made him tremble and beg for his release. Then they rewarded him by eating his cock and hole and fucking him with their tongues until he sobbed in pleasure.

And all the while their pale and crimson gazes scorched him possessively.

Like he was theirs to claim. To dominate. To break. To cherish.

Charlie found his gaze straying to their reflections again and again, unable to tear his eyes from the sinful sight of his own unmaking. His body grew sticky with sweat and cum as they broke him in thoroughly, his hole growing so lax he knew he was more than ready to take them both.

"Do it!" he gasped a while later. He was lying on his back while Reuben stood fucking Jasper on the edge of the bed. "I want you both inside me!"

Reuben and Jasper froze.

Charlie spread his thighs, no longer shocked at his brazen words and perverse desires. "I'm aching, deep inside. See?" He rocked his hips and stretched his loose entrance with his fingertips. "Fill me up!"

Reuben slipped out of Jasper, his expression as feral as the demon's. They lubed their cocks under Charlie's hungry gaze.

The angel climbed on the bed, his movements predatory. Charlie panted when he pushed his right thigh up past his ear and slicked his ass liberally before thrusting three fingers inside him. Reuben tested his passage thoroughly before yanking him up and turning him around. He pressed his broad chest to Charlie's back and held him close as he laid down.

Charlie shivered when Reuben worked his hands under his thighs, bent his knees, and spread him open, exposing every intimate inch of him to Jasper's hungry stare.

"Look in the mirror, Charlie," Reuben whispered in his ear. He nipped the shell with his teeth, drawing a gasp from Charlie.

Charlie looked at the mirror at the end of the bed. He moaned when Reuben tilted his hips and stroked the weeping head of his cock up and down Charlie's entrance.

"Watch as we take you," Reuben grated out.

Charlie trembled when Reuben entered him, his insides quivering with a hunger that would not be quenched. Jasper waited until the angel was embedded to the hilt before crowding Charlie's ass.

"*Oh!*" Charlie squeezed his eyes shut when the demon's cock pushed against his opening.

His rim stretched tautly. A sliver of fear darted through him at the hot sting.

*No! They'll tear me open!*

"Keep looking, Charlie." Reuben kissed the side of Charlie's neck, his tone reverent.

Charlie swallowed, heart pounding and body quivering. He opened his eyes and met Jasper's crimson gaze. His fear faded at the expression on the demon's face.

Jasper was gazing at him with as much adoration as Reuben's words held. He leaned down and kissed him gently.

"I know you want this as much as we do," he murmured against Charlie's lips. "Don't be afraid."

Charlie shuddered. He nodded jerkily.

Jasper smiled. Charlie's heart lurched.

His gaze shifted to the mirror as Jasper kept pressing against his entrance. He breathed in and out and forcibly relaxed his body, willing himself to take the demon.

They all gasped when the head of Jasper's dick finally breached his hole.

Charlie panted shallowly as he watched Jasper slowly slide home. His insides felt full to bursting and the ring of muscles guarding his passage throbbed and burned with the most exquisite pressure.

Jasper stilled when he was fully inside him. The demon shuddered and closed his eyes. "You feel—" he faltered and swallowed. "Jesus!"

"You feel amazing," Reuben breathed. His lips skimmed Charlie's neck.

The angel and the demon stayed motionless, giving his body time to adapt to their girths. The sharp sting in his ass receded. A slow ache replaced it.

Heat coiled inside Charlie's belly. He licked his lips and squeezed his passage slightly.

He might as well have set off a bomb the way Reuben and Jasper reacted. The angel and demon gnashed their teeth, their fingers biting in his flesh where they held him. Still they did not move.

Goosebumps broke out across Charlie's skin.

"Please," he whispered. "Fuck me!"

A ragged moan left him as they obeyed his command, his hole stretching oh so deliciously around their thrusting cocks. Reuben and Jasper took turns kissing him, their tongues lashing his with hot strokes, just as they lashed his insides with their thick rods.

"Does it feel good?!" Charlie gasped.

Jasper pressed his forehead against Charlie's. "Do you even have to ask?!" he growled, nipping at his lips.

He rocked his hips and drew a groan from Charlie.

Reuben nibbled Charlie's nape. "Your body is amazing, Charlie." His fingers flexed on Charlie's thighs. "*You* are amazing. You were made for us. For *this*."

Tension stiffened Charlie's spine at their words. His chest swelled with emotion. "I'm glad! This—*everything* you do to me—makes me feel more alive than I've ever felt!"

The angel and the demon exchanged a heated look.

"I'm happy you feel that way," Reuben said.

"Because we're never letting you go," Jasper growled.

Their thrusts accelerated.

Precum shot out of Charlie's dick as pleasure knotted his belly. He cursed when Reuben and Jasper started stroking his straining erection. He came with explosive violence moments later, his passage squeezing their cocks so hard they cursed. They rocked their hips through his convulsions and soon had him erect again.

Sobs of pleasure tumbled from his lips as they took him over the edge once more, their powerful thrusts milking his prostate dry.

Charlie's consciousness flickered when the three of them finally climaxed together. He screamed in ecstasy as Reuben and Jasper ejaculated inside him, their shouts registering dimly in his ringing ears while their hot cum flooded his passage.

They rode the devastating storm for what felt like hours, bodies locked tight, arms clutching one another, lips blinding seeking each other's mouths.

Charlie shivered and blinked dazedly when Jasper and Reuben carefully pulled out of him a timeless moment later. He moaned, feeling bereft all of a sudden. Jasper kissed him tenderly as Reuben lifted him in his arms and carried him into the bathroom.

Steam swirled as Jasper drew the gigantic bath.

He joined Reuben and Charlie in the shower. They washed Charlie's hair and body before cleaning him out intimately. Charlie gasped and sought their lips, quivers of pleasure shooting through him at their probing fingers. The angel and demon cleaned each other next before leading Charlie to the bath.

Charlie sank into the hot water to his chin and leaned against Jasper's chest, his head falling languidly on his shoulder.

"Stick a fork in me, I'm done," he groaned.

Reuben chuckled and caressed Charlie's legs under the water where he sat opposite them. "I didn't think you'd be able to take both of us so soon."

"Yeah, well, I'm not one to walk away from a challenge," Charlie murmured. The steady thrum of Jasper's heart against his back was making him pleasantly drowsy. He closed his eyes.

The demon trailed a finger along his arm. "Really?"

"Uh-huh," Charlie mumbled.

"Does that mean you'll take Argonaut's promotion exam and become a Level One enchanter?" Reuben said.

"Whatever you say." Charlie stiffened when he realized what he'd just agreed to. His eyes slammed open. "Wait! I didn't mean—!"

"No backsies," Jasper said tartly. "You're taking the damn exam."

Charlie flushed at his confident voice. "But—but I'm not good enough!"

Reuben sighed. "The enchantment you wielded tonight? We can assure you that only a Level One enchanter could pull off something like that."

"Stop holding yourself back, Charlie," Jasper said quietly. "You're a genius."

Heat flooded Charlie's cheeks. He covered his face with his hands and groaned.

"Are you blushing?" Jasper teased.

"No," Charlie mumbled.

"He is," Reuben said, self-assured.

"I am *not!*" Charlie protested.

Reuben peeled his hands from his face, chuckled at his mortified expression, and pressed a loving kiss to his lips. "Come on, let's get you out of here before you melt into a crimson puddle."

Charlie grumbled about overbearing assholes as they pulled him out of the bath. They dried him, changed the sheets, and pulled him into their bed.

A contented sigh left Charlie as Reuben and Jasper tucked him between them. "I really wish I didn't have to go into work tomorrow."

"We already took care of that," Jasper said.

Charlie raised his face from the demon's chest and stared. "What?"

Reuben kissed his back. "We messaged Morgan and told him we needed you for an urgent mission."

Charlie gaped at him over his shoulder. "And he agreed?!"

"We may have implied we knew a way to get you to take the exam," Jasper said guilelessly.

Charlie sucked in air, not sure if he felt incensed or deliriously happy at their Machiavellian tactics. "You had this all planned out, didn't you?!"

Jasper nuzzled his nose. "We weren't exactly sure how it would pan out."

"You're not exactly predictable," Reuben drawled.

Charlie shut up at that. He relaxed against them. "So, what did you guys have planned for tomorrow?"

"We thought we'd make breakfast, then go for a long drive and have a late lunch somewhere," Reuben said.

Charlie pursed his lips. "I agree with the breakfast plan. But the only things I'm intending to ride are your dicks."

Reuben burst out laughing. Jasper groaned.

"You're gonna be sore when you wake up," the demon said caustically.

"I don't care," Charlie said mutinously. "You can put some Blossom Silver on my ass."

Reuben started chortling.

"You're a stubborn mutt, you know that?" Jasper growled at Charlie.

Charlie grinned and kissed him. "Come, I need my beauty sleep if I'm gonna spend my day ravishing you two." He reached across Jasper and switched the light off.

The demon grumbled for a while longer.

"Shut up, Jas." Charlie grasped his lovers' hands and tucked them against his heart as he closed his eyes.

A singular truth resonated through him as they shifted closer to his warmth.

He wasn't sure if what he was starting to feel for the demon and the angel was love. But one thing he was certain of. He needed them, just as much as they needed him.

And no one was more shocked by that fact than him.

*Morgan's gonna have a heart attack when he finds out about us.*

A satisfied smirk curved Charlie's mouth at that thought.

He really was a temperamental asshole.

### THE END

# MORTIS

AVA MARIE SALINGER

# MORTIS

FRAGRANT BUBBLES TICKLED MORTIS'S NOSE AS HE SANK to his chin into the immense, obsidian clawfoot bath dominating the bathroom. His gaze swept the opulent white and black space.

With its marble floor and walls, dazzling crystal chandeliers, and gold and silver-gilded monochrome furnishings, it wasn't the kind of place he'd normally choose to visit. It was too lavish. Too decadent. Too... *hedonistic.*

Unease tightened Mortis's belly.

*Do I really belong here?*

As the Right Hand of the God of Death, he was accustomed to the stark ambience of the bone and ivory castle he shared with his master, and the modest domain he inhabited with his Reaper brethren. His gaze strayed to the door leading to the rest of the hotel suite at the thought of the deity who commanded him. Mortis's face flushed with more than just the heat wafting off the rose and jasmine scented water.

The Reaper God waited for him in the next room.

He squeezed his legs to his chest, acutely conscious of what was about to unfold and still somewhat dazed by it all.

*I can't believe Master wants to—wants to do that with me!*

His groin stirred when the words the Reaper God had uttered in *Occulta* just before they left the bar an hour ago echoed through his skull once more.

"*We are going to consummate our relationship. Pan has given me careful instructions and a book on the subject.*" His master had directed a laser-like look his way when he'd taken hold of his hand to guide him out of the place. "*We are going to try* all *the positions.*"

Mortis bit his lip and dropped a hand to his cock. He shivered at the prickly pleasure his own touch elicited when he stroked his swelling shaft. The body the Gods Pan and Boreas had granted him so he could navigate the earthly realm was a little too sensitive.

*Will Master touch me here?* He swallowed. *Will he—will he put* his *inside me?*

His ass twitched at that perverse thought. Mortis hesitated before dipping his hand past his taint. He stopped shy of touching the tight pucker that protected his passage, too self-conscious to explore that part of his body yet.

Though he could not recall the details of his past life, he was aware of what sex entailed, even between men. Reapers sometimes recounted the various acts they'd caught the humans whose souls they'd harvested engaging in over the centuries that he'd lived among them. Their curiosity was driven by pure academic interest, since there were innumerable humans who crossed over from the world of the living into that of the dead in flagrante delicto of the enterprise. It caused Reapers to wonder whether such fleeting pleasure was worth losing one's life over.

But there was a reason they called an orgasm "La Petite Mort." Mortis had seen the evidence of this with his own eyes when he and the Reaper God had walked in on Pan making passionate love to Demetrius during a visit to the Spirit Realm. From what Mortis had witnessed, the demigod of Spring had thoroughly relished what was happening to him despite the loud keens and tortured gasps that tumbled from his throat as Pan held his hips in a white-knuckled grip and plundered his body with savage thrusts where he'd bent him over a table.

Mortis had done his best to hide how flustered he'd been by what he'd seen. The Reaper God on the other hand looked like he'd been taking notes.

Mortis wasn't sure when he'd started looking at his master with more than just admiration and respect. He did not possess a beating heart in his Khimer form, but he was certain that if he did, his growing awareness of the Reaper God would have caused his pulse to flutter in his presence.

There were many things he had learned about his master in the time they'd spent together. Things that made it so he now cherished the deity more than his own existence.

Though his role and his appearance instilled terror

in most, the Reaper God was kind and just. He liked thunderstorms, cats, and, more recently, the lemon sherbet Pan served him on his visits to the Spirit Realm. He rarely granted second chances. He told terrible jokes. He was awful at just about any game. And he often appeared lonely, to the point there were days when all Mortis wished for was to erase the forlorn expression that haunted his master's face when he thought no one was looking. When he wanted to take him in his arms, press his head to his chest, and murmur words of comfort in his ear.

Of course, Mortis would never dare do that in reality.

It wasn't until the Reaper God was taken captive by the God of Darkness who invaded their domain that Mortis came to know true fear and was finally forced to acknowledge the depth of feelings he harbored for his master. Feelings he'd hidden inside himself for too long.

He loved the Reaper God.

He would happily have kept his one-sided infatuation a secret and continued to serve the deity in his best capacity as his Right Hand until he was no longer needed. He had no right to expect more and none knew this better than him.

Except the Reaper God had implied that he also entertained some kind of affection for Mortis. His master had not specified what his feelings for him were in so many words. The only thing he had made clear tonight was that he wished to have a physical relationship with Mortis.

It was a request Mortis could not refuse. Not that he would have wanted to anyway. He lifted a handful of bubbles and stared as they popped and vanished on his palm. Resolve had him clenching his fist.

*I shall do my best to satisfy Master!*

With that thought firmly in mind, Mortis washed his body thoroughly before rising and climbing out of the tub. He was reaching for the towel on the standing rail when he caught sight of his reflection in the floor-length mirror opposite him. He paused, mesmerized by what he saw.

With high cheekbones, an elfin-like jaw, full lips, and a broad forehead, his face was arresting, as was the lithe body he now owned. Add to this hair and eyes the soft, rich brown of chestnuts and flawless, honey-colored flesh that had taken on a dewy sheen from the bath essences he had soaked in and Mortis could not help but avoid his own gaze.

He still wasn't used to the bewitchingly handsome form Pan and Boreas had granted him. According to the two Gods, his current appearance bore a close likeness to what he had originally looked like, when he was still a human. Color stained Mortis's cheeks when his glance danced off his semi-erection. He hastily dried himself and slipped into the black velour robe hanging on the wall.

Awareness sent his heart thumping when he opened the door and entered the bedroom. Like the rest of the luxurious suite, this space was decorated in monochromes accentuated with silver and gold tones. Unlike the bathroom however, the lighting here was muted, the only illumination coming from a floor-standing lamp in the corner and some dozen, glass candle holders scattered atop a myriad surfaces.

The Reaper God stood at the far end of the room. He was looking out through the terrace doors to the bay and the dazzling bridge beyond the balcony. Ice clinked in a bucket holding a bottle of champagne on a table beside him, the candle light sparking off the drops of condensation coating the dark glass. His robe stretched across his shoulders when he lifted a flute of the drink to his lips.

An ache roused inside Mortis. Though the Reaper God was built along the same willowy lines as him, he wasn't gaunt by any means. Mortis had only ever caught glimpses of his true form through the cloak of shadows he normally wore. Heat warmed his veins as he studied his master's strong back and the defined muscles of his arms and legs for the first time.

The Reaper God was like a ballet dancer, all grace and supple limbs that still projected undeniable strength.

It wasn't just his master's body that had Mortis entranced. He itched to sink his fingers in the lustrous black hair flowing down the deity's back. He found himself wondering what it would feel like against his skin. On his lips.

Draped all over his throbbing cock.

Mortis flushed at that illicit thought. He almost bit his tongue when his master spoke.

*"Your gaze is burning a hole into my back, Mortis."* The Reaper God turned and met Mortis's nervous stare, his

own inscrutable. He observed him for a silent moment before reaching out a hand. *"Come."*

Mortis padded barefoot across the parquet floor, powerless to resist his master's command. He stopped in front of the Reaper God, his pulse racing with excitement and a degree of trepidation even as he tilted his chin to maintain eye contact with the deity.

He wasn't sure what the Reaper God intended to do after tonight. Whether he expected this to be a regular thing. Or whether he would be content with sleeping with Mortis once to satisfy his curiosity about the carnal aspect of being with a human, and resume their working relationship the next day as if nothing had happened.

As far as Mortis was concerned, he would never be able to look at the deity in the same light again. Not after being physically intimate with him. By the time morning came, the Reaper God was going to own his heart, his soul, *and* his body and damn if that didn't make him tremble in anticipation.

His restless thoughts scattered to the winds when the Reaper God raised a hand and caressed his face with gentle fingers. Mortis shivered, his eyelids drooping as he instinctively moved into the deity's cool touch. His hooded gaze dropped to his master's pale, sculptured lips.

His belly clenched on a spasm of pure need.

*I want his mouth on me.*

A crimson light flared in the pupils opposite him, as if the Reaper God had read the lewd wish that had just crossed his mind. Mortis's heart skipped a beat.

His master's face was full of a dark emotion. One that raised delicious goosebumps on Mortis's skin.

*"What are you thinking about?"*

The question was so unexpected it made Mortis blink. He stared blindly at the deity whose touch had bewitched him, too stunned to formulate a reply.

The Reaper God traced his lower lip with a thumb, his heated stare locking on Mortis's mouth.

Sparks ignited across Mortis's flesh.

The Reaper God leaned in and repeated the question. *"What are you thinking about, Mortis?"*

His velvety voice and the faint scent of camphor wafting off his body made Mortis's cock spring to attention.

"I—" he stopped and swallowed, flustered. "I—I'm too ashamed to tell you, Master," he finished on a rushed whisper.

He could never lie to the Reaper God. But there was no way in the Nine Hells he was going to admit to the deity opposite him all the filthy things he wanted him to do to him.

His master sighed. Mortis squirmed, knowing his answer had disappointed him.

If the Reaper God noticed the pulse beating frantically at the base of his throat, he gave no sign of it. He straightened and handed Mortis the champagne glass on the table.

*"Drink,"* he said imperiously.

"Hmm." Mortis stared from the flute to his master's face. "I—I'm not used to alcohol."

"*Good.*" The Reaper God's eyes flashed. "*It should help loosen your inhibitions a little.*"

Mortis hesitated before taking the glass.

*Is he trying to get me drunk?*

He squinted at his master. The Reaper God met his suspicious stare with a guileless look. Mortis tipped the flute to his lips and guzzled down a mouthful of the champagne. He realized his mistake when the bubbles tickled the back of his throat, making him cough and splutter.

To his everlasting mortification, the Reaper God patted his back as if he were a child.

"I'm—I'm sorry, Master!" Mortis choked out once the fit had passed. Dismay had his stomach sinking. He'd spilled some of his drink on his chest and robe. "I'll go wash up again."

He put the glass down and whirled around, embarrassment heating his face. A strong hand clasped his wrist.

"*No,*" the Reaper God said. "*I shall take care of it myself.*"

Incomprehension widened Mortis's eyes as his master turned him around.

Gold glittered in the Reaper God's hooded gaze when he saw his skittish expression. He put his own glass down and leaned in, his hair a glossy curtain that hid half his face.

Air locked in Mortis's throat when the Reaper God sniffed the side of his neck.

"*Did I mention that you smell utterly divine?*"

Mortis's legs almost gave out at the feel of his master's breath on his flesh. Unlike his fingers, it was hot. Then the Reaper God carefully licked the golden liquid staining Mortis's exposed skin and Mortis lost his mind.

He bit his lip to stifle a cry, his teeth pressing in so deep he almost drew blood. His hands found the Reaper God's head, his fingers sinking none too gently into hair so soft and glossy he never wanted to let go.

His master did not seem to mind his rough touch.

Mortis twitched and panted as the Reaper God laved his flesh with his tongue. It was even more scalding than his breath. And his fingers were growing warm where he still held Mortis's wrist, as if his desire for him was heating him up from the inside out.

Blood pounded heavily in Mortis's skull. His body bowed helplessly toward the one wreaking sweet havoc on his senses.

*Is—is this really happening?!*

But there was no way he was imagining the hot tongue lapping sensuously at his skin. Mortis shuddered, dropped his head back, and closed his eyes, light-headed at the forbidden pleasure the sensations were evoking and the wicked thought that immediately followed it.

He wanted his master to do that to the rest of his body, especially at the juncture of his thighs, where his sex throbbed with a hunger he had never known.

His cock jerked at that mental image. A moan fell from his lips.

The Reaper God shuddered at the sound. Mortis

blinked his eyes open when his master slowly straightened.

"*Interesting.*" The Reaper God's voice had deepened to a gravelly tone that quickened his already racing pulse. "*It tastes sweeter on your skin.*" He met Mortis's dazed stare, his own glowing with a banked heat.

Mortis gulped, unsure how to respond.

It almost seemed as if his master was...trying to seduce him.

"I—Master, I am yours," he murmured. "You need not concern yourself with foreplay. You can do with me as you wish."

The Reaper God stilled. Mortis's mouth went dry.

Though his master's expression hadn't changed, he could tell he was unhappy from the stiff line of his shoulders. Panic made Mortis swallow convulsively.

*Did I—did I do or say something wrong?!*

"I'm sorry, Master," he whispered wretchedly. Mortis lowered his gaze. "I—I didn't mean to ruin the—!"

The Reaper God gripped his chin, swooped down, and swallowed the rest of his words with his mouth, the movement almost angry.

Mortis went rigid at the first touch of his master's lips. He stared wide-eyed into the gold-laced, crimson gaze opposite and trembled at what he read there.

Irritation. Desire. Possessiveness. And...something else. Something Mortis daren't put a name to.

The Reaper God clasped Mortis's face with both hands and angled his head so as to deepen the kiss, his touch gentling. Mortis moaned breathily as his master carefully learned the shape of his lips before delving inside his mouth and exploring the heated depths past his teeth.

His breathing fairly stopped when the Reaper God twined their tongues together. Electricity sparked across Mortis's nerve endings. His entire body buzzed, as if he'd been struck by lightning.

This kiss was madness.

It was fire. It was ice. It was a blaze that would wreck his body. A storm that threatened to shatter his very sanity.

Mortis didn't realize he'd looped his arms around his master's neck and was pressing his body wantonly against him until he felt something hard poke his belly.

The Reaper God nipped at his tongue and lips with strong white teeth before reluctantly ending the kiss. He touched their foreheads together, the red flags on his cheekbones stark against his pale skin, his breathing more labored than it had been a minute ago.

*"I do not wish you to lie with me because you believe it is your duty, Mortis."*

Mortis gasped when the Reaper God took one of his hands where he still clung to his nape and lowered it to the rock solid length tenting the lower half of his robe.

*"I want you to feel what I'm feeling. I want your body to heat up and harden, just like mine is doing. I want you to want this just as badly as I do. I want you to want* me, *Mortis."*

Mortis's heart thundered erratically at his master's words and the slight quiver in his strong voice. He never knew he held such power over the deity he loved until this very moment.

He didn't realize he was crying until the Reaper God's face softened. The deity stooped to kiss the tear drops trembling on his lashes.

"Do—do you really mean that, Master?" Mortis quavered. "Do you—do you feel the same way I do?!"

The Reaper God's pupils flared at his indirect confession. *"If by that you mean I want to worship you from the top of your head all the way to the tips of your delectable toes, then the answer is yes, Mortis."* His breath danced against the shell of Mortis's ear when he leaned down to kiss the side of his neck. *"I care for you deeply, Mortis. And I want you. I want to kiss you and touch you all over. I want to explore every inch of you, especially* this part."

Mortis sucked in air when the Reaper God slipped his arms around his waist and caressed his butt.

*"I want to be inside you."*

Mortis's hole twitched and contracted hungrily, his body reacting like it couldn't wait for those words to come true. He whimpered when his master worked a hand inside his robe and trailed his knuckles along his straining erection.

*"And I want to see* this *part of you weep for me and taste your pleasure."* The Reaper God bit his ear lobe at the same time he squeezed the head of his swollen shaft.

Mortis's eyes rounded. "Oh!"

His dick jerked at the sharp prick of his master's teeth and the pinch of his fingers. He blinked when warm wetness oozed out of his cock and filled the

Reaper God's palm. To his horror, his master lifted his hand and stared at the sticky fluid now coating his pale skin.

"*So, this is precum,*" the Reaper God said solemnly.

Mortis's mouth rounded on an O of pure mortification.

"*M—Master!*"

He grabbed the Reaper God's hand and wiped hurriedly at the evidence of his disgraceful act with the edge of his robe, his face flaming.

A low chuckle had his head snapping up.

Though the Reaper God was keeping a straight face, his shoulders were quaking with mirth.

"You're laughing," Mortis said, stunned.

The Reaper God took his hands and kissed his knuckles, looking mighty pleased with himself. His tone dropped to a husky rasp that did all sorts of wicked things to Mortis's pulse. "*I feel I will experience many firsts with you, Mortis.*"

Mortis went weak at the knees. He'd never known his master act like this before.

He blurted out the first thought that came to his mind.

"Pan—Pan has corrupted Master! He's—he's turned Master into a Casanova!"

The Reaper God sobered. A frown puckered his brow. "*I find myself experiencing an unpleasant, prickly feeling at the mention of that God's name,*" he told Mortis coolly. "*In fact, I would very much like it if you refrained from talking about another male when we are being intimate. Or a female, for that matter.*"

Mortis opened and closed his mouth soundlessly.

*Wait. Is—is Master jealous?!*

The Reaper God tipped Mortis's chin with a knuckle, his expression flinty. *"Is that clear?"*

Mortis nodded jerkily. Instead of feeling chastised, he found himself experiencing a feverish thrill. The Reaper God taking control of their love making was so titillating it was filling his mind with dirty fantasies of dominance and submission.

*"Good,"* the Reaper God murmured. He cocked his head to the side. *"Still, I should punish you for speaking his name."*

Butterflies swarmed Mortis's stomach at his master's blistering gaze.

The Reaper God took a step back and folded his arms across his chest. *"Strip."*

Mortis's breathing quickened at the terse order. His hands trembled when he undid the knot at his waist, excitement making his fingers clumsy. His cock throbbed painfully as he allowed the robe to fall open.

He knew his master could see his naked arousal.

It should have made him feel awkward. But it didn't.

The Reaper God looked on unblinkingly as he shrugged out of the thick material. The robe pooled silently at Mortis's feet when he dropped it. He lowered his eyes, struggling to keep still beneath his master's heated stare.

A low growl brought his gaze right back up.

The Reaper God's nostrils were flaring, the light in his pupils predatory. Mortis shivered.

*"Lie on the bed."*

Mortis caught sight of the enormous erection denting his master's robe. His passage spasmed, eager for something he had never experienced but that he wanted more than anything right now.

He climbed onto the cool, obsidian sheets covering the giant bed and lay on his back in the center. The mattress dipped when the Reaper God followed and knelt above him. Mortis's heart pounded heavily as his master's gold and crimson eyes raked every inch of his quivering body.

The Reaper God was studying his slender form like he was committing it to memory, his silken hair teasing Mortis's sensitive skin where it touched his flesh.

*"Beautiful,"* he said thickly. *"You are beautiful, Mortis."*

Mortis barely had time to register his master's reverent tone before the Reaper God traced his twitching cock with a finger.

*"Ah!"* Mortis gasped and thrust into his master's touch.

He pressed his knuckles to his mouth, mortified at the wanton sound he'd made and the way his body had instinctively reacted.

The Reaper God leaned down and kissed his palm, the red in his eyes so bright it scorched Mortis's senses.

*"Move your hand, Mortis. I want to taste what's mine."*

Mortis shuddered, desire sending his pulse into the stratosphere. He lowered his hand. Then his master's lips were on his and he forgot about everything else.

The Reaper God explored his mouth at a leisurely pace, like they had all the time in the world. He kissed and sucked and gently bit Mortis's lips until they were pleasantly swollen. Then he used his wicked tongue to drive him out of his mind all over again. And all the while, he gently caressed Mortis's erection.

Mortis trembled as the Reaper God rained soft kisses on his eyes. His cheeks. His ears. He nudged Mortis's chin up with his nose and worked his way down his neck, his hot breath raising goosebumps on Mortis's skin and sending shivers down his spine even as his fingers wreaked havoc on his sensitive organ.

Mortis moaned as the Reaper God feasted on the pulse beating frantically at the base of his throat and stroked him with a feather light touch. He could feel something building deep inside his belly. A tension he'd never experienced before. A hot pressure that begged to be released.

It gripped his balls. His cock. His spine.

It filled his ass with an ache that could not be assuaged and had his hips jerking off the bed.

"Ah! Master! I feel—I feel strange!"

"*How so?*" the Reaper God murmured, his own breathing unsteady where he nibbled on Mortis's skin.

"It tingles. Everything—everything feels tight! *Hmm!*" Mortis bucked against the hand torturing his swollen shaft with exquisite tenderness. "My body feels like it's gonna snap! I want to—I want—*Master, I don't know what I want!*" he whimpered.

The Reaper God's gaze seared his face when he raised his head and looked at him. "*You're about to climax, Mortis. Don't fight it.*" He pressed a hot kiss to Mortis's lips. "*Just listen to your body.*"

Incoherent sounds left Mortis as he did just that. He heard the slick friction of the Reaper God's fingers on his aching organ when he started rolling his hips. He took a peek at where his master was touching him to distract himself from the tightness gripping his entire body and nearly swallowed his tongue.

His engorged cock had gone a deep, rosy hue where he pumped it shamelessly through his master's fist. Creamy liquid pearled at the tip and oozed down his shaft. The Reaper God used it to lubricate his grip.

The sight proved too much for Mortis.

Fire filled his veins and blinded his vision as he finally crested the peak of pleasure the Reaper God had expertly guided him to. He was barely aware of grabbing the Reaper God's shoulders and sinking his nails into his robe as he came on a loud cry, his ejaculation so forceful his cum splashed into his master's hand. Mortis's consciousness wavered as he convulsed beneath the being who'd brought him such devastating ecstasy, unable to control the erratic, thrusting motion of his hips or the lustful sounds rising from his throat.

It was some time before his awareness returned.

Mortis blinked when he felt a tender touch upon his face, his breaths still shuddering in and out of his heaving chest. He'd collapsed on the bed at some point and lay pliant and loose limbed beneath his master's curious gaze.

The Reaper God moved aside a damp lock and gently kissed his brow. *"Was that good?"*

Mortis nodded numbly, too sated to speak. Gone

was the tension that had possessed every inch of his body. He felt more relaxed than he could ever recall being in his entire existence.

*"You know, I have to agree with Pan. Your O face is most delectable."*

Mortis's eyes rounded.

The Reaper God pursed his lips. *"I wonder what Benjamin would think if I have it immortalized in a painting and we put it in the main entrance of the castle?"*

Mortis sucked in air, horror vibrating from every line of his body.

The Reaper God burst out laughing at his expression.

Mortis's heart clenched at his dazzling smile and the faint lines crinkling the corners of his eyes, his outrage all but forgotten.

*How could anyone be scared of him? He is just...lovely.*

The Reaper God finally stopped chuckling. He glanced at Mortis's spent cock, his eyes gleaming. *"Why don't we get started for real this time?"*

"But—you just made me come!" Mortis blushed hard.

The Reaper God arched an eyebrow. *"That was the hors d'oeuvres. We haven't even gotten to the starters yet."* He sat back on his heels and shrugged out of his robe, exposing a pale, toned chest and well-defined abs.

Mortis's gaze dropped. His eyes bulged. "Master?"

*"Yes?"* The Reaper God cast his robe on the floor, oblivious to the fresh apprehension underscoring Mortis's voice.

"That's not gonna fit," Mortis croaked.

The Reaper God looked down at his enormous erection. *"Pan's is as big as mine and it appears to fit rather well inside Demetrius."* He met Mortis's dazed stare and arched an arrogant eyebrow. *"Besides, don't you just love a challenge?"*

"Not when it involves my butt, I don't," Mortis mumbled before he could help himself.

He wasn't going to ask his master under exactly what circumstances he and the Wild God compared the size of their dicks.

The Reaper God blinked at Mortis's grumpy tone. Mortis stiffened, realizing his blunder.

His master laughed again before he could apologize.

*"I like that,"* the Reaper God chuckled.

Mortis eyed him warily. "You like what, Master?"

The deity pressed down onto Mortis and trapped his wrists above his head with one hand, the other falling to his hip so he could align their frames. Mortis's eyes nearly rolled into the back of his skull at the full body contact.

He could feel every hard inch of the Reaper God's body, especially the thick rod nudging his own stirring cock. It made him feel hot and cold, like he was in the grips of a fever.

*"I like that you're finally being honest with me. I want more, Mortis. I want you to tell me everything you want me to do to you. And everything you want to do to me."*

Mortis's pulse stuttered at the expression on his master's face. Emotion squeezed his heart.

The Reaper God was looking at him as if he were the most precious thing in the world.

*"I want you to tell me what you like and what you don't like. I want to please you, Mortis. Just as you please me."*

Then his master kissed him senseless and all Mortis could do was hang on for dear life.

He shivered and arched as the Reaper God wreaked the sweetest havoc upon his mouth before slowly working his way down his throat and chest. The Reaper God worshipped every inch of him just like he'd promised, his burning lips and scorching tongue following the path his fingers had made upon his trembling flesh.

The Reaper God rubbed and played with his chocolate colored nipples when they crossed his path. Mortis squirmed, not certain if he liked the feeling. Then his master pinched one of his nubs between his thumb and forefinger and tugged on the other with his teeth.

*"Oh!"* Mortis cried out, his eyes flying wide open and his cock hardening in an instant.

The Reaper God laved his stinging flesh with his tongue and observed him with a sultry look full of curiosity. *"Did that hurt?"*

Mortis met his master's gaze, dazed. "It did. But— but it also felt good." Heat flooded his face at this sinful confession.

A wicked smile stretched the Reaper God's mouth. *"Want me to do it again?"*

Mortis hesitated before nodding, his ears hot. "Yes."

His master's eyes flared with satisfaction. *"Good boy."*

Mortis groaned as his master tortured his breasts

for long minutes. By the time the Reaper God reached down and cupped his quivering sex, he'd made a mess of their stomachs with his precum.

"*You're full again.*"

Mortis moaned when the deity squeezed the swollen sac beneath his cock. The Reaper God dipped his fingers lower and caressed his taint with a feather light touch all the way to the rim of his twitching hole.

"*This part of you must be hungry too.*"

Mortis shuddered. It wasn't just his master's taut voice and the crimson and gold blazing in his pupils that told him he was deeply aroused. His skin was growing slick with his master's precum where his rock hard organ probed his thigh.

Mortis's belly twitched and trembled when the Reaper God kissed his abs before working his way south. He teased Mortis's belly button with his tongue, licked his faint treasure trail, and pushed his thighs open. Mortis blinked when his master finally settled in the cradle of his body.

*Don't tell me he's planning to—?!*

"*Put your legs over my shoulders, Mortis.*"

Mortis's heart hammered a frantic tempo against his ribs when he met his master's hot gaze. The Reaper God's expression was feral with lust. Mortis knew what was about to happen.

His master was going to fulfill one of his filthiest fantasies.

Never in his wildest of dreams could he have believed this possible.

Mortis swallowed and did as he was told. His

heels settled against the Reaper God's back, the new angle tilting his hips forward so his cock jutted toward the deity's face. The Reaper God reached for a pillow and slipped it under Mortis's butt, raising his lower body even higher off the bed.

*"Do you know what I'm going to do to you, Mortis?"*

Mortis nodded jerkily, his gaze locked unblinkingly on the deity staring at him intently from between his legs.

*"Tell me."*

Mortis panted, so turned on he felt he would explode at the slightest touch. "You're—you're going to suck me."

*"Suck...what?"*

Mortis whimpered when the Reaper God's hot breath teased his sensitive shaft. "Master, you're being —you're being mean!"

The Reaper God ignored his protest. *"Say it, Mortis,"* he ordered silkily.

Mortis's fists clenched on the sheets. "My—my cock! You're going to suck my cock!"

Fire blazed in the Reaper God's eyes at his hoarse reply. *"That's right, Mortis. Now be a good boy and watch while I eat you."*

A silent scream locked in Mortis's throat at the first flick of the Reaper God's tongue on his quivering organ. He released a guttural sound, one hand finding his master's head while the other grasped the silken hair draped over his thigh.

The feeling of the deity's mouth on his sex was a

hundred times more pleasurable than he'd imagined it would be.

The Reaper God carefully licked him from the root of his shaft all the way to his leaking tip before circling his slit. He ignored the incoherent noises tumbling from Mortis's lips and repeated the motion again and again. His fingers soon came into play, his touch made slick by his own spit and Mortis's precum.

Mortis's eyes rolled back into his head when the Reaper God finally took him inside the velvety depths of his mouth. The delicious tension he'd experienced before started building up rapidly inside him. It was sharper this time, as if his body had memorized the sensation and was keen to experience it all over again.

"*Master!*" he mewled. He sank his nails into the Reaper God's scalp and tugged him closer.

But his master couldn't reply, not when Mortis was filling his cheeks so well. He dug his heels into the Reaper God's back as the latter started bobbing his head up and down and sucked his dick with powerful contractions of his jaws, his torrid gaze locked on Mortis's face. Mortis's hips rolled of their own volition, soon matching the sinful rhythm his master established.

Ecstasy overwhelmed him once more. He came on a scream, his vision flickering, the loud buzzing in his ears drowning out his desperate voice. And still the Reaper God ate him. His cock soon hardened under his master's skillful ministrations, the pleasure overloading his senses so fierce it was almost pain.

It was only after he'd climaxed a third time that his master finally let go of his dripping cock.

Sweat drenched the sheets beneath Mortis as he collapsed on the bed, so weak from the rapture that had been visited upon his body he could hardly move. The Reaper God rose and reached for a small, glass vial on the side table, his face taut with lust and his erection raging. He knelt between Mortis's legs once more and poured some of the liquid in his palm.

"What's that?" Mortis mumbled.

"*It's the nectar of the Fenoa flowers.*" The Reaper God met his curious stare as he placed the vial next to him. "*It will help with what we're about to do.*" He pressed Mortis's left knee open onto the bed, braced his right leg against his shoulder, and stroked his hole with a slippery finger.

Mortis stiffened.

"*Relax, Mortis,*" the Reaper God murmured. "*Keep looking at me.*"

Mortis shuddered and did as he was told. His ass tingled and throbbed as he kept his gaze on his master. The Reaper God rubbed the potion across the tight folds protecting his entrance, his cheeks flushed with passion.

Mortis wriggled a little, not sure if he liked the sensation or not.

The Reaper God leaned down and kissed him. Mortis sighed, his body melting into the bed and his mouth opening eagerly to welcome the tongue probing his lips.

His master pushed the tip of a finger inside him.

Mortis gasped and went rigid.

The Reaper God's eyes blazed as he continued kissing him. *"You're tight."*

He slipped his finger out and pushed it back inside Mortis's passage. Except this time he went deeper.

Mortis moaned, a different kind of tension seizing him. Heat was spreading through his entire body from where his master had entered him. He hooked his arms around the Reaper God's shoulders and wrenched his mouth from his lips.

"Master?"

*"Yes?"*

"I—I like it." Mortis flushed and buried his face in the crook of the deity's neck, too mortified to look at him. "M—more! I want more!"

The Reaper God stilled. A low growl left him. He removed his finger, spread Mortis's thighs wide, and hitched him high so he could lick his hole.

Mortis arched and cried out, his toes flexing in mid air. He stared dazedly at the dark ceiling as the Reaper God flicked his pucker with his scalding tongue.

He would be lying if he said he hadn't fantasized about his master performing this most wicked of acts on him.

It was everything he'd imagined it to be and more.

His entrance spasmed and unfurled as the Reaper God rimmed him with lustful groans, the sounds almost drowning out Mortis's moans and pants. Then his master's tongue was inside his body and Mortis's sanity scattered to the winds.

He couldn't even begin to describe what it felt like

to have the deity he loved worship him so. He sobbed, overwhelmed by the exquisite sensations assailing his virgin body.

His orgasm swept over him like a storm, as unexpected as it was sudden. A guttural shout left Mortis as he crested the peak he hadn't even seen coming.

The Reaper God kissed and tongued his twitching folds while he shuddered and ejaculated violently all over himself. It wasn't until Mortis had gone limp in his arms that he finally straightened, his long dark hair cascading sensuously on Mortis's inner thighs.

Mortis blinked sweat out of his eyes, his labored breaths loud in his ears. He shivered when he saw his master's face.

The Reaper God's expression was raw with need.

Mortis whimpered when his master began thrusting two fingers in and out of his hole. The Reaper God grabbed the Fenoa nectar and poured some of the liquid directly onto Mortis's opening, lust making his movements awkward. Mortis hissed when the cool liquid splashed across his sensitive entrance. It was soon warmed by the fingers probing him.

Mortis groaned and bowed his head back into the bed when the Reaper God slipped a third digit inside him, stretching him deliciously open. He licked his lips.

It felt good. Much better than he'd thought it would considering this was his first time. He could feel himself growing loose down there. Then the Reaper God did something with his fingers and Mortis saw stars.

*"Master!"*

He grasped the Reaper God's arms. The deity slowed his thrusting and met Mortis's stunned stare. He leaned down and took his mouth in a sweet kiss.

*"That was your sweet spot, Mortis."*

He hooked his fingertips and touched the exquisitely sensitive bump inside Mortis once more.

Mortis's passage spasmed violently around the hot intruders within it. A guttural sob left his throat.

He didn't realize he'd come until he felt the new stickiness coating his belly. He blinked sweat and tears from his eyes before meeting the Reaper God's heated stare, his heart thundering so rapidly he felt it would leap from his chest.

"More, Master!" he breathed. "I want you to do that again!"

A savage expression twisted the Reaper God's face at the husky command. He gave Mortis exactly what he asked for, plundering his ass with his fingers, stroking the place that drove Mortis out of his mind over and over again until he almost passed out from the ecstasy.

By the time the Reaper God removed his fingers from his slack, quivering body, Mortis's throat was hoarse from screaming in pleasure. The Reaper God hooked Mortis's legs around his hips and leaned down to kiss him, his cheeks flushed and his eyes burning bright. He linked their fingers together and trapped Mortis's hands on either side of his head.

Mortis stilled when he felt something hot and hard press against his hole. He locked gaze with his master, his breath freezing on his lips at this delicious overture of what was still to come.

"I want to touch you."

The words were out of his mouth before he could help himself.

The Reaper God froze, surprise widening his eyes. He licked his lips and carefully guided Mortis's right hand to the thick rod jutting from his groin.

Mortis shivered as he caressed the solid length about to impale him. The Reaper God's cock pulsed beneath his touch, silky smooth but for the veins snaking beneath his hot skin.

Mortis didn't know what possessed him to do what he did next.

He lifted his head off the bed and placed his mouth close to his master's ear.

"Master?"

"*Yes?*" the Reaper God said, his tone tight.

"I really want *this* inside me," Mortis whispered. He tugged on the broad head sitting against his loose pucker. "Promise you'll fuck me hard and good, Master."

The Reaper God reared back, like he'd been struck by lightning.

His nostrils dilated violently as he stared at Mortis, his expression feral with lust. He grabbed Mortis's wandering fingers and laced their hands together again.

"*I know I told you to be honest about your feelings, but I fear you're going to be the death of me,*" he groaned.

Mortis grinned. "Wouldn't that be something?" He

leaned up and nipped at his master's jawline with his teeth. "By the way, after you come inside my hole, I want you to come in my mouth and in my hand."

The Reaper God's eyes rounded with shock and desire. Then he growled and punched his hips forward.

Mortis gasped when his master's cock breached his entrance.

He could tell from the Reaper God's taut expression that he was teetering on the edge of losing his self-restraint.

The deity closed his eyes, his head drooping until his hair formed a silken curtain around Mortis. A ragged breath shook his body as he fought for control.

Mortis danced his lips across the Reaper God's brow. "It's okay. I'm ready."

The Reaper God blinked and stared into his eyes. He rocked his hips gently, sinking in inch by delicious inch, his gaze roaming Mortis's face like he was looking for any sign of pain. Mortis swallowed at the burn of his first penetration.

They both hissed when the Reaper God reached the tightest part of him.

His master stilled. "*Are you okay? Should I stop?*"

Sweat beaded Mortis's brow. He shook his head and licked his lips. "Just…just give me a minute."

He inhaled and exhaled shallowly, forcing his body to relax. A gasp shuddered out of him when the Reaper God finally punched past the taut ring of muscles with a fierce grunt.

Then his master was buried inside him to the hilt. The deity froze before staring dazedly at the spot where their bodies were fused together, looking fairly stunned.

Mortis bit his lip at the impossible fullness of the thick cock stretching his passage. He ached and burned and tingled. But it wasn't just discomfort he was feeling.

There was a trace of something else there. A pleasure he had yet to know awaited him still. He was sure of it.

Then there was no more time to think.

For the Reaper God had pulled out and pushed back in, spine bowing and mouth stretching on a fierce grimace.

"Ah!" Mortis's nails scored the back of the Reaper God's hands where they clasped each other's fingers. *"Master!"*

Sparks lit his insides as the Reaper God began plundering his passage with powerful thrusts. Mortis rolled his hips, instinctively matching the cadence he set, seeking the pleasure he'd just tasted.

*"Does it feel good, Mortis?"*

Hot drops splashed onto Mortis's chest. Sweat crowded the Reaper God's brow and snaked down his face. He gazed intently at Mortis, the muscles of his thighs bunching powerfully as he moved.

Mortis met the crimson gaze burning into his face and nodded shakily, too overwhelmed to speak for a moment. The slick sound of flesh entering flesh was making his cock throb.

"It feels—it feels good!" he finally gasped.

The Reaper God let go of one of his hands and grasped his waist.

The new angle had the broad head of the deity's cock hitting Mortis's sweet spot.

"Oh!" he cried out. "*Yes!* Right *there!*"

"*Mortis!*" the Reaper God groaned as he pounded him into the bed.

Their harsh breathing and throaty sounds filled the suite as their bodies fell into a rhythm as old as time.

The Reaper God's pants grew labored, the points of color on his cheekbones bright against his snow white skin. His face glazed over with his growing pleasure. His grip tightened on Mortis's hand and waist. His movements gained in ardor, rocking the bed frame even as they lifted Mortis's body off the sheets.

Mortis welcomed it all, his heart swelling with so much joy he felt it would burst. This sweetly savage mating was everything he could have wished for and more. It was bliss. It was rapture. It was a connection no one else could forge with the deity who was possessing him with passionate strength, his expression radiating a bone deep hunger that would consume him.

A buzzing sound filled Mortis's ears as the dizzying pleasure he was experiencing neared its crest. He convulsed on a guttural groan, back bowing and heels digging into the Reaper God's lower back. His cock pulsed violently, anointing the Reaper God's belly and his own stomach with sticky streaks of musky cum.

The Reaper God hissed when the strong contractions rippling through his passage squeezed and milked his erect length. His motions grew erratic. Crimson bloomed in his eyes.

Mortis could only watch in breathless wonder as the God he loved finally went rigid above him. His master threw his head back, his long hair swaying beautifully as it cascaded down his spine. His neck corded and his mouth opened on an animal noise that was almost pain.

Mortis's passage swelled as the Reaper God climaxed inside him. The deity's hips jerked fitfully, ramming his ejaculating cock deep within Mortis's pleasantly used body. He let go of Mortis's hand and gripped his hip, fixing him to the bed while he pumped out his pleasure with harsh grunts.

Mortis shivered. His master's seed was hot. So hot it scorched his insides and all his senses.

It was some time before the Reaper God stilled and sagged above him. He blinked hazily, pupils constricting and dilating as his awareness slowly returned. He stared at Mortis as if he were seeing him for the first time.

*"Mortis?"*

"Yes, Master?"

The Reaper God leaned down and kissed him with aching tenderness. *"I love you."*

Mortis trembled. His vision blurred, his heart so full to bursting he wanted to sob.

*"I should have told you that before I touched you,"* the Reaper God confessed, his tone somewhat remorseful.

The deity looked at Mortis expectantly in the

silence that followed, a sliver of worry dancing in his eyes.

Mortis swallowed a smile, hooked his arms around his master's neck, and whispered the words he very much wanted to hear against his lips. "I love you too, my one and only Master."

The Reaper God drew a sharp breath at his tremulous confession. Something swelled inside Mortis. He blinked before flushing.

His master was hard again.

The Reaper God shuddered and closed his eyes briefly. *"I'm sorry, Mortis. I'm afraid I cannot stop."* He rolled his hips, his growing erection stretching Mortis's passage as he resumed their sensual mating dance.

*"Master,"* Mortis sighed. Tingles spread though his insides, his body eagerly reacting to the fresh possession. He groaned when the deity's feverish gaze dropped to his own burgeoning cock. "Touch me. Please!"

The Reaper God did just as he asked, his fingers moving expertly on Mortis's aching flesh. Mortis gasped when he lifted him up and sat back on his heels. He blinked as he found himself riding his master's sex, his arms looping instinctively around the deity's shoulders.

The new angle deepened the penetration and drew a lustful groan from them both.

*"I will never tire of this,"* the Reaper God whispered against his throat. *"So, you better prepare yourself, my sweet Mortis."* His pupils flared crimson and gold under

his hooded gaze as he grasped Mortis's hips and moved him up and down his hot length.

Mortis moaned and clung on for dear life, his erection bobbing between their bellies as his master plundered his body over and over again, as eager for the sinful act as the God who held him was.

By the time dawn poked pale fingers on the horizon, they'd mastered several of the positions in the sex manual Pan had given the Reaper God. At the latter's insistence, they stayed five more days in the earthly realm so they could explore all the others the Reaper God had been keen to try.

Mortis did not protest too much, especially since his master let him touch him and eat him to his heart's content.

### THE END

# NIGHTFALL

## AVA MARIE SALINGER

# NIGHTFALL

Theophile Serrano studied his reflection nervously as he adjusted the knot in his tie.

The man staring at him in the mirror with his curly, chestnut hair slicked back and his green eyes sparkling above a navy check suit with a rust-colored waistcoat looked like a stranger.

A wry grimace tugged at Theo's lips.

*It's amazing what a thousand dollar suit does to your appearance.*

His cell phone chimed on the dresser, reminding him of his appointment. Not that he needed reminding.

He'd been counting down the days to his date with Victor Sloan.

Theo headed out of the master bedroom and walked down a hallway to an open plan living space. The setting sun painted riotous colors across the sky filling the outlook of the glass wall to the right, the fading light turning the River Thames and the London skyline a flaming red. Theo stopped and stared, as mesmerized by the sight as when he'd first seen it.

His new apartment was in the same converted granary in Bermondsey where Cassius Black, his blood brother and fellow Guardian of the Nether, owned a place. Theo had moved into it three weeks ago, following the events that had seen Inner London trapped in the Seventh Hell and his identity as a newly awakened demigod revealed to the world.

There were days when Theo still had to pinch himself to check if all of it had been a dream. He only had to sense the soul of the demigod who'd reincarnated inside him and feel the sacred connection that bound them to Victor Sloan to know this was very much his new reality.

He took his car keys from the tray by the front door and headed out of the apartment. A private lift took him down to the underground garage.

The lights of his new Maserati flashed when he neared it.

Theo climbed nervously into the luxury car. Though his recently appointed position in the Order of Rosen came with an eye-watering salary and perks that were usually reserved for diplomats and royalty, he still wasn't used to his newfound fame and glory or the lavish lifestyle that accompanied it. His body may house the soul shard of the previous South Star, but his human origins were a humble one.

Theo pursed his lips as he settled in the leather seat and scanned the opulent interior of his ride. The car had been a gift from Victor.

The demigod head of Cabalista had showered him with plenty of expensive presents since they'd started going out, but even Theo had protested when he'd given him the keys to the custom-made Maserati on their third date.

"I can't accept this, Victor," Theo had objected where they'd sat eating in an expensive hotel in the West End.

"You need a new car," Victor had replied with a dismissive shrug before taking a sip of his wine.

"Who the hell buys his boyfriend a Maserati?" Theo had groaned.

"I do," Victor had said arrogantly. His expression had softened at Theo's scowl. He'd reached across the table and taken Theo's hand, his thumb caressing Theo's knuckles. "Besides, it's to make up for missing our last date."

The apology in his blue eyes had had Theo falling silent.

With the capital still recovering from the disaster that had befallen it, the local bureaus of the agencies governing the otherworldly had seen an unprecedented rise in requests for assistance. Victor's workload had more than doubled and he often spent late hours at the Cabalista headquarters in Finsbury. He'd ended up not just missing their second date, but their fourth and fifth ones too.

Tonight was different though. Victor had promised he would make their rendezvous come hell or high water. Theo had been able to tell from the frustration lacing his voice when they'd last spoken that he loathed not being able to see him. Not least because it meant Victor couldn't touch Theo.

Heat warmed Theo's cheeks as he drove out of the garage and headed west into London. Though he and Victor had kissed and indulged in some heavy petting after their dates, they hadn't progressed beyond that. Victor had always taken Theo home and bade him goodnight like a perfect gentleman before leaving.

It was a state of affairs Theo found increasingly difficult to fathom. He and Rohengar were Victor's soulmates. That much had become inherently clear when they'd battled the dark God Elios and rescued London from the Seventh Hell. Yet Victor didn't appear as eager to consummate their relationship as Theo was.

Which had led Theo to finally decide to take the bull by the horns.

*Tonight. I'll make him make love to us tonight. Even if I have to ambush him!*

Though Rohengar harbored some misgivings about his plan to seduce Victor, he'd not protested too strongly. If anything, he seemed fascinated by Theo's determination to get his man.

*Don't worry Rohengar,* Theo had promised. *You're finally going to get your wish. I'll make sure Coraos eats you tonight.*

Rohengar had sighed heavily at this.

Theo's pulse quickened when he crossed Westminster Bridge.

Victor had booked a table for them at a swanky restaurant in Soho.

He navigated the narrow streets of the West End and pulled up outside an elegant building with a dark and gold frontage moments later. A parking attendant came out and took his keys when he stepped out of the Maserati.

Theo became aware of the curious stares of passersby as he crossed the curb and headed for the entrance. Excited murmurs sounded when several people recognized him. A camera flashed.

Theo flushed and ducked his head.

Even the doorman couldn't completely hide his awe as he welcomed him inside the building and guided him to a private lift. Theo emerged in a small, resplendent foyer on the third floor a moment later. A maître d'hôtel stood behind a mahogany reception desk. He brightened at the sight of Theo.

"Ah, the guest of honor is here."

Theo gave him a puzzled half-smile. "Hi. My partner made a reservation. His name is Victor Sloan."

"Of course," the man said effusively. "Follow me, Mr. Serrano."

Crystal chandeliers shed an artfully subdued lighting around Theo as he headed through an arched doorway into the restaurant. The place was the definition of opulence, the oak paneling and gold-quartz speckled terrazzo floors complementing the black leather chairs and marble tables, and the rich colors of the Victorian furnishings.

It took Theo all of three seconds to clock that the place was deserted. He glanced at his watch.

It was past seven o'clock on a Friday night. He'd expected the place to be packed.

The maître d'hôtel spied his confused expression.

"Oh. Did Mr. Sloan not tell you? He reserved the entire restaurant."

Theo's stomach dropped. "He did what?!"

The man smiled. "We don't usually accept requests to secure the whole place, especially on a Friday night, but we couldn't refuse a deity who helped save the city."

Theo became aware of the not so subtle stares of the handful of waiters and waitresses around him. Even the bartender was trying his best not to ogle him as he pretended to clean a glass.

To his surprise, the maître d'hôtel led him to a private dining room at the back of the restaurant. Theo's eyes widened when he saw the vases of flowers and glittering candelabras crowding the sideboards. The scent of roses filled the space, adding to the intimate mood.

His mouth dried.

The place looked like the perfect setting for a grand, romantic gesture.

Excitement buzzed through Theo's veins as he accepted the glass of champagne the maître d'hôtel poured him. Tonight was going to be special. He could feel it in his bones.

*I'm glad it's my birthday.*

He'd deliberately not told Victor about the special date. Knowing the demigod, he would probably give him an island. Theo would rather just spend time with him.

*That's the best gift he could ever grant me.*

The thrill Theo was feeling slowly died as an hour ticked by and Victor failed to turn up. He checked his messages and voicemail and even tried calling the demigod, to no avail. The maître d'hôtel gave him an awkward glance when he served him a second bread basket.

By ten o'clock, Theo was certain Victor wasn't coming. He apologized to the maître d'hôtel and the staff and left a large tip for everyone before walking out of the restaurant with his ears flaming.

*I can't believe he bailed on us!*

Victor had always contacted Theo beforehand when he'd been unable to make their date.

*Is he—is he bored with us?!* Tears blurred Theo's vision as he got behind the wheel of his car. *Or is it that we are of so little importance to him that he couldn't even be bothered to grant us an excuse for standing us up this time?*

The warm scent of summer flooded his senses as Rohengar's presence rose inside him, the demigod doing his best to soothe him.

*Don't make excuses for him, Rohengar!* Theo clenched his jaw and wiped his eyes. His disappointment was turning to fury. *The only way he's coming anywhere near us is if he gets down on his hands and knees and begs us for our forgiveness!* His knuckles whitened on the steering wheel. *No, make that crawl on his belly like the mangy dog he is!*

Theo gunned the engine and drove out of Soho.

Instead of heading across the river, he skirted the northern embankment and turned east.

He didn't want to go back to his empty apartment right now.

Theo drove through Whitechapel and soon entered Spitalfields. He pulled up outside an old, brown brick building ringed on three sides by a park, turned off the engine, and looked up at a dark window on the second floor.

He still had the keys to his old studio.

Theo quietly let himself inside the building. Silence greeted him when he entered the place he'd rented when he'd first come to the city. He flicked on a floor lamp next to a couch.

The soft light revealed a practically bare room, the only furniture beside the couch a metal bed and a small dining table with two chairs. A door to the right opened onto a tiny bathroom overlooking the street.

Theo's shoulders drooped. The anger he'd felt on the drive over had drained away, leaving him weary. Concern gnawed at his insides.

*Did something happen to Victor?*

He suspected he and Rohengar would have felt it in their soul core had the demigod been in a danger. And his newborn instincts as the South Star would have warned him had Elios's dark forces invaded the city. Still, he'd checked the radio channels for live news updates while he'd been driving and had been relieved to find out nothing untoward had happened in London that night.

Which only served to highlight the fact that Victor had thoroughly dumped him and Rohengar.

Theo kicked off his shoes, climbed on the bed, and closed his eyes, his throat tight and his chest hot.

✿

RELIEF MADE VICTOR SLOAN WEAK WHEN HE SPOTTED the Maserati parked in the shadows of some trees on the road below.

The maître d'hôtel had been about to lock up when he'd arrived at the restaurant in Soho. The man told him Theo had left an hour ago. Victor had immediately flown to Theo's new apartment in Bermondsey, only to find the place dark and empty.

He'd been racking his brain trying to figure out where the demigod could have gone when he'd remembered his old studio in Spitalfields.

Victor was conscious he'd abused his authority as the head of Cabalista by using his wings in a non-combat situation, but he honestly couldn't care less about that right now.

He pulled up sharply above the building housing Theo's old apartment and levitated to a window overlooking the park.

The soft light of a lamp washed over Theo where he lay sleeping on a metal bed.

Victor closed his eyes and shuddered.

*Thank Heaven he's here!*

He knew Theo was likely furious with him for standing him up. Though Victor had a decent excuse for his absence, he suspected the demigod would not forgive him easily this time around. He hesitated before knocking on the window.

Theo stirred. He rose on an elbow and rubbed his eyes blearily with the back of a hand. He froze when he spotted Victor through the glass.

Fury darkened his face. He jumped off the bed, stormed over to the window, and yanked the curtains closed in Victor's face.

Victor sagged, wings dipping. He knocked on the window again.

"Let me in, Theo. We need to talk."

"Go talk to yourself, asshole!" Theo yelled.

Lights were coming on in the rest of the building. A window opened below Victor. He snapped his wings and rose.

There was an access door on the rooftop.

He broke the lock, walked down a narrow flight of stairs, and reached the front door of Theo's studio seconds later.

"I'm not going away until you let me in, Theo," Victor said through the heavy wood.

His answer was a muffled curse.

A door opened farther along the passage. A woman peered out, a frying pan in her hand.

"What—what's going on?!"

Theo's door opened abruptly. The scowling demigod grabbed Victor's wrist and tugged him across the threshold.

The woman gasped. "Oh! Aren't you that Victor—?!"

Theo's door slammed closed, shutting the world out.

Victor's breath got knocked out of him when the furious demigod grabbed him by the throat and slammed him up against a wall.

"At least do me the fucking decency of leaving me alone when I ask you to!" Theo hissed, his pupils flaring gold. "You seemed to ignore me just fine these last couple of weeks so I don't get why—!" He froze in the next instant. The color drained from his face. "Why is there blood on your clothes?" he mumbled numbly.

Victor winced at the itching on his left shoulder and arm. His injuries had almost finished healing.

"A maintenance team found a monster's den in an abandoned section of the underground," he explained as Theo let him go, the demigod's green gaze locked on the crimson-stained claw marks on his suit. "It looks like they'd been there since London was in the Seventh Hell. I got the call when I was on my way over to the restaurant." Victor grimaced and ran a hand through his hair. "I'm sorry, I should have called you before I headed into the underground. I was confident it wouldn't take me and the Cabalista agents who were there long to get rid of the creatures, but they were fire monsters. I was the only one who could fight them. One of them crushed my phone when it hit me."

Theo shuddered.

Victor's chest tightened at his ashen face.

"It looks worse than it feels, honestly," he reassured. "The wounds are nearly gone." He faltered. "I'm truly sorry, Theo. I—*Argh!*"

Theo's fist had smashed into Victor's gut. He wheezed, shocked.

"You should have asked me to help you," Theo grated out, hands clenched tightly at his sides and chin trembling as he glared at Victor. "Isn't that what partners are for?! Isn't that what," the demigod stopped and swallowed, "what *soulmates* are for?!"

A tear overspilled Theo's eye and trickled down his cheek.

Victor tugged him in his arms, guilt twisting his insides. "Don't. Don't cry, please." He burrowed his face in the crook of Theo's neck. "It breaks my heart to see your tears."

Theo's hands found his back, his fingers clenching tightly on Victor's suit. His voice came out in a quivering whisper.

"Does that mean you still love us?"

A heavy feeling pooled in the pit of Victor's stomach. He straightened and took hold of Theo's shoulders as he stared into his glistening eyes, his pulse pounding heavily in his veins. "Why would you even say that?" He clenched his jaw. "Does Rohengar feel the same way?"

Theo sniffed and shook his head. "He told me to be patient but I—I thought you might be getting be bored with us."

Victor took Theo's hand and led him to the couch. He sat him down, their knees touching as they faced one another.

"I love you, Theophile," Victor said quietly. "And

Coraos loves Rohengar. Those two facts will never change for as long as we have breath left in us."

The way Theo searched his face made Victor feel like an utter bastard.

"Do you—do you really mean that?"

"Yes." Victor kissed Theo's eyelids tenderly and pulled him into his arms. "I swear it in the name of Heaven."

"Then, why haven't we had sex yet?" Theo mumbled against his chest.

Victor flinched. He met Theo's faintly accusing expression guiltily as the demigod looked up at him.

"Are Rohengar and I not to your liking?"

Victor groaned. *He is killing me.*

Having Theo this close after so many days apart was sheer torture. From the heaviness pooling in his dick, his body felt the same.

"I want to take things slow," he confessed stiffly.

Theo's eyes widened when Victor straightened, clasped his hand, and pressed a hot kiss to his knuckles.

"I want to woo you."

Theo blinked. "Woo be damned. I want sex."

Victor choked on a bark of laughter.

Theo chewed his lip and cocked his head. "Is this because you took Cassius to bed two weeks after your first date?"

Victor drew a sharp breath. "He told you that?"

Theo shrugged. "I was curious, so I asked him."

Regret knotted Victor's belly. "I should have treated

him better." Determination hardened his voice. "I won't make the same mistake with you and Rohengar."

Theo frowned. "Look, I get that you want to court us, but Rohengar and I are about at the end of our patience. Me more than Rohengar. I'm honestly surprised that guy didn't jump you before the Fall." He paused and narrowed his eyes as he listened to whatever it was Rohengar was telling him. "Oh, please," Theo scoffed. "You and I both know exactly what you wanted Coraos to do to you."

Victor's lips twitched.

"What?" Theo said suspiciously.

"You guys are cute when you argue with one another."

Theo bristled at his grin. "Look here, asshole. No one wants to hear they're cute. And I'm telling you we want you to—*hmph, hmph!*"

Victor swallowed Theo's recalcitrant words with his mouth.

The demigod stiffened before melting in his hold. A moan left him when Victor probed his lips with his tongue and slipped inside. The fire that had been smoldering in Victor's gut for the past few weeks ignited at the way Theo responded to him.

It took all his willpower to end their torrid kiss.

"Are you sure?" Victor whispered. "Because once we start this, I won't be able to stop, however much you or Rohengar beg me to."

Theo nodded tremulously. "Yes. It's not midnight yet, so it's still my birthday. I want this as my gift."

Victor froze. "What?"

Theo lowered his gaze sheepishly. "I knew you'd buy me something ridiculous if I told you, so I kept quiet about it," he mumbled.

Victor inhaled raggedly. "That...makes me a little upset."

Theo peeked at him hopefully from beneath his lashes. "Upset enough to punish me?"

Victor groaned. Theo's sparkling eyes made it clear the demigod wouldn't mind if Victor disciplined him in bed.

"Has anyone ever told you you have a one-track mind?"

"Most virgins do," Theo confessed, not in the least bit abashed.

He yelped as Victor slung him over his shoulder in a lightning fast move and carried him across the room.

A gasp whooshed out of him when Victor dropped him on the bed.

Victor climbed on the sheets and knelt above Theo. "This isn't exactly what I had in mind for your first time." He glanced around the spartan room.

Theo swallowed. "I don't mind where we do it."

"I do." Victor trailed a finger from the pulse beating frantically at the base of Theo's throat all the way down his chest and quivering belly to the telltale bulge in his pants. "You deserve satin sheets strewn with rose petals and candlelight." His voice dropped an octave, lust heating his own flesh. "Every delectable inch of you merits to be wooed and worshipped."

*I AM GOING TO LOSE MY FREAKING MIND.*

Theo shivered when Victor traced a lazy pattern on his rock-hard cock. He grabbed Victor's face and tugged him down to kiss him, his soul core throbbing as desire seared his senses.

Victor made a low sound of approval when Theo melded their tongues in a hungry, heady dance. Black flames flickered into life around him, the haze warming Theo's fingers where he clasped the demigod's hard jawline.

Victor straightened, sat back on his heels, and reached for the knot in his tie, his erection tenting his trousers and his cheekbones flushed with passion.

Theo's mouth dried as he watched Victor undress.

The demigod's body was even more spectacular than he'd imagined it would be, his muscles sharply defined and toned to perfection, every hard line and angle an ode to his devastating masculinity.

Theo gulped when Victor's manhood sprung free. It had been a while since he'd seen that part of him.

*I can't wait to have him inside me.*

The heat suffusing his insides told him Rohengar was just as enthralled by the sight of Victor's thick cock.

Victor took Theo's mouth in hot kisses as he stripped him of his three-piece suit.

"By the way, I forgot to tell you how handsome you look in that."

Theo nodded distractedly, too focused on Victor's hands where he was undoing his belt buckle to pay attention to much else.

"Are you listening to me?" Victor nibbled on the inside of Theo's left knee as he yanked his boxers and trousers down his legs.

Theo shuddered at the love bite, his dick jutting proudly from his groin.

"I want to suck you," he told Victor bluntly.

Victor cursed. He grabbed their neckties from the bed and secured Theo's wrists to the metal bars making up the headboard in the blink of an eye.

"Oh."

Victor smiled smugly at Theo's shocked look. "Bet you weren't expecting that."

Theo licked his lips. "That was number three on my fantasy list. Number four for Rohengar."

Victor stared. He burst out laughing in the next instant.

Theo's mouth pressed to a thin line.

"I'm sorry," Victor snorted, his eyes crinkling at Theo's annoyed look. "It's just—you never fail to surprise me. I really love that about you. Both of you."

Theo's stomach flip-flopped at his heartfelt words.

The air thickened with sexual tension as they looked at one another.

Theo's breath stuttered when Victor raked his body with a heated gaze, his stare scorching his skin and leaving a trail of fire in its wake.

"You are so beautiful."

The demigod's hoarse voice sent a shiver down Theo's spine.

Victor bent down and sucked Theo's right nipple into his mouth.

"Oh!" Theo bucked his hips, precum oozing on the tip of his cock.

Victor's nostrils flared at the musky scent. He straightened and traced the stickiness trailing down Theo's shaft with a light finger.

"This part of you is especially pretty." Gold flared in his eyes. "Doubly so when it's wet."

Heat warmed Theo's cheeks. His flesh tingled as Victor caressed him with a featherlight touch. Victor wrapped his hand around Theo's cock and began stroking him in earnest.

Theo bit his lip on a sound of pure pleasure, the sweet friction everything as thrilling as he remembered it.

A dangerous smile stretched Victor's mouth as he watched Theo squirm on the bed and punch his cock through his fingers.

"This is your first punishment, Theophile."

Confusion shot through Theo. It wasn't until Victor worked him close to an orgasm and let go of his straining cock so he could watch from hooded eyes as Theo rolled his hips helplessly off the bed and sought his release that he understood Victor's meaning.

Blood thundered in Theo's skull as he held Victor's scorching gaze.

He couldn't have looked away from the demigod even if he'd wanted to in that moment.

The feral expression on Victor's face.

The naked lust burning in his glowing eyes.

All of it told Theo he was finally seeing Victor's true

carnal self. A side of him he'd never shown to Theo for fear of scaring him.

But Theo wasn't scared. And neither was Rohengar.

They accepted Victor's every caress as he teased and edged them over and over again until a pool of precum formed on their belly and their breathless pleas for release filled the room.

"What were your number one and number two fantasies, Theo?" Victor growled as he began rubbing his exquisitely sensitive flesh again.

"I—I wanted you to make me come with your tongue in my ass! *Oh!*" Theo squeezed his eyes shut and hissed at the electrifying tingles throbbing through his cock and making his passage clench. "And—and I wanted you to take me from behind, doggy style! *Ah!*"

"And Rohengar?"

"*Hmm!*" Theo hummed. "That feels—*argh!*"

Victor pinched the tip of his shaft with just enough pressure to make him feel a sliver of pain but not enough to hurt him.

"Tell me, Theophile," the demigod demanded, his voice rough with passion.

"He—he wanted you to touch and lick him all over!" Theo whimpered and bit his lip so hard he almost broke the skin. "Victor! *Enough!* We—we want to come!"

"That was just fantasy number one," Victor said, unrelenting.

Agonizing tension spiraled through every inch of Theo's body.

"Rohengar—Rohengar wanted you to take him

hard," he gasped. "Hard enough to make him scream. And he wanted to ride you!"

"Good boy," Victor murmured.

He lowered his head and sucked Theo's cock inside his mouth.

A buzzing sound filled Theo's world as he finally crested the towering peak of ecstasy Victor had brought him to. Sound and sight faded as he convulsed on the bed, his cock spurting fitfully in the hot confines of Victor's cheeks, his wrists straining against the ties binding him.

He came to to find Victor licking his lips with a sinful expression where he knelt between his legs. Victor gave his own cock a few tugs before undoing Theo's restraints. He kissed Theo, flipped him on his front, and worked a pillow under his belly.

Theo's pulse stuttered as Victor moved down the bed. He gripped the sheets when Victor spread his butt cheeks and gave the demigod a wild look over his shoulder.

"Here comes fantasy number one," Victor promised sultrily.

He ducked his head and flicked his tongue across Theo's tight folds.

"*Aaah!*" Theo squirmed, hips punching his stirring cock into the bed.

Victor pinned him with a strong grip and spent several torturous minutes lavishing his hole with teasing strokes of his wicked tongue as he softened his entrance. He sucked his pucker and blew air across his tingling nerve endings, making him gasp and groan.

Theo's eyes almost rolled back in his head when Victor finally spread him open with his thumbs and speared his tongue inside his body. His knuckles whitened, the incoherent sounds falling from his lips echoing in his ears as he worked his hard cock helplessly on the sheets, the beautiful tension heralding his orgasm spiraling through his spine and limbs once more.

Their soul cores resonated with a heat that drew a savage growl from Victor and a tortured sob from Theo and Rohengar both.

Victor hitched Theo's hips higher and fucked him with his tongue, each thrust driving him deeper inside his quivering passage. He reached under Theo's body and fondled his dripping cock and trembling balls.

The dual stimulation tipped Theo over the edge, the sounds he and Rohengar made as they came making his face grow even hotter.

His hole twitched when Victor extracted his tongue from his body. The demigod gave his convulsing pucker a final kiss before letting him go.

"You can tick that fantasy off your wish list," Victor murmured. "Let's move on to the next one, shall we?"

"Oh!" Theo's eyes rounded as Victor spread the cum he'd spilled in his palm across his loose opening.

Victor slipped a finger inside him and probed around until he found the spot that made Theo see stars.

"There it is."

Theo shivered, sweat beading his face as Victor worked his passage open with steady thrusts. Victor slipped a second finger inside him, then a third, making him hiss with pleasure.

Victor kissed Theo's back. "Does that feel good?"

Theo hummed and nodded jerkily.

"I'm glad," Victor said, his tone gruff with desire. "My cock is going to feel ten times better."

Theo bit his lip. He'd never imagined sex with Victor would be this filthy or this sinfully good. The way Victor played with his body was so erotic he knew having his cock inside him would wreck him in ways that would practically make him swoon with pleasure.

Victor scissored his fingers and spread Theo as wide as he could.

Then he pulled Theo up on his hands and knees, crowded his back, and parted his butt cheeks.

"Here I come." Victor took hold of Theo's chin so he could twist his head around and claim his mouth as he pressed his cock to his opening.

Theo's heart thundered violently as Victor entered him, their gazes locked unblinkingly on one another.

He winced when Victor reached the tightest part of him.

"Breathe, Theophile." Victor nibbled on his lower lip and worked his hand around Theo's front so he could stroke his quivering cock.

Theo moaned and panted, forcing his body to relax. His eyes flared when Victor breached the taut ring and filled him to the hilt.

Victor stilled and closed his eyes. "Fuck! You're so tight!" He gnashed his teeth, his fingers sinking into Theo's skin where he gripped his waist.

He withdrew a little and nudged his cock back in, his expression pained, like he was barely holding on to his self control.

Theo gasped at the hot friction. He instinctively squeezed his passage. The motion elicited a heartfelt curse from Victor.

Victor pulled out even more and plunged back in, his thrusts slow and steady as he established a sensual rhythm that fairly robbed Theo of his senses.

"The way your hole is squeezing my dick tells me you're really enjoying this," Victor hissed.

"I am," Theo confessed breathlessly. "You were right. Your cock feels ten times better than your fingers!"

Victor groaned.

The warm scent of summer filled the room as Rohengar made his presence felt.

*"Harder, Coraos!"*

Victor growled and bit Theo's shoulder as he gave in to the demigod's command. The bed creaked when his movements grew more forceful.

Theo grabbed the metal headboard and rocked to and fro, each slick motion of Victor's cock inside his body making bright spots burst across his vision.

Rohengar's lustful moans merged with Theo's throaty gasps and cries as Victor fulfilled both their fantasies and claimed their bodies with untamed passion, his grunts savage and his grip painful where he clutched their waist.

Their climax when it came made their soul cores blaze and scorched the room with dazzling beams as

divine power blazed from their eyes, their shouts of
pleasure tortured and wild.

Theo panted when Victor pulled out of his body,
flipped him on his back, and plunged back inside him,
the black flames simmering around him cocooning
them in a sultry heat that made every inch of Theo
tingle.

Tension knotted Theo's spine and belly as he and
Rohengar approached the crest of their next orgasm.

Victor's features distorted on a feral expression, his
climax hitting him at the same time they convulsed
around his plundering cock. He withdrew a moment
later, grabbed Theo's wrist, and tugged him up.

"Ride me!"

Theo's chest heaved with his breaths when Victor
sat back on his heels and guided him so he straddled
his groin. His every nerve ending sizzled and tingled
from the overwhelming pleasure he and Rohengar had
experienced tonight.

But there was still plenty more to feel.

Because just as he and Rohengar hungered for the
devastating ecstasy they had found in Victor's arms, so
did Victor's desire for them seem unquenched.

Sweat dripped off Theo's face as he took hold of
Victor's hard cock and slowly impaled himself upon it.
He let Rohengar take over their fused souls as he rose
and sank sensuously, the demigod finally claiming the
pleasure he had only ever dreamed about in his past
life.

Violent pulses of light throbbed from Victor's eyes

as Coraos rode his soul and fucked Rohengar hard and deep, his mouth ravishing Rohengar's lips hungrily.

A wondrous expression washed across his flushed face as he watched Rohengar explode in his arms. He pressed hot lips to the column of Theo's throat, his hips thrusting passionately through the convulsions of the demigod quivering in his embrace.

*"Rohengar!"*

Dawn was poking pale fingers across the night sky above London when they finally succumbed to sleep in each other's arms, bodies limp and sated.

Theo woke up hours later to Victor's lips dancing lightly across his nape.

"Hmm." He wriggled and sighed. "What time is it?"

"It's two o'clock."

Theo's eyes snapped open. He gasped and bolted upright. "Shit! We're late for work!"

Victor stared at him blankly before bursting out in a belly laugh that filled the room.

"I—I wished I could claim I fucked you for three days straight, but it's still Saturday, Theo," he wheezed.

Theo flushed and rubbed the back of his neck awkwardly. "Oh."

Victor arched an eyebrow at his embarrassed expression and trailed a finger down his back. "It was that good, huh?"

Theo narrowed his eyes a little. "You're looking awfully smug."

Victor grinned and folded his arms behind his head. "That's because I'm confident about my skills. Besides, your croaky voice is enough evidence of how splendidly I made you and Rohengar—"

He groaned when Theo climbed on top of him and kissed him.

"Yeah, yeah, your dick is a wonder of the world."

Victor palmed his butt cheeks and rolled his hips.

Theo sucked in air as their stirring cocks brushed.

"Just this world?" Victor nibbled on Theo's lower lip.

Theo gave him a pitying look. "Wow. So you're saying your dick is a wonder of all the realms?"

"I think I have a fighting chance of claiming that position," Victor declared arrogantly.

Theo laughed. Then he moaned and hissed and gasped as Victor flipped him on his back and worked his wicked hands and mouth down his body.

THE END

# BELOVED

AVA MARIE SALINGER

# BELOVED

THE DULCET CORDS OF HARPS AND LYRES FILLED THE AIR, the harmonious sounds underscoring the clear, bright tones of flutes rising from an invisible celestial orchestra. The soft tinkling of water added to the beguiling melody, the jets spouting from the hundred crystal fountains adorning the open-roofed banquet hall and the gardens sparkling magically under the shimmering constellations and swirling galaxies stretched across an endless night sky.

Icarus observed the Gods and demigods circulating through the reception over his glass of nectar where he sat in a private arbor suspended above a small lake. It was the second day of the week-long banquet all divine beings were required to attend every one hundred years and was as much a social gathering as it was an opportunity for new demigods to be introduced and pay their respects to the Gods of Old.

It was Icarus's fourth time attending the function since he'd taken the seat of the North Star.

*Not much has changed since we were last here.*

He was not sure if this was a good thing in view of the rumor that had been circulating of late.

Icarus became conscious of the avid stares he was drawing from the busy crowd. It was the reason the Guardians had requested a private pergola outside the main hall for the duration of the festivities. Though he had long grown accustomed to the naked longing with which many of the guests who attended the banquet openly regarded him, it was still uncomfortable to be the focus of such heated gazes.

He was distracted from his aggrieved thoughts by a low grumble.

"Like peacocks showing off their plumes," someone groused under their breath.

Icarus glanced at the hulking, red-haired demigod leaning against a marble column beside him. Archon, the West Star and custodian of the war hammer Echo, was scowling at the glittering figures below.

"Better not let our Heavenly fathers and mothers hear you utter such blasphemy," Icarus told his brother-in-arms drily.

"I shall give them blasphemy," Archon scoffed. "Look at them! Tarted up to the eyeballs and acting like they have nary a concern in this world." He narrowed his eyes, outrage simmering in the tawny depths. "Of course they don't, the damn fools. We're the ones working our armors off keeping them safe from the dangers lurking outside the Nether."

Icarus swallowed a sigh. Arguing with Archon when he was in this mood was about as productive as trying to convince war demons not to be the monsters they were born to be.

"Why does Archon look like he's about to eat someone?"

A beautiful, dark-haired demigod holding two platters loaded with succulent fruits and fine meats had alighted onto the arbor. Icarus smiled softly at his blood brother Rohengar, the South Star and wielder of the Spear of Light.

Nildar, the East Star and keeper of the divine bow Sky Piercer, landed gracefully in Rohengar's wake, not a drop spilled from the drinks he carried. He gave one to Archon.

"Here, how about you down that and relax? Rohengar and I could feel your murderous vibes from the other side of the banquet hall. Even the Winter God was shuddering."

Archon accepted the glass grudgingly. "Yes, well, maybe Boreas should stop being a giant baby and help us out in the Nether."

"You're the biggest baby here," Nildar pointed out.

Archon sucked in air.

Translucent wings shimmered out of the corner of Icarus's eyes as Archon and Nildar launched into one of their caustic exchanges. Several attendants hovered close by, their expressions nervous as they peered at the four Stars. Though they were meant to serve all the Gods and demigods at the banquet equally, the reputation of the Guardians was such that most weren't sure how to behave around them.

Archon's glares and Nildar's icy stares hadn't helped matters thus far.

Rohengar sighed. "Stop fighting you two. You're scaring the servants."

"We're not scaring them," Archon scoffed.

Nildar's green eyes glinted with cold menace as he glanced at the loitering figures. "If this is enough to frighten them, they shouldn't have signed up for the position."

A Naiad overheard his remark. Her face crumpled. She darted into some bushes, her wings trembling like jewels as she sobbed. Her friends arrowed toward her to console her.

Rohengar pinched the bridge of his nose. "Great. You made her cry."

"She'll get over it," Nildar said dismissively.

Archon smirked.

"Daphne won't be pleased," Rohengar warned.

Nildar and Archon sobered. Even the Guardians knew not to cross the queen of the Naiads. Daphne might come across as sweetness and light, but she was a Goddess who had annihilated entire battlefields in the past and was fiercely loyal to her kin.

"Maybe I should apologize," Nildar muttered.

"By the way, where did you find that?" Archon indicated the bottle the East Star had brought from the banquet hall.

"This?" Nildar's lips tilted in a mocking smile as he waved the bottle. "It's a present. A specialty of the Spirit Realm. I've been meaning to try it for a while."

Archon's eyes flashed. "You got that from that horned bastard?!" he spat.

"If you mean the Wild God, then the answer is yes," Nildar replied blithely.

Rohengar studied the East Star with a trace of concern. "Be careful, brother. Pan isn't one to bestow gifts without asking for something in return."

"Indeed," Archon groused. "That son of a goat loves nothing more than forcing people into his service in exchange for a favor."

"You are correct." Nildar shrugged. "I had to promise him something."

Archon stiffened. He fisted his hands, brows lowering in a fierce glare. "What kind of god-awful request did that brute make of you?!"

"I owe him a sexual favor," Nildar said nonchalantly.

Icarus choked on his drink. Rohengar dropped the piece of fruit he had just pierced with a fork.

The glass in Archon's hand exploded into glittering shards.

"You fool!" Nildar rushed over, grabbed Archon's hand, and used a napkin to dab at the cuts on the West Star's palm.

Icarus leaned toward Rohengar.

"He knows Archon can just heal himself, right?" he whispered sotto voce.

Rohengar hushed him.

"Did you—" Archon stopped and swallowed, unheeding of his wounds. "Did you really tell Pan he could bed you?!" His frozen gaze remained locked on Nildar.

Nildar scowled. "Of course not! I was only jesting. Besides, you know as well as I do that becoming a Guardian practically means taking a vow of celibacy."

"Oh." Archon sagged. "That's—that's right." His cuts began to mend as he came to his senses.

Silvery laughter drew Icarus's gaze to the main banquet hall. A group of Goddesses had just arrived. From the way the crowd converged on them, their company was sought-after.

"It's the Moirai and the Hesperides," Rohengar observed, a hint of surprise underscoring his voice.

Nildar and Archon wandered over to his side.

Icarus studied the Goddesses greeting old friends and acquaintances with bright voices and tactful smiles. Their beauty was dazzling even for deities and their confident bearing spoke of the power they wielded.

Nildar blinked. "Oh."

Archon raised an eyebrow. "Now *that's* one for the books."

Icarus followed their stares.

A second group of Goddesses had entered the hall behind the Moirai and the Hesperides. Though just as physically stunning, their wings were as black as night and their austere auras signaled the darker nature of their divine abilities.

Icarus knew without being told that he was looking at the Furies and the Black Fates, blood sisters of the Moirai and the Hesperides.

The reticent manner in which the dark winged Goddesses were being welcomed was in sharp contrast to the reception their bright-haired and white-winged siblings had earned.

Icarus frowned slightly.

*Their presence may be daunting but still, it is rather rude not to show them the same respect as their blood kin.*

"It has been a good five hundred years since I last saw all of Nyx's daughters gathered under one roof," Rohengar murmured.

Icarus glanced curiously at his brother. Rohengar had left Rain Vale and assumed the seat of the South Star long before he himself was chosen to be a Guardian.

"I thought all deities were obliged to attend the centennial banquet."

"They are, if their duties allow," Rohengar replied. He exchanged a troubled look with Nildar and Archon.

"It seems the daughters of Nyx have been busy behind the scenes, just as we have been in the Nether," Nildar said broodingly.

Lines wrinkled Archon's brow. "We should talk to them. See if they have heard the same whispers that have reached our ears."

Unease prickled Icarus's scalp as he probed the Goddesses' neutral expressions.

*Could the reason that they have scarcely attended the banquets of late have something to do with what we've heard? That a God might be planning some kind of rebellion?*

Movement behind the Black Fates captured his gaze. Icarus's eyes widened.

Rohengar drew a sharp breath beside him.

Two figures had alighted at the entrance of the banquet hall. One was a handsome demigod with fair hair and dark wings that sizzled with stygian flames. The other figure was barely visible where he was wrapped in a storm of black wind.

Icarus's belly tightened when the inky currents parted to reveal the second demigod's form.

Jet-black hair crowned the deity's tall, imposing frame. His eyes shone the color of purest cobalt and his sharply chiseled features would challenge even the prettiest Moirai's charms. A shimmering tunic hugged his powerful body, the hem stopping just short of his knees and hinting at the muscular thighs beneath.

Icarus swallowed.

He flinched when Archon spoke. Heat warmed his ears when he realized he'd nearly been caught staring at the dark demigod below like a lovestruck fool.

"Who's that with Coraos?" Archon was frowning at the new arrivals.

Icarus recognized the name he had uttered. Coraos was a demigod son of Nyx.

*He must be the one with the gold-spun hair and dark flames.*

"I believe that is Ivmir," Rohengar replied.

Something in his brother's voice had Icarus looking over at him. The South Star was still watching Coraos. A faint flush of color crept upon Rohengar's cheeks.

Surprise swept through Icarus.

He had never seen that expression on his brother's face before.

Rohengar took a shallow breath and recovered his composure.

Icarus hesitated before choosing to maintain his silence. It was not his place to question what he had just glimpsed in Rohengar's bright, sapphire eyes.

Nildar pursed his lips. "So that's the demigod Nyx sired with Queen Atlanteia's son," he muttered, his focus on Ivmir. "It explains the Dryad magic I can feel from him." The East Star brightened in the next instant, the glee in his green eyes telling Icarus he had just recalled something that had tickled his funny bone. "Wait. Wasn't he the one who got banned from attending the banquet when he was a child?"

Icarus blinked. "What?"

Nildar flashed a grin his way. "You likely won't know this story. You were still in Rain Vale at the time."

Rohengar sighed at Icarus's questioning look. "Apparently, there was an...incident when Ivmir was still a juvenile demigod."

"What kind of incident would warrant a ban from the divine banquet?" Icarus asked, aghast.

"One in which a star got destroyed," Rohengar replied reluctantly.

Nildar chuckled.

Icarus's secret esteem for the demigod he had been admiring from afar faded a little.

"I don't like him," Archon stated bluntly.

They all turned to the West Star.

Archon was wearing a mutinous look.

"Not that this surprises me, considering your frequent lapses in judgement in such matters," Nildar said patiently, "but why, pray tell, do you dislike Ivmir when you have not even met him?"

Archon ignored Nildar's unsubtle dig. "He looks like a lady killer. There, see?" He pointed, peeved. "All the female deities and attendants are already fawning over him." His mouth twisted in a moue of disgust. "Good Heavens, even the males are trying to ingratiate themselves with him."

Icarus looked over. Half the crowd had indeed peeled away from the Moirai and their sisters and were busy trying to engage the dark-winged demigod. From the tense looks on the Furies and Black Fates' faces, it looked like they had half-expected this. The Moirai and the Hesperides joined the dark-winged Goddesses as they approached their demigod brother, the guests parting diffidently in their way.

A whispered exchange took place between the siblings.

Ivmir frowned. His annoyed voice reached Icarus's ears.

"Why should I?"

Several of the Goddesses' mouths flattened to thin lines. More words were traded.

Ivmir listened for a moment before crossing his arms, his expression growing even more irate. "And how is that my problem exactly?" He glared at the deities lurking close by. "I was born with this face. It's not my fault these fools can't stop gawking at it."

Icarus choked on an involuntary chuckle. He bit his

lip and smoothed his features into an impassive impression at Rohengar's curious glance.

Over on the banquet floor, the eldest Moira Atropos and the Black Fate Tenebra were pinching the bridge of their noses. One of the Furies muttered something under her breath and looked beseechingly at the night sky. Coraos's shoulders drooped, like he'd heard all this before.

A Hesperis patted Ivmir's back, a gentle yet determined smile stretching her lips as she spoke quietly to him.

Ivmir brightened. "Really? You'll let me fight Ladon?" His voice rang across the banquet hall, his tone full of passionate enthusiasm.

Hesperia scowled.

"I said I would let you *ride* him, not fight him!" she snapped. She seemed to recall where she was and pasted a demure expression across her face once more.

Ivmir deflated a little. "Oh." He rubbed his chin thoughtfully. "I guess I can settle for that." He bobbed his head. "Alright, it's a deal."

Coraos and the Goddesses breathed sighs of relief.

"I wonder what they asked him to do," Nildar mused as Ivmir disappeared in the direction of the gardens.

"Judging from his temperament, they probably told him to lie low," Rohengar said in a resigned tone. He cast a pointed look at Archon.

The West Star shrugged. "What?"

To Icarus's surprise, the daughters of Nyx flew over to their arbor a short while later.

"It is good to see you, Guardians," Atropos greeted with a graceful curtsy after she landed on the marble floor. Her sisters followed suit, their wings dipping as a sign of due regard.

Rohengar rushed forward. "Please, Goddesses," he said, flustered. "It is us who must lower our heads to you."

Icarus followed his brother and the other Guardians' lead as they bowed to the twelve Goddesses. He straightened to find Atropos smiling kindly at him.

"It is a pleasure to meet you, North Star. The tales of your accomplishments have already reached our ears."

The corners of Icarus's mouth tilted upwards. "The pleasure is mine, Goddess."

Atropos blinked. Interest sparked in the eyes of several of her sisters.

"That smile of his is lethal," Nildar muttered to Rohengar.

Icarus glanced at them, confused. One of the Furies drew a sharp breath.

Icarus followed her gaze. The hairs lifted on the back of his neck.

A sudden stillness had come over Atropos. Her eyes flared gold and her expression took on a far-away look.

Though he'd never witnessed the phenomenon, he could tell the Goddess of Fate was receiving some kind of portent.

The brightness slowly faded from Atropos's pupils.

The Goddesses beside her exchanged wary glances, as did Rohengar and the other Guardians.

The eldest Moira observed Icarus for a silent moment, her expression solemn. He stiffened when she closed the distance to him and took his hands. Even her sisters looked surprised at the act.

"I hope we shall become good friends, Awakener." She squeezed his fingers and peered into his eyes, as if hoping to unravel a mystery. "I may be risking the wrath of the Gods of Old by saying this, but I must be frank with you. Your fate and those of myself and my siblings will be intertwined in the near future."

A fraught silence descended upon the arbor.

Apprehension clouded Rohengar's eyes.

Atropos registered the South Star's unease with an apologetic half-smile. "Do not fret, Rohengar. I do not mean your brother harm."

Rohengar hesitated before dipping his head. "Thank you for allaying my fears, Goddess." He traded a cautious look with Icarus, Nildar, and Archon before directing a guarded stare upon Atropos and her sisters. "I think we should converse further at your leisure." He glanced at the deities circulating through the banquet hall and the gardens. "Maybe at a more opportune and private moment? We have...some information that may be of interest to you."

Atropos's face tightened a little. Tisiphone, the eldest Fury, narrowed her eyes.

"Then we shall look forward to our next meeting, Guardians," Atropos said quietly.

The Goddesses took their leave. Icarus blinked

when one of the Black Fates winked at him over her shoulder.

"What was that about?" Archon said gruffly.

"I have no idea," Icarus murmured.

He had a feeling the words Atropos had spoken would linger in his mind for some time to come.

"You need to tell him to dampen down his pheromones," Nildar told Rohengar. He cocked a thumb at Icarus. "I'm pretty sure Alecto means to have her wicked way with him at some point during this banquet."

Icarus's stomach dropped. *Wait. Is that why she winked at me?!*

Rohengar's expression grew resigned. "You know as well as I do that Icarus cannot help it."

"Cannot help what?" Icarus said, perplexed.

Rohengar, Nildar, and Archon all gave him the same brooding, pitying look.

Nildar sighed and took hold of Icarus's shoulders. "Just...try not to get yourself eaten by a wolf." He squinted at the deities in the banquet hall. "There are many of them around."

Icarus was still puzzling over the East Star's warning as he strolled through the gardens a couple of hours later. He'd slipped away to get some fresh air when Pan had come over to rile Archon.

To his relief, the section of the gardens he had come to was as deserted as it had been during his last trip here. It was in a remote part of the grounds, where only stars served to light up hidden paths and secret places that could be unearthed by meandering through gaps in the thick hedges and shrubbery.

To Icarus's delight, he found yet another magical spot when he ducked under some heavy, fruit-laden boughs. He picked an apple from a tree and wandered over to a pretty gazebo gracing the center of a pond covered in lotus flowers, in the midst of a secluded glade.

The music from the banquet was a faint, pleasant melody in his ears as he crossed the path of rocks floating on the water to the open-aired pavilion. It wasn't until he entered the shadows of the structure that Icarus realized he wasn't alone.

A lone figure was perched on a balustrade, his back against a column and one arm propped lightly on a bent knee as he gazed at the distant stars.

"Oh," Icarus murmured. "My apologies. I did not know someone was here."

He was about to retrace his steps when the figure turned his head and pinned him with a cobalt stare.

Awareness slammed into Icarus as he met Ivmir's eyes. His breath caught.

Ivmir slowly unfolded his long legs and swung them over the edge of the railing, his curious gaze still locked on Icarus's face. The way the demigod scanned his body with slow insolence made Icarus's skin grow hot.

"I have not seen you before." An impudent grin curved Ivmir's mouth. "This is good. I was starting to get bored. You can stay and entertain me."

Icarus's pulse spiked at his sultry stare. Heat pooled

low in his belly, the sensation so alien he couldn't help but inhale sharply and press a hand to his body.

*What—what is this?*

Ivmir's pupils flared, gold flashing in the dark depths. His smile widened to a smirk brimming with arrogance.

"I see the attraction is mutual." He chuckled as he rose to his feet and strolled over. "This should make bedding you easier."

Icarus blinked, the tension sparking through the pavilion so thick he was finding it difficult to draw air. The words Ivmir had just uttered finally sank in. He straightened to his full height, appalled.

"What in Heaven's name do you mean?!" Icarus blurted out angrily.

"Oh hush, now." Ivmir slipped a hand behind Icarus's neck and took hold of his waist so he could tug him close. "I know we have only just met, but I prefer my lovers quiet and docile."

Icarus gasped and shivered at his touch. He felt weak all of a sudden, like his strength had been sapped out of him. In its place was a smoldering fire that swept through his veins in an uncontrolled blaze he feared would soon consume him.

Ivmir leaned down until his lips were a scant hairbreadth from Icarus's mouth.

"Besides, if you're here, it must mean you're trying to escape that infernal banquet too. So why don't we enjoy each other's company for a while?"

This close, Icarus could see dazzling specks in Ivmir's eyes. He stared, too dazed to react.

*They look like stars.*

Rationality fled when Ivmir claimed his lips.

Icarus was faintly aware of dropping the apple he'd been holding. He stared into Ivmir's hooded eyes as it rolled by their feet, unsure if this was reality or an absurd flight of fancy. Then Ivmir suckled on his lower lip, angled his head, and fused their mouths.

Icarus swayed, his sanity fading as new sensations assaulted his body.

*This is definitely not a dream!*

He wasn't aware he was clinging to Ivmir's shoulders until he felt the firm tension of his flesh beneath his fingers and heard the demigod's low sound of approval.

The softness and heat of Ivmir's mouth. The intoxicating scent of his breath and his skin. The strength in his hands as he fixed Icarus in place and aligned their bodies until nary a space was left between their straining frames.

All of it washed over Icarus in scalding waves that drowned him in a sea of wanton feelings he had never known, leaving him trembling.

Ivmir slipped a bold tongue inside Icarus's mouth. His fingers tightened on Icarus as he lashed their flesh together, each sinful motion drawing a muffled gasp from Icarus's throat. A growl of pleasure escaped Ivmir at the sounds. He dropped a hand to Icarus's behind, pressed a solid thigh between his legs, and molded their groins together.

Icarus stiffened when he felt the evidence of Ivmir's arousal. He shivered, not sure if it was disgust he was experiencing or something else. Something he dared not put a name to for fear it would expose the lewd fantasy playing across his inner mind.

One where the demigod who held him did all sorts of wicked things to him.

Ivmir shuddered and raised his head. He lifted a hand and rubbed Icarus's lips with a gentle thumb, his expression hungry and a little glazed as he stared into his eyes.

"You taste divine," he said, his tone gruff with desire. "Tell me your name."

Icarus's heart thudded painfully against his ribs as he stood frozen in Ivmir's arms. He knew he should push the demigod away and chastise him for his unseemly behavior. Yet he…couldn't.

Instead, Icarus found himself craving Ivmir's touch and the beguiling flames licking at his insides.

*I must be losing my mind. This is—this is wrong!*

Icarus took a shaky breath and was about to wriggle out of Ivmir's arms when a thunderous roar shook the trees around the lake and sent ripples across the water, making the lotus flowers dance.

Archon flew into the pavilion, his expression murderous.

*"Unhand him, you vile beast!"*

Ivmir grunted as the West Star yanked him away from Icarus and swung a fist back to punch him. He blocked the blow with his forearms, snapped his wings open, and retreated to a safe distance.

"What in the Hells is your problem?!" Ivmir barked at Archon.

Rohengar and Nildar alighted beside Icarus, their expressions tense.

"Are you unharmed?" the South Star asked Icarus stiffly. His eyes flashed as he frowned at Ivmir.

Icarus nodded, his senses slowly returning. "Yes." He swallowed, his face warm. "I am—I am alright, brothers."

He couldn't very well admit to them that he had just been ravished and had even contemplated giving in to Ivmir's ridiculous demand.

*Was I really going to let him bed me?!*

A shiver raced through Icarus. Apprehension tightened his chest as he studied the dark-winged demigod scowling at Archon.

*What did he do to me? Is it—some kind of spell?!*

Rohengar misunderstood his shudder. He wrapped a comforting arm around Icarus's shoulders, the soothing scent of summer flowing from him.

"Brothers?" Ivmir sneered at the far end of the pavilion. "How uncouth of you to interfere in your sibling's love life." He observed the three Guardians mockingly before glancing at Icarus. "He may be your brother, but he is not a child."

"Wait." Archon's jaw dropped. "Does this buffoon not know your identity?!" he asked Icarus with an appalled expression, one finger pointed shakily at Ivmir.

Doubt clouded Ivmir's face for the first time. "What do you mean?" He cut his eyes to Icarus. "Who are you?"

Motion in the sky distracted them before anyone could reply.

Coraos was winging his way over to the pavilion. The demigod landed beside Ivmir. He took in Icarus's flushed face and the other Guardians' angry expressions, and directed a suspicious look at his brother.

"I only went to get us drinks." Coraos placed the two glasses of nectar he was carrying on a ledge. "What in Heaven's name happened?"

Ivmir crossed his arms. "A pretty little lamb wandered into my enclosure," he explained with a dismissive shrug. "I was enjoying a taste when his harebrained brothers decided to turn up and ruin things."

Fury ignited Rohengar's eyes. Sky Piercer appeared in Nildar's hands.

Icarus swallowed a mortified groan.

*I can't believe he just admitted that!*

Coraos's face darkened. "You little—" He stopped, jaw clenched and fisted hand dropping to his side. He grabbed Ivmir by the back of the neck and forced him into a half-bow. "Apologize. *Now!*"

Ivmir struggled in his brother's hold, a hurt expression flashing in his eyes. "What? Why?!"

Golden light brightened the night behind them. Icarus looked around. His stomach sank.

Ivmir's sisters were arrowing toward them at great speed.

Atropos alighted first. Her gaze swept the pavilion before landing squarely on Ivmir.

"What did you do, brother?" she said icily, her eyes so bright with power the radiance scorched black spots across Icarus's vision.

"Nothing that concerns you or anyone else here, *sister*," Ivmir snapped. He finally freed himself from Coraos's grip and indicated Icarus. "All I did was kiss him. Why is everyone so up in arms about it?"

Atropos's eyes bulged.

"Oh the divinity," Coraos mumbled numbly.

"Was tongue involved?" someone asked in an innocent voice. "Inquiring minds wish to know."

Tisiphone hushed a bright-eyed Alecto.

"Of course tongue was involved," Ivmir grunted.

The heated look he gave Icarus made his breath quicken.

Some of the color had drained from Rohengar's face. He cut his eyes to Icarus.

"Did he—did he force himself on you?!"

"What? No!" Icarus protested. He hesitated and glanced at Ivmir. "I mean…he *did* take my lips without my express permission."

Atropos started quivering, jaws clenched and nails sinking so hard into her palms Icarus feared she would cut her own flesh.

Archon ground his teeth. "What else did he do?"

Nildar was shooting daggers at Ivmir.

Icarus swallowed. There was no point shying from the truth. Not when he was in the presence of the Goddesses of Fate.

"He, er, touched my behind and said he wanted to bed me," he confessed reluctantly.

The silence that descended upon the pavilion was so profound Icarus heard a leaf fall in the gardens.

Coraos groaned and dropped his face in his hands.

"Argh, that dimwit," Lachesis moaned.

"He's gone and done it now," Tenebra said glumly.

"Was he born an idiot?" Hesperia asked Erytheis.

"Maybe it's because of that time Tisiphone dropped him on his head," Megaera muttered.

Atropos marched across the pavilion, took Ivmir by the shoulder, and forced him down until his knees hit the ground. The floor cracked beneath the demigod under the force she was exerting.

She bowed deeply to Icarus, her sisters and Coraos following suit.

"I beg your forgiveness, Awakener," the eldest Moira said in a tone full of remorse. "My fool of a brother has caused you great offense. I shall discipline him as you see fit."

Ivmir paled. He raised his chin and leveled a stunned stare at Icarus, his neck cording as he struggled against his sister's overwhelming strength.

"You are the Awakener?!"

"Shut up, you idiot!" Tenebra hissed.

"Please," Atropos ground out, her fingers sinking into Ivmir's flesh until he winced. "Tell me what punishment you would like me to meter out, Awakener."

Icarus chewed his lip worriedly. He could tell from the Moira's expression that Ivmir would be getting the walloping of his life after this. Despite Ivmir's outrageous transgression, Icarus didn't want him to get hurt. He took a deep breath, crossed the floor, and stopped before the dark-winged demigod.

"Do you know what you did wrong?" he said sternly.

"I kissed you without your permission," Ivmir replied promptly.

Icarus arched an eyebrow. "And?"

"And I was remiss in touching your behind." A smirk stretched Ivmir's mouth. "Which, by the way, is the nicest bottom I have ever—*Ouch!*"

Tisiphone had dinged him around the ear.

Icarus flushed as several of the Goddesses stared at that part of his anatomy with renewed interest.

"Let me kill him," Archon pleaded with Rohengar.

"Not if I kill him first," Nildar growled.

Rohengar rubbed his forehead, his expression still pinched. He gazed at Icarus.

"Is this really alright, brother?"

"Yes." Icarus faltered at his anxious mien. "It was just a mistake. I'm sure Ivmir has learned his lesson. I see no need to punish him further."

"But," Rohengar directed another irate look at Ivmir, "—he stole your first kiss."

Icarus suddenly wished the ground would open up and swallow him.

The Goddesses watched with bated breath. Even Atropos seemed fascinated.

Ivmir's eyes widened. "That was your first kiss?!"

Irritation shot through Icarus. From the experienced way Ivmir had claimed his mouth, he was willing to wager it hadn't been Ivmir's first kiss. The smile that lit up the demigod's face in the next instant scattered Icarus's thoughts and made his soul core throb.

"Now I want to bed you even more," Ivmir said fervently.

Archon punched him in the jaw.

❧

"For the hundredth time, I am sorry, alright?" Ivmir pleaded in a beleaguered voice.

Icarus whirled around. "Stop following me," he snapped.

He turned and resumed his walk, only to halt when Ivmir took flight and landed in front of him. Cobalt blue eyes that had haunted his sleep and his every waking moment for the past week studied him in earnest hope.

"Not until you tell me you forgive me and agree to have a drink with me."

Icarus sighed and rubbed his forehead tiredly.

It was the penultimate day of the banquet. Ivmir had pretty much stalked him since the night they'd first met. Though he never approached Icarus when he was in the company of the other Guardians, his brooding eyes had followed his movements when Icarus had been obliged to mingle with the other deities attending the celestial banquet.

Distance and the passage of time had made Icarus question all he had felt when Ivmir had taken him in his arms. He'd come to the conclusion that it had been a folly brought about by strange circumstances. As a Guardian, his duty was to lead an ascetic life and abandon all interest in the pleasures of the flesh. It was not so much a written rule as it was an inevitable consequence of possessing a Guardian soul core: the power it bestowed overrode most base instincts and emotions, allowing Guardians to ascend to a level of spirituality in keeping with their roles.

Icarus was confident Rohengar was as chaste as he was. Nildar and Archon on the other hand were much older than them and had both had relationships before they were chosen as Guardians. Icarus had never once heard them express regret as not being able to experience physical love again. Whether they privately lamented the loss he would never know without asking them.

*And that is* not *a conversation I am ever going to have.*

Ivmir fidgeted restlessly as he waited for an answer.

Icarus's lips twitched. "I forgive you. But I shall not have a drink with you."

"Why not?" Ivmir almost wailed.

Icarus swallowed a snort.

Ivmir stared. "Did you just laugh at me?"

The demigod looked so incensed Icarus couldn't help but burst out laughing.

Ivmir crossed his arms and pouted.

Icarus doubled over.

"I'm sorry," he chuckled once he got his breath back. He straightened, wiped away his tears, and gave Ivmir an apologetic look. "You looked like a child just now and I remembered the story Nildar told me."

Suspicion darkened Ivmir's gaze. "What story?"

Icarus scratched his cheek. "About the time you got yourself banned from the banquet."

Ivmir drooped. "Oh. That story."

Icarus smiled. Ivmir stilled, his gaze locking on Icarus's face as if he'd just unearthed the most wonderful treasure. Icarus tried not to squirm under his heated stare.

"I need to make something clear. I cannot reciprocate your feelings for me."

Ivmir frowned. "Why not?"

"Because I'm a Guardian," Icarus explained patiently. "We are not allowed to engage in physical relations."

Ivmir cocked his head to the side. "Who says I want to have physical relations with you?"

Displeasure tightened Icarus's jaw. Ivmir's mouth quivered.

Icarus squinted.

*He is definitely teasing me. Well, two can play that game.*

Icarus took a few bold steps and closed the distance to Ivmir. The demigod had a couple of inches on him, which meant Icarus had to raise his head to look him in the eye.

"Do not lie, Ivmir," he murmured. "This part of you is more honest than your tongue." He lifted a hand and trailed lazy fingers down Ivmir's rock hard chest and stomach.

Ivmir's eyes flared. He grabbed Icarus's wrist when he reached the area under his belly button. His heat cocooned Icarus when he leaned in and brought his lips to his ear.

"You're dancing with fire, Awakener."

Icarus shivered as Ivmir's breath teased the delicate shell, his pulse beating frantically under the demigod's fingers.

*What am I doing right now?! I just told him I couldn't respond to his desires.*

But his body wasn't listening to his mind. Icarus was helpless against the instinct that made him tilt his neck to the side, exposing the column of his throat.

Ivmir froze for a breathless moment at the silent invitation.

The kiss he pressed to Icarus's skin was as tender as it was hot.

Icarus moaned.

The sound galvanized Ivmir. He wrapped his arms around Icarus, nosed his chin up, and took his mouth in a savage kiss. Every inch of Icarus tingled and throbbed as Ivmir claimed his lips with a passion that would not be quenched. It was only when he felt Ivmir's erection probe his belly that he realized he'd looped his arms around Ivmir's neck and was clinging to him wantonly.

"*IVMIR!*"

They flinched and wrenched their mouths apart as a Goddess's roar swept through the gardens.

Tenebra was winging her way through the sky toward them, her expression dark.

"You little wretch! I am going to wring your neck!"

Ivmir groaned. "My sisters are going to be the death

of my libido." He released Icarus, pressed a peck to his lips, and shot up into the sky. "I'll see you soon, Awakener!" he yelled over his shoulder.

Icarus brought a trembling hand to his mouth, unaware that the flames Ivmir had lit inside him would make him ache in places he had never ached before for days to come.

ॐ

ICARUS BLOCKED THE SPEAR OF LIGHT WITH HIS SWORD and darted out of the way of Nildar's blade. It skimmed his shoulder, causing him to lose his balance.

He froze when the Spear of Light stopped an inch from his throat.

Rohengar straightened and lowered the weapon. "You are distracted, brother."

Nildar looked equally troubled beside him.

Icarus averted his gaze from their probing stares. "I'm just a little tired."

He wiped the sweat from his brow and looked around, his chest heaving and his heart racing from their practice session. The beauty of the Nether struck him once more, causing his breath to catch all over again.

The star that graced the sky bathed the vast kingdom in a sparkling, golden light. Verdant islands floated amidst soft, white clouds all around them, the forests, mountains, rivers, and lakes upon them full of life and resplendent with their unique charms. Flocks of birds danced above the towering trees and sailed across the firmament, their colorful wings bright as they soared through the crystal clear air, their silvery calls a sweet song Icarus would never tire of hearing.

He never expected the forbidden domain that few could enter to be so majestic. It made him glad he had been chosen as a Guardian, even though the role came with heavy duties.

"Is Ivmir the reason you cannot focus on your training?" Nildar grunted. "I heard he was like a bull with a sore head when his sisters banned him from saying his goodbyes to you."

Icarus swallowed a sigh. The East Star was too shrewd for his own good.

It had been two weeks since they had returned from the celestial banquet. Though Ivmir had promised Icarus they would see each other again, he had not laid eyes on the demigod since they'd kissed that second time in the gardens. It was only afterward that Icarus had learned the demigod had been ambushed by his sisters and practically gagged and trussed up before being hauled off the grounds.

*I can't blame him for not keeping his promise. It's not like he can enter the Nether at will.*

A figure appeared in the distance before Rohengar and Nildar could question Icarus further. Archon approached, four deer swung on a giant shoulder and a net full of freshly-picked fruits in his hand.

He'd been out patrolling the Nether's borders.

"Come, let us take a break, brothers."

Night was falling by the time Icarus returned to his island and the pale palace that graced its center. Bright orbs darted out from the building and appeared from between trees and flower bushes when he landed in the gardens, the spirits who served him assuming ethereal cherubic forms as they converged on him.

"Master, you have returned!" they sang merrily.

Icarus smiled as they flitted and danced around him, their touches soft and warm where they caressed his hair and face. "I'm back, little ones." He gave them the deer Archon had gifted him. "This is a present from the West Star."

"Let us prepare Master's bath and meal!" the spirits chanted animatedly to one another.

They zoomed toward the palace with the game Archon had hunted, golden sparks trailing in their wake.

It wasn't until he'd retired to the open-roofed observatory that graced the north dome of his palace and his bed chambers later that evening that Icarus's thoughts turned to Ivmir once more. He hesitated before tracing his mouth with a hesitant finger. Heat warmed his cheeks and pooled in his belly when he felt a stirring in his groin.

Icarus flushed and lowered his hand as the memory of the torrid kisses they had shared danced through his mind for the umpteenth time.

To his embarrassment, he'd woken up to an erection most mornings since he'd returned from the banquet, the heat and hardness of his flesh a direct consequence of the sordid dreams that had filled his every night. Dreams where Ivmir delivered on the wish he'd made to bed him.

Icarus was aware of the practicalities of how two males mated. He'd seen enough depictions in the books on sexual arts his sister Kalliste used to sneak out of the royal library in Rain Vale to make him blush. Though it had surprised him to no end that males found such an act pleasurable, he'd never envisaged himself in that position.

He was not a stranger to physical attraction. He had sometimes felt a tightness in his chest and butterflies in his stomach in the presence of certain Nymphs and Potamoi, back when he was still a prince of Rain Vale. But none had tempted him enough to want to explore those feelings further.

It was not frowned upon for male Gods and demigods to enter into relationships. The practice was indeed widely accepted in all the realms and had been from Heaven's very inception. As far as deities were concerned, the souls of their partners carried more importance than the physical bodies they inhabited.

A wry smile curved Icarus's mouth then. The Wild God was possibly the only exception to that edict. As Archon had once declared, barring war demons, Pan could fornicate with just about anything with a pulse.

Icarus took a sip of his honeyed tea and sighed as he watched the stars twinkling far above.

*I wonder if I will see Ivmir at the next banquet.*

He was lost in contemplations when the hairs suddenly lifted on his arms. Icarus stilled, his pulse quickening.

His gaze swung west and found the spot where he

could sense a disturbance in the sky. Something was coming. Something that did not belong in the Nether.

Brightness flashed high above his palace. Icarus's stomach twisted.

A portal had opened in the Nether's wall.

Something fell through it as it closed. Something with dark wings.

Icarus jumped to his feet.

*Is that a war demon?!*

Divine power flooded his veins, bringing with it Heaven's Light. It bloomed on his skin and hair and made the air crackle as he prepared to unleash his armor and sword.

Icarus flinched when a distant expletive reached his ears.

"Oh, the Hells!"

The falling figure crash landed in a lake a short distance from the palace. Icarus froze for an instant before spreading his wings and darting in that direction, his heart slamming against his ribs.

He knew that voice.

Spirits swarmed Icarus as he arrowed to where the figure had emerged from the water and was swimming steadily for the shoreline.

"No, Master! Run away!" the orbs pleaded. "We will take care of the intruder!"

They shifted, their new forms no longer that of sweet cherubs but the deadly warriors they had once been. For the spirits who inhabited the Nether belonged to fallen soldiers who had once served in a divine army.

"At ease, my old friends," Icarus said soothingly. "I know this demigod. He means me no harm."

The spirits traded anxious glances. Still, they obeyed his command and fell back to a safe distance, their suspicious stares swinging to the figure in the shallows of the lake.

Icarus landed in the shadows of a grove of trees in time to see Ivmir rise from the water. Air locked in his throat.

"I'm going to murder that Wild God the next time I see him," the demigod grumbled under his breath, ripples sloshing around him. He ran a hand through his wet hair and stepped onto the bank, his sandals squelching under his feet.

Icarus barely heard Ivmir, his enthralled gaze raking every inch of his sharply defined anatomy where his see-through tunic clung to his flesh. He swallowed when he glimpsed the shape and thickness of Ivmir's manhood. The fire that had been smoldering in his veins since the demigod last held and kissed him ignited with a vengeance.

Ivmir stilled when he noticed Icarus's presence. The smile he gave Icarus lit up his face and made Icarus's heart throb.

"I kept my promise."

ॐ

IVMIR ADJUSTED THE TOGA ICARUS'S SERVANTS HAD given him awkwardly. Truth be told, he loathed wearing the things. Since Icarus's clothes would not fit his frame, it was the best they had been able to offer him.

Judging from their mistrustful stares, Ivmir suspected they would rather have seen him dressed in rags.

He followed one of the spirits as it led him from the guest quarters to Icarus's chambers in the north wing of the palace. The spirit closed the door after him when he entered the suite. Ivmir looked around curiously.

Icarus's residence was nowhere near as lavish as it ought to be, considering his status. Though the place was beautifully furnished, the inherent simplicity of the decor spoke of someone who cared not for appearances.

He spied a large, white bed through the archway to his right as he crossed a sitting area and a dressing room. It was covered with a gossamer canopy and strung with gauzy curtains that added to its privacy.

Ivmir's pulse quickened. He could smell Icarus's scent the strongest from that direction.

He stepped inside a circular, north-facing room. A star-filled night sky spun above him, the light the celestial bodies shed sparkling on the surfaces of the lakes and rivers that dotted the island.

Books lay scattered on a desk to his left. A reclining seat stood next to it, its surface similar laden with piles of texts and scrolls.

Ivmir's gaze skimmed the star-gazing instruments gleaming in the half-gloom before landing on the figure to his right. Icarus sat on a window seat loaded with soft cushions, a glass of steaming tea in his hand.

Ivmir's breath caught as the Awakener's beauty struck him all over again.

Icarus's features were perfectly symmetrical and exquisitely refined, the sharp lines of his cheekbones softened by his jawline and his elegant nose. His long, fair hair shimmered where it hung loosely past his shoulders, a pale curtain that draped a solid physique which was not overly muscular. His limbs were long and graceful, their form lissom despite the strength Ivmir knew they possessed.

*Every inch of him is breathtaking.*

Icarus turned his head, as if he had read Ivmir's mind. His gray eyes rooted Ivmir's feet to the ground, the emotion he glimpsed in their silver depths masked behind a neutral stare in a heartbeat.

"Come," Icarus said quietly. He indicated the spot opposite him. "Have a drink with me."

Ivmir hesitated, feeling strangely nervous all of a sudden. He crossed the floor and sat down. Icarus poured him a glass of tea from a carafe. Ivmir accepted it with a wry grimace.

Icarus eyed him quizzically. "What is it?"

"This isn't quite what I had in mind when I said I wanted to share a drink with you."

Icarus arched an eyebrow. "Don't tell me you were planning to get me intoxicated with liquor so you could take advantage of me?"

"I was, actually," Ivmir said bluntly.

Icarus's eyes rounded. He burst out laughing in the next instant.

Ivmir gave him a vexed look. Icarus laughed harder.

"I'm sorry," he chortled. "It's just, I didn't think you'd be so honest about it."

"Yes, well, I would rather avoid any more misunderstandings between us."

Icarus's eyes twinkled as he took a sip of his tea. "Your faux pas was the talk of the banquet."

"Don't remind me," Ivmir groaned. "Coraos makes it a point to tell me how much of a dolt I was every time we see each other."

Icarus chuckled. His breath stuttered when Ivmir leaned over and gently fingered a lock of his hair.

"I've never seen you with your hair down before."

Flags of color painted Icarus's cheekbones a pretty pink. "I—I only have it like this at night."

Ivmir glanced in the direction of the archway. Icarus's blush grew.

"I like your bedroom by the way." Ivmir brought the lock of hair to his lips, his hooded gaze on Icarus's flushed face.

The way Icarus shivered and his pupils dilated told Ivmir he was just as aroused as he was.

Ivmir reluctantly let go of Icarus's hair. He'd promised himself he wouldn't rush the Guardian.

Icarus blinked. Something that looked like disappointment flitted in his gaze.

Ivmir hid a satisfied smile behind his glass as he took a sip of his drink.

"How exactly did you get into the Nether?" Icarus asked.

Ivmir stiffened.

*Drat. I thought he'd forgotten about that.*

"I...would prefer not to reveal that detail."

Icarus narrowed his eyes slightly. "Was Pan involved?"

Ivmir sucked in air. "How did you know?!"

"You were grousing about him when you were coming out of the lake."

"Oh." Ivmir lowered his glass to his lap and scratched his cheek awkwardly. "I didn't realize you'd overheard me."

Icarus's face tightened. "So, Pan has a way of getting in and out of the Nether without the Guardians' knowledge?"

Ivmir sighed. He had a feeling Icarus was not going to let this go until he got an answer.

"Who do you think keeps giving the East Star liquor from the Spirit Realm?"

Icarus flinched and gasped. "Nildar knows?!"

"From what Pan said, they've been in cahoots for centuries," Ivmir drawled.

A muscle jumped in Icarus's cheek.

"Relax, Awakener," Ivmir murmured. "Pan is not your enemy."

Icarus's expression grew pinched. "Still, there are rules for a reason."

Ivmir couldn't resist anymore. He put their glasses on a side table, clasped Icarus's cheeks, and kissed him.

Everything Icarus did. Each expression and gesture. How his lips moved when he spoke and the corners of his eyes crinkled when he smiled. All of it stoked his desire for the Guardian.

The way Icarus responded made Ivmir want to drag

him to his bedroom and make a mess of him and the pristine sheets he'd glimpsed a moment ago. Icarus's lips parted eagerly to welcome Ivmir's probing tongue, the breathless little moan Ivmir swallowed full of hunger and pleasure.

It took all of Ivmir's willpower to end the kiss and lift his mouth from Icarus.

Icarus's fingers clenched on his shoulders. His chest heaved with heavy pants as he stared dazedly into Ivmir's eyes.

"What have you done to me?" he whispered.

Ivmir traced his glistening lips with a finger, his belly tight and his cock hard. "The same thing you have done to me. You have bewitched me, Awakener." He pressed his forehead to Icarus's brow, his flesh tingling where it met Icarus's hot skin. "You have beguiled me, body and soul, and I fear I never wish to be rid of this spell." Ivmir shuddered. "I want you, Icarus. I want your everything."

His heated confession filled the space between them.

Ivmir realized he had never been as honest with someone he wished to bed as he was in that moment.

*No. Not just to bed.* He traced Icarus's cheek with a trembling hand as a shocking realization rocked him to the core. *This is not just about sex. I want to own this deity. I want him to be mine forever more.*

Icarus took a ragged breath and squeezed his eyes shut, as if he found Ivmir's gaze scorching. "I—"

Ivmir stayed his words with a finger. "You don't

need to give me your answer right now. I do not wish to pressure you into a decision you might regret."

Icarus swallowed and nodded tremulously. "Alright," he breathed.

"Good." Ivmir smiled. "I'm going to woo you, Prince of Rain Vale." He tilted Icarus's chin with a knuckle and kissed the tip of his nose. "Look forward to it."

"DID SOMETHING HAPPEN?" ROHENGAR QUIZZED ICARUS.

They'd just put away their weapons and were wiping their faces with a cloth. Dull clashes rose from the island where Nildar and Archon still sparred below them.

Guilty tightened Icarus's throat. "Not particularly. Why do you ask?"

"You are full of smiles these days."

Icarus blinked. "I am?"

"Yes." Rohengar patted his shoulder, his expression warm. "Not that I mind in the least. It makes me happy to see you happy, brother."

The lie he'd just told the South Star burned Icarus's stomach. He knew he was going to have to tell the other Guardians about Ivmir eventually.

It had been a month since Ivmir began sneaking into the Nether to visit Icarus's palace. So far, all they had done was share drinks and meals and gone for walks on the island. The spirits serving Icarus had finally warmed to the demigod and even greeted him affably when he arrived for his night time visits.

Ivmir hadn't touched him since the first night he infiltrated the realm of the Guardians. Icarus was conscious he was waiting for an answer to his confession.

*The problem is me.* Icarus frowned as he and Rohengar flew down to the island where Nildar and Archon had just finished their training session. *I...don't know what I want to do.*

His inner voice mocked him at that disingenuous thought. Icarus bit his lip.

Truth be told, it wasn't that he didn't know the desires of his own heart and soul. He just wasn't sure he was allowed to fulfill them.

The role of Awakener was a most sacred one. Only a few were ever chosen for it. To wish for more seemed the very definition of selfishness and arrogance.

Yet, Icarus couldn't stop longing for Ivmir.

*Is it a dereliction of my duty to crave him? To want a relationship with him? One that will consume my very being?*

Saying yes to Ivmir would mean giving his everything to the demigod, just as he had articulated that night he'd first come to him. Ivmir had made it clear how serious he was about him during the long hours they'd gotten to know one another since. And Icarus had never once doubted his sincerity.

*Once we cross that line, there will be no going back.*

Still, there was one thing Icarus was confident about. Ivmir would never become a liability to his role as Guardian and Awakener. If anything, he would become a pillar of strength that would support him, just as the other Guardians did.

The day ended faster than he'd expected, his tumultuous thoughts making haste of the hours of training the Guardians went through when they weren't busy patrolling the borders of the Nether. Nildar came over to him as they prepared to leave for their respective domains.

"Can we talk?"

Icarus studied the East Star's inscrutable expression before glancing to where Rohengar and Archon were talking. "Sure."

Nildar led the way to a willow tree dipping its branches into a lake. It was far enough that Rohengar and Archon would not overhear them.

"Here. This is for you." He slipped something out of his tunic and gave it to Icarus. "You only need a tiny amount of it."

Icarus stared at the glass vial. It contained a shimmering, golden oil.

"What is this?"

"It's the nectar of the Fenoa flowers. It comes from the home of the Naiads." Nildar sighed at Icarus's puzzled expression. "It makes penetration easier." He made a graphic gesture with his fingers.

Icarus gasped and almost dropped the vial.

"It has analgesic properties, so it should soothe the sting and burn of having a giant manhood rammed into your hole," Nildar continued bluntly.

Icarus covered Nildar's mouth with his hand and hushed him, mortified.

"How," he stopped and gulped, his face hot, "—how did you know?!"

Nildar peeled Icarus's fingers away from his lips. "The Wild God blabbed." He shrugged. "I swear, that horned bastard almost burst an artery trying to keep the fact that Ivmir was visiting you a secret from me."

Icarus groaned and closed his eyes. He snapped them open a second later and pierced Nildar with a frown. "I can't believe you taught Pan how to enter the Nether."

"I lost a bet," Nildar confessed glumly.

Icarus stared. His stomach plummeted. "Wait. He didn't—?!"

"Oh, please," Nildar scoffed. "The only way that beast's cock is going anywhere near my behind is over my rotting corpse. Since I'm pretty certain Pan isn't into necrophilia, I think I'm safe."

Icarus breathed a sigh of relief. He pursed his lips as he studied Nildar. "You know, in all the years we've known each other, I never realized your mind and mouth were quite so filthy."

Nildar stared. His shoulders drooped.

"What?" Icarus said worriedly.

"Ivmir is going to eat you alive," Nildar mumbled. "I sure am going to miss that sweet innocence of yours."

Icarus rolled his eyes and sighed. The thought that had troubled him the past few weeks rose to the forefront of his mind. He hesitated. "You do not find it wrong?"

Nildar tilted his head, puzzled. "Find what wrong?"

Icarus rubbed the back of his neck. "Ivmir and me?

I...can't help but feel I'm being selfish even entertaining entering into a relationship with him."

A soft smile stretched Nildar's mouth. "There is no rule that says you cannot be a Guardian *and* be happy, Icarus."

The vial the East Star had given Icarus almost burned a hole in his tunic as he flew to his palace. His spirits greeted him with their usual ebullience when he landed in the gardens. Heat flared through Icarus's belly. He blinked.

"Is Ivmir here?"

"Yes," the spirits sang. "He awaits your presence in your chambers, Master."

Icarus swallowed. He was still getting used to the strange sensation in his soul core. The one he'd started experiencing during Ivmir's visits lately.

"Can you prepare my bath?" he requested breathlessly.

"As you wish, Master."

Icarus headed slowly inside the palace, his mind spinning at the decision he'd finally come to. By the time he reached the open air bath that graced the center of a private courtyard, the surface was already steaming and the fragrant scent of herbs and flowers suffused the air. Icarus stripped and headed down a set of shallow steps.

The water made his skin tingle when he sank into it. Icarus submerged himself to his chin, his face hot. He was already sporting a splendid erection and he hadn't even seen Ivmir yet. He counted stars until his aroused flesh settled and had nearly finished washing himself when a voice came from somewhere above him.

"I was wondering where you were."

Icarus whirled around and looked up, the water sloshing around his hips where he stood in the bath.

Ivmir was leaning his elbows on the balustrade of the second-floor gallery that encircled the courtyard. "I sensed your presence." He vaulted over the railing and landed lightly on the terrace.

Icarus looked blankly at Ivmir, the demigod's words echoing in his mind.

*Wait. Does that mean he feels the same thing I do in my soul core?!*

He didn't realize he'd said the words out loud until Ivmir drew a sharp breath.

"You can feel it too?"

Icarus dipped his head, his pulse racing.

"Oh." A strange expression came over Ivmir.

Icarus realized he was staring at his body. More precisely, he was studying Icarus's revived erection where it broke the surface of the water with the kind of rapt focus that indicated he was immortalizing this moment in his mind.

Icarus gasped and spun around, mortified.

He squeezed his eyes shut when Ivmir's footsteps came closer.

There was a soft splash. Ripples washed against Icarus's skin.

Then Ivmir's heat was all around him as he embraced him from behind.

"Don't hide from me," Ivmir whispered in his hair.

He parted the damp strands clinging to Icarus's nape and pressed his lips to his skin. "You are the most beautiful thing I have ever seen. Every inch of you takes my breath away. I could look at you for hours, nay, days."

Icarus shivered, the storm of emotions and physical sensations sweeping through him so intense he had to bite his tongue to contain a whimper.

Ivmir squeezed him with his arms. "Tell me, Icarus. Tell me what I long to hear. Tell me you will be mine." His husky tone was laced with a desperation that tugged at Icarus's heart as he pressed his brow against Icarus's quivering nape.

An ache built inside Icarus when he felt Ivmir's erection against his buttock. The only thing separating their naked flesh was the tunic Ivmir wore. And Icarus wanted desperately to be rid of it.

Icarus shuddered. He could no longer deny the wishes of his heart.

He opened his eyes, twisted in Ivmir's hold, and clasped the demigod's face with trembling fingers. He stared into his sparkling, cobalt gaze and whispered,

"Yes. I will be yours."

The heat that seared Icarus's core in the next instant drew a gasp from his throat and was reflected in Ivmir's widening pupils.

Icarus was confident then that their meeting had been predestined.

That their connection would be something special.

Because he could feel a bond forming between their souls.

*We are—*

"Soulmates," Ivmir breathed reverently. His voice shook as he beheld Icarus. Tears of joy and wonder pooled in his eyes. "You are my soulmate."

Icarus's vision blurred and his breath hitched.

Ivmir lowered his head and gently kissed the silver tears tumbling down Icarus's cheeks. Icarus grasped the demigod's shoulders, rose on his toes, and fused their mouths in a frenzied kiss.

"Make love to me!" he begged brokenly against Ivmir's lips. "I want to feel you!"

Ivmir flushed with desire. The hungry sound that left his throat making Icarus weak at the knees. Then Ivmir's tongue was inside his mouth and his hands were on his naked body and the world faded around Icarus on a sparkling, white wave.

Ivmir's lips. His tongue. His fingers.

They ravaged Icarus and seared his nerves until he became a being of pure sensation, at the mercy of his lover's whim. He moaned wantonly when Ivmir nosed his chin up and pressed a hot trail down the column of his throat to the pulse beating frantically at the base.

Icarus cried out when Ivmir sank his teeth into his skin.

Ivmir grazed his nipples with his nails, the contact so electric Icarus couldn't help flinching as his belly clenched painfully.

"I knew they'd be pink," Ivmir mumbled.

Icarus's eyes rounded when Ivmir ducked his head and sucked his left nipple into his mouth. His cock throbbed. Something thick and sticky oozed from his body.

Icarus pushed Ivmir away, stunned. "What—what was that?!"

Ivmir's gaze dropped. A smile stretched his lips. "That was your pre-ejaculate."

To Icarus's everlasting shock, Ivmir traced the pearly drops crowning his quivering manhood with a fingertip before bringing to his mouth and sucking on it.

Ivmir grinned. "Sweet, like the finest nectar."

Icarus dropped his hot face into his hands.

"My soulmate is a pervert," he groaned.

Ivmir burst out laughing. He pulled Icarus into his arms and kneaded his buttocks with his hands.

"We'll be doing more perverted things than this before the night is over," he promised in a heartfelt voice.

A wanton shiver raced down Icarus's spine when Ivmir's erection pressed into him.

Ivmir turned his attention to Icarus's nipples once more, his lips, tongue, and teeth teasing the stiff nubs until they were swollen and exquisitely sensitive. All the while, he ground their groins together, his hips mimicking the act of sex as he slowly rocked his pelvis.

"More," Icarus moaned. He tipped his head back, his blind gaze lost in the night sky as Ivmir taught him pleasures he had never known before.

A savage growl erupted from Ivmir. He ripped his tunic off his body and cast it on the terrace before grabbing the back of Icarus's thighs and lifting him up so he could hook his legs around his waist.

"*Oh!*" Icarus's eyes almost rolled into the back of his head as their naked bodies kissed intimately from their chests to their groins.

Ivmir's manhood was hard and thick and hot where it pressed against his trembling stomach.

"Icarus, my Icarus," Ivmir chanted huskily. He worshipped Icarus's face and throat and chest with his lips.

Icarus's hole twitched. An ache was growing inside him, one that centered on his lower half and parts of him that had never known another's touch.

Ivmir carried Icarus across the open air bath, lifted him out of the water, and sat him on the edge. Icarus gasped when the cool marble ledge kissed his heated flesh.

Ivmir claimed his mouth hungrily before taking hold of his erection and stroking him.

"*Ah!*" Icarus hissed at the electrifying friction. He looked down and flushed at the sight of Ivmir working his stiff member.

"Does it feel good?" Ivmir nipped at his chin.

"Yes." Icarus's body was growing hotter with every beguiling motion of Ivmir's hand. "I—I want to do that to you too!"

"Later," Ivmir said. "If you touch me right now, I'll go off like a shooting star."

Icarus glanced at Ivmir's erection. He gulped.

"Ivmir?"

Ivmir nibbled on his collarbone. "Yes?"

"Hmm, Nildar gave me a vial of nectar from the Fenoa flowers. I still don't think *that* is going to fit inside me though."

Ivmir froze. "Where?"

Icarus blinked. "What?"

Ivmir raised his head and narrowed his eyes, his fingers stilling on Icarus's straining cock. "Where's the vial?"

Icarus indicated his tunic where it lay at the side of the bath. "It's in my pocket."

Ivmir lunged for his clothing and removed the item Nildar had gifted Icarus. He clenched it tightly and squeezed his eyes shut briefly.

"Thank you, East Star!" Ivmir met Icarus's confused stare. "I've been trying to get hold of some for ages," he confessed. "I'm in Daphne's bad books at the moment, so it hasn't been easy finding this stuff."

"Do I want to know why you are in her bad books?" Icarus said in a resigned tone as Ivmir returned to his side.

"Not right now," Ivmir admitted guiltily. He put the vial next to Icarus and clasped his rock hard cock once more. "Where were we?"

Icarus sighed as he surrendered to the wicked sensations Ivmir was eliciting from his hot flesh. He flushed when his member oozed more of the pearly evidence of his pleasure, slicking Ivmir's strokes.

A feverish tension ignited inside him. It stiffened his spine and thighs and belly. Icarus moaned and started rocking his hips, powerless to resist his body's instinct.

"Ivmir!" Icarus gasped. He met his demigod lover's intense stare, his fingers digging into his solid shoulders.

"You're close." Ivmir kissed him softly. "Come for me, Icarus."

Icarus's body tightened like a bow as Ivmir quickened his motions. Wanton sounds left him as he thrust his sensitive manhood shamelessly through Ivmir's firm grip, reaching for something.

Something he knew would wreck him yet that he still craved.

Fire blossomed in his soul core, the flickering flames matching the tautness washing and ebbing through him. Icarus whimpered as he neared the dizzying crest of what he'd been seeking.

His hole contracted and his stomach knotted painfully when he finally tumbled into an ocean of devastating pleasure.

Icarus was barely aware of his shout of ecstasy as the pressure in his lower body exploded into streaky, pale jets that spurted from his cock and anointed Ivmir's fingers. His wings snapped open, the feathers trembling violently as they reached for the sky.

Icarus sobbed and gasped, his hips jerking fitfully and his passage pulsing as he rode the endless waves of blinding sensation, the world fading until all that was left was his body and mind and soul drowning into a river of red, hot pleasure.

It was a while before Icarus's awareness returned. He roused to find Ivmir raining tender kisses down the side of his neck. He was clinging to the demigod, his heels digging into the back of his thighs, his arms and wings wrapped tightly around his shoulders.

Ivmir straightened and wiped Icarus's sweat-soaked brow. "Was that good?" he asked huskily.

Icarus nodded numbly. "It was so good I—I thought I was going to die!"

Ivmir bit his lip. His shoulders trembled.

Icarus squinted. "Are you laughing at me right now?"

"No," Ivmir denied in a strangled voice.

Icarus punched him lightly on the shoulder.

Ivmir grinned and collected the vial of nectar. "How about we take this to the bedroom?"

Icarus's breath caught when he swung him up into his arms and walking out of the bath in all his naked glory.

"I can walk," Icarus mumbled.

Ivmir kissed him tenderly as they entered the palace. "Your legs are still shaking."

Icarus flushed. Truth be told, he'd never felt so weak-limbed and sated in his entire life.

He became aware of his spirits peering at them curiously from behind columns and the corners of the hallways they were navigating.

"Do not disturb us," Icarus told them with flaming ears before burrowing his hot face in Ivmir's chest.

"Yes, Master," they murmured glumly.

Icarus groaned when the spirits' low whispers reached him.

"Poor Master is going to get violated," one mumbled dispiritedly.

"That's one giant cock," another said, sounding more than a little impressed.

Ivmir swallowed a snort. He winced when Icarus pinched his chest.

"I told you that demigod was up to no good," another spirit hissed. "Now look! He's going to insert his enormous manhood inside Master and wreck him."

Icarus bit his lip. Being wrecked by Ivmir was exactly what he wanted. Not that he'd ever admit that out loud.

"You know, I don't think Master minds," another spirit observed shrewdly. "You heard the sounds he made just now. He was definitely not in pain."

Then Ivmir and Icarus were inside his chambers.

Ivmir kicked the door closed and burst out laughing.

"It's not funny," Icarus grumbled. "They are going to lose all respect for me."

"Yes, it is. And no, they won't." Ivmir grinned and put him down on his feet. "They love you." He walked Icarus backward into the bedroom, his lips landing hotly on Icarus's eyelids and cheeks and lips.

Icarus gasped when Ivmir pushed him down on the bed and dropped the vial of nectar next to him. Ivmir climbed atop the sheets and studied Icarus broodingly where he knelt on all fours above him.

"Touch me," he commanded gruffly.

Icarus hesitated before raising his hands and stroking Ivmir's chest lightly. Pleasure painted red flags on Ivmir's cheekbones. He hissed when Icarus touched his nipples, his pupils blowing until they were dark pools of desire.

His reaction made Icarus grow bolder.

Icarus lifted his head off the pillow and kissed Ivmir's throat. He caressed his shoulders and arms and his wide, strong back before working his way down the solid ridges of his abdomen, his fingers tracing invisible patterns on Ivmir's twitching skin as he teased a path to his groin.

Ivmir jerked and hummed when Icarus cupped him. "By the Gods, that feels good!"

Icarus swallowed at the weight and feel of Ivmir's erect manhood. Though he found it impossible to imagine how his thick girth would fit inside his body, he very much wanted to experience Ivmir's possession.

Icarus explored the veins and silken skin of Ivmir's shaft for breathless moments, learning his shape and the way he liked to be touched.

A lustful groan left Ivmir, his expression telling Icarus he was reaching his limits. He kissed Icarus before clasping his errant hand and pinning it above his head with his other wrist.

Icarus moaned when Ivmir lowered his frame and pressed him into the bed. He discovered that he relished the feeling. Being subjugated in this fashion, his arms trapped and his pliant body crushed and exposed to his lover's touch, felt sublime.

And touch him Ivmir did.

Icarus gasped and trembled and whimpered as Ivmir explored every inch of him with his fingers and mouth. The demigod played with his nipples until

Icarus begged him to suck them, only for him to cry and dirty the sheets with his pre-ejaculate when Ivmir gave in to his pleas.

By the time Ivmir kissed a path down his quivering belly, Icarus was a hot mess. His trembling cock had oozed a sticky, pale pool that had gathered around the root of his shaft and trickled down his balls and taint.

Ivmir's hooded gaze locked on Icarus's feverish stare as he worked his hands under his knees and lifted them.

Icarus sucked in air when Ivmir parted his legs and kissed the inside of his left thigh. Ivmir settled on his belly, propped Icarus's knees on his shoulders, and stretched him nice and wide, exposing his most sinful part to his gaze.

Icarus licked his lips as Ivmir studied his hole with a devout look.

"This part of you is so pretty I want to immortalize it in a painting," Ivmir declared in an impassioned voice.

Icarus dropped his head on the pillow and covered his eyes with his hands.

"How in Heaven's name can you say such things with a straight face?" he groaned.

He stiffened in the next instant.

Ivmir's breath had just danced across his erection.

"Ivmir? What are you—?! *Ah!*"

Icarus's shout echoed across the bedroom as Ivmir licked a scalding path from the root of his engorged cock to his twitching tip. His hands found Ivmir's hair and his gaze Ivmir's sultry stare.

Ivmir repeated the motion, heedless of Icarus's fingers digging into his scalp, his clever tongue tracing the veins on the underside of Icarus's shaft.

Icarus had read of this practice. He'd just never imagined anyone doing it to him.

It was filthy. Obscene. Wicked.

And Icarus loved it.

He hissed when Ivmir circled the head of his erection with his tongue before flicking his oozing tip.

Then Ivmir swallowed him inside his mouth and Icarus fairly lost his mind.

All he could do was feel as Ivmir worked his rigid member with his lips and tongue and the most exquisite suction of his powerful jaw and cheeks.

Icarus's body soon fell into a rhythm as old as time as Ivmir continued his ardent ministrations, his hips undulating sensuously off the bed.

Pleasure soon blinded him. He gripped Ivmir's hair and began thrusting his cock wantonly inside his mouth. Fire pooled in the pit of his belly, bringing with it a tension that made Icarus's every nerve ending tingle.

"Ivmir! Please, I beg of you!" he panted.

Ivmir reached for something as he continued eating him to his heart's content. Icarus heard the pop of a lid and gasped when a few drops of a warm liquid anointed his hole.

The sweet scent of flowers assailed Icarus's nostrils.

He stiffened, his eyes rounding.

Ivmir was stroking the slick pad of a finger across the tight folds protecting his entrance.

Icarus bit his lip and shivered at the sinful sensation.

His body tightened like a bow as Ivmir worked his front and his back, the demigod sucking him lustfully while he rubbed and circled his twitching hole.

Then Ivmir widened his jaw and swallowed Icarus's throbbing manhood all the way to the back of his throat at the same time he pushed a finger past his softened folds and inside his body.

Icarus's core flashed as he detonated like a star.

He ejaculated violently inside Ivmir's hungry mouth, his guttural cry of pleasure echoing in his ears, his passage clenching fiercely around the stiff intruder piercing him with gentle thrusts. Ecstasy wreaked havoc upon Icarus's senses as he convulsed on the bed, his cock throbbing and jerking inside the hot confines of Ivmir's cheeks.

Ivmir gulped and swallowed his seed, his finger still working Icarus's entrance.

He finally let go of Icarus's pleasantly spent cock and straightened so he could sit back on his knees, his cheeks flushed and his eyes dark with passion.

The look he gave Icarus as he poured more of the Fenoa flower nectar on the place where he was penetrating him made Icarus shudder as he lay panting on the bed, his legs propped on Ivmir's shoulders and his body weak with pleasure.

Then Ivmir stretched his opening with his thumbs and ducked his head to flick his tongue across his quivering folds.

"*Ivmir!*" Icarus gasped, shocked.

Ivmir growled, a sound full of need. He grabbed Icarus's calves, spread him wide, and hitched his lower body off the bed so he could feast on his hole.

Sparks of electricity stabbed Icarus's passage as Ivmir rimmed him thoroughly. His cock swelled with fresh arousal, his toes curling in mid-air at every sinful motion of Ivmir's wicked tongue.

Icarus whimpered when Ivmir lifted his head and lowered him to the bed before pushing two fingers inside him. To his surprise, they went in easily, his hole and insides slick with the nectar of the Fenoa flowers and Ivmir's spit. He met Ivmir's torrid stare as the demigod plundered his body, getting him used to the feeling of being penetrated.

A hiss left Icarus as Ivmir scissored his fingers, spreading him even more open.

"I'm coming in," Ivmir said gruffly a moment later.

Icarus's heart thudded violently as he watched Ivmir slick his cock with a generous amount of nectar.

Then Ivmir crowded the cradle of Icarus's body, spread his thighs wide, and wrapped his legs around his hips. He leaned down and took Icarus's mouth in a scorching kiss as he pressed the head of his cock to his entrance.

Icarus moaned when the rock hard intruder pierced his body, his hole stretched impossibly wide. A burning sensation scorched his rim. He winced.

"Breathe, Icarus," Ivmir whispered against his lips. "I promise, this gets better."

Icarus panted and nodded tremulously. He gazed into Ivmir's breathtaking eyes and did as he instructed, focused on loosening his body. His passage prickled when Ivmir finally breached his entrance and sank inside an inch.

"Ivmir!" Icarus whimpered. His nails scored red lines on Ivmir's arms where he'd pressed them on either side of Icarus's body.

Ivmir groaned and squeezed his eyes shut as he stilled and waited for Icarus's body to adapt to his girth.

"It feels so good inside you," he mumbled.

Sweat dripped from his face and splashed onto Icarus's belly.

Icarus's heart clenched at Ivmir's taut expression. He could tell he was holding back so as not to cause him pain. Icarus raised a hand and caressed Ivmir's face.

"More," he whispered. "Give me more, Ivmir."

Ivmir opened his eyes. The fire smoldering in the blue depths should have scared Icarus. Except it didn't.

"Are you really alright?" Ivmir asked.

"I won't lie to you," Icarus said softly. "It hurts. But I still want this."

Ivmir swallowed. He clasped Icarus's wrist and kissed his palm as he nudged his hips forward. Icarus's mouth opened on harsh gasps as Ivmir slowly filled him, their gazes locked on one another.

Then Ivmir was in to the hilt. The demigod took a shuddering breath, his body quivering with tension.

Wonder danced through Icarus at the fullness inside him.

It felt alien and hot and a little painful still. He could

feel the Fenoa flower nectar working its magic as it soothed the soreness.

There was something else there.

A banked heat that throbbed in tandem with his soul core.

It expanded when Icarus tentatively squeezed Ivmir's cock with his passage.

"Icarus," Ivmir groaned. A bone deep shudder shook him.

"Yes?"

"I'm trying to be gentle," Ivmir pleaded, "so keep still."

Icarus licked his lips. "I can't." He gripped Ivmir's thick member with his hole and was rewarded with a colorful curse.

The pain had faded. In its stead was a slow growing fire.

Then Ivmir pulled out and punched back inside Icarus in a motion that stoked the blaze inside him and drew a shout from his lips.

"*Ah!*" Icarus's hands found the sheets above his head as Ivmir began rocking his hips in a tempo that scorched his senses and sent his mind spinning. "Oh! *Hmm!*"

Ivmir grunted and gnashed his teeth as he thrust in and out of Icarus. Their heated gazes met.

"Tell me this feels as good for you as it does for me!" Ivmir leaned down and sucked on Icarus's lower lip. "Because I have never experienced pleasure like this before!"

Icarus clasped Ivmir's face and kissed him hard, his

heart thundering and his ears ringing with the sound of his pounding blood as he lifted his hips and met Ivmir's thrusts.

"It feels—it feels wonderful!" he panted. "I don't want you to stop! *Ah!* Fill me up, Ivmir!"

A wild look came over Ivmir. He fixed Icarus's hips with his hands, his thrusts growing increasingly savage as he plunged his rigid manhood in and out of Icarus's hungry body.

Icarus matched him stroke for stroke, his heels digging into Ivmir's buttocks.

"*Yessss!*" he hissed. "Like that! Harder, Ivmir!"

"By the Gods, Awakener!" Ivmir growled. "You would have me turn into a rutting beast!"

Icarus flushed and bit his lip as he beheld Ivmir's untamed expression. Seeing Ivmir lose control was the most singularly arousing thing he had ever seen.

The flames licking Icarus's insides set his nerve endings ablaze as Ivmir claimed him with ruthless passion. His cries and moans filled the bedroom at the exquisite pleasure pulsing through his passage.

Gold flashed in Ivmir's pupils, his own face growing taut with ecstasy.

"Let's come together!"

Icarus whimpered when his soul core throbbed with sweet violence. From the way Ivmir gasped, so did his. The bed rocked as their motions accelerated, their bodies bowing and straining as they ascended the towering cliff of pleasure they'd created with their lovemaking.

Ivmir's animal shout underscored Icarus's scream

when they peaked the heady crest and fell into an oblivion of wild ecstasy. Heat flooded Icarus's face as the scalding evidence of Ivmir's pleasure filled his insides. His own seed anointed Ivmir's belly in pearly jets, his manhood jerking as it throbbed and emptied itself.

Icarus trembled at the powerful convulsions quaking through him.

Ivmir continued moving.

It took Icarus a moment to realize the demigod was still hard.

"Ivmir?!" he mumbled.

Ivmir leaned down and kissed him, his expression desperate.

"More! I need more of your sweet taste! I swear I will lose my sanity if we stop doing this right now!"

Icarus shivered. He clung to Ivmir as he claimed him again, drowning him in ecstasy so fierce his throat soon ached from shouting.

Ivmir flipped Icarus onto his front and showed him the pleasure of being taken from behind, his hand tugging Icarus's long hair until his back bowed beautifully where he knelt on the bed. He plundered Icarus against the wall, in a chair, and with him standing and leaning forward at the waist while he gripped the footboard of the bed, the demigod rutting wildly as he pierced him repeatedly from behind.

Time whiled away as they returned to the bed and mated with wild abandon, the sheets growing damp with their sweat and seed. Every wave dragged Icarus under, every time his conscious flickered, Ivmir was there to bring him back to life with a savage thrust.

Taking him. Wrecking him. Driving him senseless with ecstasy.

Ivmir's motions gentled when he finally appeased the frenzied hunger that had come over him. His lovemaking grew slow and sensual, his touches and kisses so tender Icarus could not help but shiver. Ivmir's eyes sparked gold as he danced above him, his hips rolling at an unhurried pace, as if they had all the time in the world. He stared in wonder as Icarus shattered under him again and again, at times lowering his head to swallow his sultry moans and gasps with his mouth.

It was a few hours before daybreak when they finally collapsed onto the sheets, their limbs entangled and their bodies heavy as they succumbed to a deep slumber.

Icarus stirred at first light. It took him a moment to register who was in his bed.

Ivmir's chest rose and fell softly with his breaths where he dozed soundly beside him.

Icarus's cheeks grew warm at the memory of the wicked things they had done together. He shifted and winced.

An unfamiliar soreness throbbed through his nether half.

Even though they'd used over half the vial of nectar Nildar had given him, he could still feel Ivmir's shape inside him. The demigod had done a splendid job of deflowering him, showing him little mercy even though it had been his first time.

Icarus pursed his lips. He pinched Ivmir's nose lightly with his fingers.

It took a moment for Ivmir to stir, his brow furrowing a little in his sleep.

Icarus let go and propped his chin on his hands where he lay on his front, his lips curving in a wry smile.

*You wouldn't think he was such a beast looking at him now.*

He moved carefully so as not to wake Ivmir and braced himself on an elbow so he could watch him sleep.

Dawn soon poked pale rays inside the bedroom. Bird song sounded in the gardens as the light fell on Ivmir's face.

Icarus's heart ached as he observed his handsome features. He traced the hard line of Ivmir's nose and the rigid angle of his cheekbone with a featherlight touch before pressing his lips tenderly to his mouth.

He was a storm that had blown into Icarus's world. A fool of a demigod who had changed his entire existence with a single kiss. Loud, reckless, brazen. And yet so precious Icarus could hardly breathe as he gazed upon his sleeping form.

"I make a promise to you," Icarus whispered. "I shall love you always, across the eons and through the ages. And I vow, with my power as an Awakener, that I will protect you whatever may come. That I will save you when you need me the most."

Icarus blinked. Wonderment resonated through him at the heat that flared inside his belly.

He could feel a spell forming between his and Ivmir's cores.

Icarus took a shaky breath.

"None will break this bond," he pledged. "Even if our souls were to shatter, even if Heaven or Death were to tear us apart, we will reunite, in another world and another life." Icarus kissed the spot over Ivmir's heart, the love searing his being so overpowering his breath hitched. "I am yours for eternity, my beloved."

The divine spark that bloomed into life inside Icarus's core was reflected by an answering flash deep within Ivmir.

Ivmir stirred. His eyelids fluttered open, exposing his hauntingly beautiful irises.

A dazzling smile curved his mouth. "Good morning, my love."

THE END

BECAUSE I KNOW YOU
WONDERED WHAT HAPPENED AFTER
THE END...

# AFTERSTORY

AVA MARIE SALINGER

# AFTERSTORY

ARCHON FLINCHED WHEN NILDAR SLAMMED HIS HANDS on either side of his head, trapping him against the wall.

"We're doing this, Archon," the East Star growled.

"I—I don't know what you mean," Archon protested. His gaze roamed the chamber frantically, seeking an escape route.

Nildar narrowed his jade green eyes. "I finally have my hands on a vial of Fenoa flower nectar, so you can ditch your excuses."

The demigod grabbed Archon's wrist, hauled him across the suite to the bedroom, and pushed him down on the pale sheets.

Archon nearly swallowed his tongue at the scorching look Nildar gave him while he undressed. He'd known this day would come since the time the East Star first kissed him, after the war with Elios ended. But he'd never imagined he'd be so nervous about the whole affair. He wasn't a stranger to the pleasures of the flesh, after all.

A particularly solid piece of flesh captured his attention.

Archon's ass twitched as he beheld Nildar's rock hard member.

Though Nildar was slender compared to Archon's beast-like physique, that part of him was anything but.

Archon swallowed and scooted up the bed. "I don't think this is gonna work."

Nildar undid the silk tie holding his ponytail and shook out his long, brown hair, his expression unrelenting. "It'll fit." He climbed on the bed, tugged Archon toward him by the ankle, and stripped him naked.

Archon's pulse pounded as Nildar trapped his hands above his head.

"Now, how about you behave and let me eat you?" the East Star said with a wicked expression.

And eat Archon he did, from his head all the way to his toes.

By the time Nildar pulled his fingers out of Archon's slicked-up hole, the demigod was a hot, trembling mess.

Nildar pushed a pillow under Archon's lower body, locked Archon's thighs around his hips, and spread him nice and open.

"Say it," the East Star commanded. He teased the head of his erection against Archon's twitching pucker.

Archon whimpered and covered his face with an arm.

"Don't hide from me." Nildar tugged Archon's wrist and leaned forward to take his mouth in a scalding kiss. "Tell me what you want, Archon."

Archon's belly knotted as he beheld Nildar's smoldering gaze.

"I want—I want your cock inside me!" he admitted breathlessly. "Pierce me with your thick stick, Nil— *Ah!*"

❦

"—AND THAT'S HOW I IMAGINED THINGS WENT DOWN between you two," Suzie Myers said with a wave of a hand as she worked a cocktail shaker in Cassius and Morgan's kitchen.

Archon's mouth rounded on a gasp of horror.

"That's—that's not how it happened at all!" he protested.

Suzie arched an eyebrow. "Oh. So, you're not denying it *did* happen?"

Zach Mooney's shoulders trembled where he'd poked his head inside a cupboard in search of a salad bowl. Nildar hid a smile behind the drink Suzie handed him.

Jasper Cobb sneered at Archon. "This guy's an idiot."

The West Star stared daggers at the demon as he mixed batter for a cake.

Cassius scowled at Suzie, his hands still pressed to Noah's ears where the little boy sat on his lap.

"How could you?" he berated. "There are children present!"

Noah wriggled out of Cassius's hold.

"Is Aunty Suzie being a foul-mouthed witch again?" he asked Cassius innocently.

Suzie's expression fell. "Who told you I was a foul-mouthed witch?"

"Dad did." Noah pointed at Morgan.

The demigod was rubbing the back of the fair-haired baby girl he was bottle feeding. He arched an arrogant eyebrow at Suzie's frown. "It's hardly a lie."

"He's right," Reuben Fletcher murmured.

The angel passed Jasper a glass of wine before turning his attention to the pots simmering on the stove.

Elisha Rose Atlanteia Black-King burped contentedly on Morgan's shoulder.

Loki returned from where he'd been changing Elisha's twin Isameine in the nursery. "What'd I miss?"

Phebei tugged Lilaia's hands from her ears.

"Aunty Suzie was describing how Uncle Archon rode Uncle Nildar like a wild—" she started excitedly before her mother muzzled her.

The Nymph glared at her daughter while Loki rolled his eyes and plopped Isameine down on her play mat.

"What did I say to you?" Lilaia asked Phebei sharply.

Phebei peeled her mother's fingers from her mouth and gave her a wise smile. "That it isn't the size of their peepee that matters, but what they do with—*ouchie!*"

Lilaia had boinked her on the head.

"Not that!" the Nymph snapped.

"Bibi's in trouble again," Noah muttered.

"When is she not in trouble?" Charlie Lloyd said drily. The enchanter was helping Reuben cook.

Bostrof sighed wearily while Lilaia pinched Phebei's cheeks and stretched them wide. His and Lilaia's son Orthelis giggled on the Lucifugous demon's knee.

A portal opened on the terrace. Theo and Victor stepped out and wandered inside the apartment through the sliding doors.

"How's my favorite nephew?" Theo ruffled Noah's hair and pressed a peck to his brow after greeting Cassius.

"I'm your only nephew, Uncle Theo," Noah pointed out.

"Morgan's personality is starting to rub off on your kid," Victor muttered, kissing Cassius's cheek.

Cassius smiled. Morgan's eyes shrank to slits.

Theo studied Archon curiously as he headed into the kitchen and grabbed a couple of beers from the refrigerator. "Why is your face bright red?"

Archon indicated Suzie belligerently. "Because that woman is spreading vile lies about me!"

"To be fair, bar the bit about you asking me to pierce you with my—" Nildar paused and glanced at Phebei, "you-know-what, she was pretty much bang on the money."

"Peepee," Phebei contributed helpfully while Lilaia continued pulling at her cheeks, except it came out as "Pheephee."

"Oh, that." Theo grimaced and passed Victor a beer. "Yeah, I heard the evidence when I was flying home one night."

Nildar gave the North and South Stars a jaundiced look. "Why do you guys even have separate palaces? You're at each other's place practically every night."

"Because sometimes, a demigod needs his own space," Theo replied. "Especially when his boyfriend won't leave his ass alone," he muttered into his drink.

"This is unfair," Phebei told Lilaia petulantly. "How come Uncle Theo can say ass and I can't say peepee?"

The doorbell rang before the Nymph could berate her precocious daughter.

"It's open!" Morgan called out.

Eden and Cedric Esteban appeared, a young boy at their side. Eden's younger half-brother Julián brightened at the sight of Noah and Phebei. The kids moved over to the coffee table and started playing the board game Kalliste had gifted Noah.

"How was the honeymoon?" Suzie asked Eden and Cedric with a grin.

Eden refused to fall for the bait and graciously accepted the cocktail the witch offered her. "It was great. We loved Europe."

"The hotel in Venice had the most amazing waterbed," Cedric said bluntly.

Eden choked on her drink. She flushed and pierced the Dryad prince with a dark look.

"Everyone's talking about peepees," Noah observed at the coffee table.

Isameine rolled toward him and bumped into his

leg. He picked his sister up absent-mindedly and sat her on his knees.

"Watch closely, Isie. This is how you annihilate war demons."

Isameine blew bubbles as a group of tiny war demons perished on the game board in thin wisps of black smoke at a flick of Noah's fingers.

"It's peepee season," Phebei said confidently. She moved her army of Lucifugous demons opposite Julián's mage troops, the armored figures grumbling as they jostled one another and waved clubs the size of toothpicks.

"What's peepee season?" Julián asked curiously as he re-arranged his magicians in a defensive formation.

Eden's eyes bulged.

Adrianne and Bailey Green arrived before Phebei could launch into an explanation guaranteed to give Eden a heart attack. Bailey was holding a bright-eyed blond boy in his arms.

"God, I feel like a balloon," Adrianne groaned. She lowered herself next to Cassius with some difficulty.

Bailey put their son Sylvester on the play mat with Elisha before hovering close to his heavily pregnant wife. "Can I do anything for you, honey?"

"You can pledge a vow of chastity," Adrianne grumbled. "I can't believe you impregnated me twice in eighteen months."

Bailey made a face. "Yeah, that one's a no go, I'm afraid."

Elisha started commando crawling toward a wide-eyed Sylvester. Orthelis wriggled off Bostrof's knee and tottered over to them.

Julia Chen and Francis Strickland arrived just before the Reaper God and Mortis. A haze of golden light heralded the appearance of Morgan and Victor's sisters just as the sun started to sink toward the horizon, the dragon Ladon perched on Hesperis's shoulder in his lizard form.

Pan and Boreas were arguing about something as they emerged from the portal behind the goddesses. Demetrius followed in their wake, the demigod wearing the expression of someone who wanted to smash the two deities' heads together.

Warmth and laughter filled the apartment as they sat down to eat.

Cassius's heart constricted when he looked around the table at the humans and otherworldly surrounding him. Seven years had passed since his return from the Nether. And they were the seven happiest years of his current life.

Bar Kalliste and Galatea, everyone he loved was in that room.

It had taken over six years for the queen of the Nymphs to fulfill her dream of falling pregnant. Now nearing the end of her confinement, she wasn't allowed to travel outside Rain Vale.

To everyone's surprise, the Tree of Esnant had born fruit three times after Cassius and Morgan had spent their honeymoon inside the sacred sanctuary it hid. Kalliste and Galatea's first attempt at producing a child had failed, so the next fruit had gone to Cassius and Morgan.

Cassius's cheeks warmed as he recalled their second time in the sanctuary. It had only taken them a week to conceive the twins.

Elisha stirred on the mat where she was sleeping with her sister, Orthelis, and Sylvester. Atropos rose, picked up the little girl, and stroked her back gently as she went into the nursery to change her diaper.

Cassius's eyes misted.

*I will protect them. Even though I am no longer the Awakener. I will do everything in my power to make sure this happiness never ends.*

Noah tugged on his arm.

Cassius wiped his eyes and smiled at his son. "Yes, Noah?"

Noah pulled Cassius down.

"Don't worry, Papa," Noah whispered in his ear. "My sisters and I will protect you all."

THE END (really, this time!)

# AFTERWORD

I hoped you enjoyed the surprise Afterstory I included in this short story collection. I really couldn't leave you hanging! I would be incredibly grateful if you could leave a review of Wicked on the store where you purchased it or on Goodreads. Reviews help readers like you find my books and I truly appreciate your honest opinions about my stories.

Ready to discover my next series?
Welcome to the world of The Mage and His Brute, where magic and passion collide in an alternate Victorian London brimming with mystery and danger.

Get the first book Arcane Entanglement today.

Make sure to sign up to my store newsletter for special deals on my books and new release alerts.

Or you can sign up to my author newsletter instead to get upcoming release notifications, sneak peeks, and giveaways.

# BOOKS BY AVA MARIE SALINGER

### FALLEN MESSENGERS

Fractured Souls - 1

Spellbound - 2

Edge Lines - 3

Oathbreaker - 4

Harbinger - 5

Crimson Skies - 6

Wicked - Fallen Messengers Short Story Collection

### THE MAGE AND HIS BRUTE

Arcane Entanglement - 1

### CONTEMPORARY ROMANCE WRITTEN AS A.M. SALINGER

### NIGHTS

One Night - 1

The Escort - 2

Tokyo Heat - 3

Sweet Obsession - 4

Sweet Possession - 5

The Proposition - 6

## ABOUT THE AUTHOR

Ava Marie Salinger is the pen name of an Amazon bestselling urban fantasy author who has always wanted to write MM urban fantasy romance. When she's not dreaming up hotties to write about, you'll find Ava creating kickass music playlists to write to, spying on the wildlife in her garden, drooling over gadgets, and eating Chinese food. She also writes contemporary MM romance as A.M. Salinger.

Visit Shop AD Starrling and buy all of Ava's ebooks, paperbacks, hardbacks, and exclusive special edition print books direct.